THREE WOGS

Alexander Theroux

THREE WOGS

Gambit
INCORPORATED
Boston
1972

FASCINATING RHYTHM (George & Ira Gershwin)
© 1924 by NEW WORLD MUSIC CORP.
Used by permission of NEW WORLD MUSIC CORP.
All rights reserved

Copyright © 1972 by Alexander Theroux
All rights reserved, including the right to
reproduce this book or parts thereof in any
form.
Library of Congress Catalog Card Number: 75-137019
International Standard Book Number: 87645-055-9
Printed in the United States of America

FIRST PRINTING

SPIRITVI SANCTO
OMNIS SCIENTIAE ET SAPIENTIAE FONTI
HIC LIBER DEDICATVS EST

MRS. PROBY GETS HERS

O why do you walk through the fields in gloves,
Missing so much and so much,
O fat white woman whom nobody loves
Why do you walk through the fields in gloves?

—Frances Crofts Cornford

1

I

Picric, antagonized, scuffing
forward with a leer, Fu Manchu readily
confirmed a common fear: a distorted mind proves that
there is something on it. A girl in a diaphanous shift squirmed
to bounce free of the ropes which held her, like a network of
fistulae, to a scaled gold and emerald table, a simulated dragon
of smooth wood; a purple gag she was unable to spit free. The
yellow, moonshaped face of Fu Manchu, poised between in-
scrutability and simple lust, both of which disputed for mastery,
twitched in a decisive way and then his ochre fingernails, as if
plotting a map, curved over her arm, onto her shoulder, up to
her clavicle. Suddenly in the midst of depositing into the ashtray a slice of cellophane from her second pack of cigarettes,
Mrs. Proby screamed. An usherette came running down the aisle
and ranged various shocked groups of people with the long
beam of her flashlight. Several annoyed watchers, a few rows
back, indicated with thumbs and umbrellas a quivering Mrs.
Proby, her face the colour of kapok, hunched down into her
seat, mumbling to herself, and puffing smoke. The beam caught
her. She jerked her head toward the light; again she screamed.
Mrs. Proby stood up quickly, faced the dark audience, and, like
a fat statue come alive and gone mad, she swung her arms high
and sent out a highpitched, terrifying howl. Then she stamped
up the aisle, demanded her ticket back, and flung out of the theatre. "Simples," said Mrs. Proby as she sat on the No. 22 bus
which took her back to the Brompton Road roundabout, where
she lived. It was her neighbourhood.

"Mrs. Cullinane, *everyone* has a neck," Mrs. Proby concluded
firmly, digging into the purse of her red handbag for a saccha-

rine tablet and obviously piqued at her friend's ridiculous suggestion that the Chinese head sprouts, *mutans mutandis*, out of his shoulder blades, "even your Chinee." It was high tea: the perfervid ritual in England which daily sweetens the ambiance of the discriminately invited and that nothing short of barratry, a provoked shaft of lightning, the King's enemies, or an act of God could ever hope to bring to an end. "On top of that neck is a head between the ears of which is a yellow face, and that's what made me scream, say what you will, dear, and you jolly well know I don't just open my mouth at the first drop of rain."

"You wouldn't say boo to a goose." Mrs. Cullinane was trying to be helpful.

"Not at the pictures I wouldn't, would I?" Mrs. Proby asked archly and stirred her tea white. A blocky, cuboidal head, faced in pinks and whites and ruled in a fretwork of longitudes and latitudes which showed a few orthographic traces of worry, surmounted a body that made Mrs. Proby look like a huge jar or, when shambling along as she often did, something like a prehistoric Nodosaurus. In a neck somewhat like insipid dough showed occasional fatty splotches, her hair sort of a heap of grey slag scraped back into a lumpish mound at the back. Her eyes had a russet, copperish hue that recalled garden thistles or cold glints of steel, depending, as so much did, upon her moods. She was paradigmatic of those fat, gigantic women in London, all bum and elbow, who wear itchy tentlike coats, carry absurd bags of oranges, and usually wheeze down beside you on the bus, smelling of shilling perfume and cold air. She wore "sensible" shoes, had one bad foot, smoked too much, and cultivated a look as if she were always about to say no. In all, she was a woman with the carriage and studied irascibility of a middle-aged prebendary in the Church of England, executrix of self-reliance, lawgiver, Diocletian reborn.

"The cinema today is different. So much is, isn't it?" Mrs.

Cullinane philosophized. "It was only last week I took me to the cinema. The daily told me they were running a Conrad Nagel thing with what's-her-name, you know, the one I love, but let me tell you there was precious little Conrad Nagel that afternoon, Mrs. Proby." She brushed the shine on her skirt and struck a match for her friend's cigarette. "The picture I saw was about a garage mechanic and another git, excuse me, but git he was, in a plastic suit, who spent all their time taking drugs and forcing grammar-school youngsters to take baths with them. Now, really. I blame the Queen."

"The Bishop."

"The Queen."

"*The Bishop.*"

This froggy voice seemed convinced.

"Well," meekly offered Mrs. Cullinane in an inert and foam-sounding recovery, flustered but just managed, "it could be the Queen. It's her must be allowing all this rubbish into the country in the first place. George the Fifth, sick as he was, wouldn't have counted to seven before he sat down on the whole lot of them, looked up, and said, 'That, for Dicky Scrub!' "

Mrs. Cullinane had the pinched comic face of Houdon's marble of Voltaire, a sort of thin, wide-mouthed suffragist who existed on an ounce of biscuits, the odd celery heart, and, as well, the persistent need to support and maintain ever fiscal sanity in Britain, a brave and full-time concern. She was the kind of woman who seemed to be always holding back a constant urge to knit, the type of person who believed that the statement, "When the Going Gets Tough, the Tough Get Going," was an utterance of the highest magnitude, its speaker invariably the impresario of a dreamland that alone could reshape the world and which surpassed, making quite superfluous, every single volume of philosophy, law, science, theology, literature, and general humanity through the long history of mankind, down to the last. She was a bottomless fund of those insane sermonizing anecdotes which explained, for instance, how big-city hoodlums and czars of the underworld, when riddled by bullets in the street, gasped only for their ice skates in the final minute; how there was a broken heart for every light in Piccadilly; how turtles would never do tinkle in public; and how ladies who worked in the large sweet factories actually hated, yes, hated sweets, to which *credenda*, then, were often added precious and reverently delivered, if not memorable, didactic poems produced, she invariably felt, in the nick of time from the ragbag of tumbling skeltonics she kept at her easy disposal, like shewbread at a fair.

"We never had any trouble, mind you, until America began to send over shipfuls of dirty books and whole potloads of those smouldering films with toreadors, enormous b-e-d-s," Mrs. Cullinane spelled, "and girls in masks and open dust-coats down in Florida in the sunshine, winking at the plumber who came there just *because* and is supposedly fixing the dip-bulb in the w.c., but *we* know better, dear, and I wish we didn't, I wish we did not." Mrs. Cullinane paused, thinking nostalgically perhaps on those old, harmless sepia-tinted reels of "Movietone News" or the long lost three-handkerchief weepies. "Fancy someone like Elizabeth Two, once a princess, mind you, watching something like *Erotic Nights in Dewsbury, Miss Rod Shrieks, The Woolwich Turk*, or *Motel Wives of Pigwiggen*, never mind hearing about them. It makes one want to go sick."

"It's a dicey business, that. It's not enough in the street they're calling her Lizzie, Liz, Betsy, and Bess. Pretty soon it'll be Libby," Mrs. Proby grunted. "Beth, please and thank you. Or maybe just Betty the Mop."

"I've heard Tetty."

Exasperated, Mrs. Proby threw out an arm thick as a cutlet bat.

"No doubt, no doubt. Mrs. Cullinane, no doubt you've heard

Tetty. It's a very coarse word. But, tell me this, haven't you also heard Eliza? Lisbeth? *Elsie? Elsie, for godsakes?* Come on, own up to it. Show a little bone."

"Well, Elspeth."

"You've never heard Elspeth."

"Elspeth," Mrs. Cullinane assured her, "yes."

"A pipe dream, Mrs. Cullinane."

"I'm certain of it. Elspeth."

"*Never.*"

And Mrs. Proby glared at Mrs. Cullinane, who nipped some biscuits which were dipped, self-consciously, in the tea, several times, again—in jerks.

Mrs. Proby quickly interrupted Mrs. Cullinane who had begun humming "When the Old Dun Cow Caught Fire."

"I'm afraid to go out, Mrs. Cullinane. Even with my Weenie. I mean, if he should stop to go doo-doo by a post, who's to guarantee some big hairy thing in a mask won't come flashing out of a doorway and do me god-knows-what kind of brain damage, bash me with a cosh he might, snatch me handbag, even tamper about here and there in the you know." Mrs. Proby nodded knowingly and licked a bubble of tea off an upper lip whistle-split and slightly mystacial.

"You're smarter than Mrs. Shoe."

"Mrs. Shoe goes out?"

"Frequently."

"Alone?"

"This is my point."

"God."

"That's what I said."

"My God."

"That's just what I said."

Mrs. Proby set her tea and saucer down on the tray, walked to the door of the living room, shut it, and sat down again. She

7

shrugged, shook her head slowly, and leaned forward. "Mrs. Cullinane, I'm not sure I know how to say this to you, you wouldn't either." Biting the inside of her cheek, she threw a glance toward the aspidistra in her window and joined the tips of her fingers. "The reason I screamed, the reason you, I, anybody—even Prince Andrew himself—would scream was this: I thought of Mr. Yunnum Fun."

"Mr. Yunnum Fun?" Mrs. Cullinane stopped her jaws, her mouth full of scone.

"Mr. Yunnum Fun *downstairs*." Mrs. Proby's eyes narrowed. She nodded gravely, waiting for the shock of recognition. It came and was gone. Mrs. Proby's eyes widened as a reinforcement. "Their how is not necessarily our how, nor is yours theirs."

"He's only a simple twit."

"He's sneaky."

"He just sells rice."

"He's got things on his mind."

"He's harmless, Mrs. Proby."

"He's Chinese, Mrs. Cullinane."

The small Chinese market and its proprietor, Mr. Fun, hadn't become an object of interest for Mrs. Proby until about five or six months ago, when, at that time, a highly publicized altercation took place between the police and a body of cultural attachés at the Chinese Embassy. Not that, previous to this, harmony reigned between the English lady and the Chinese merchant; they had harrassed each other for years (listening at doors, depositing curt notes, leaving footprints on each other's mail).

A dot of a man, Mr. Fun had owned the grocery store and, in closed circuit, had lived on-premise at the back of the bottom floor of the building for eight years. Mrs. Proby, widowed and full of the spurge of the no-longer-attached, occupied the first floor for three years, a period of time that had passed slowly without the companionable, if occasionally warlike, dialectic

she had found in her husband. Mr. Proby faulted her only occasionally, never, certainly, by low dodges of the heart, but
merely on the odd Saturday night when, out on a toot, he would
lurch home glassy-eyed under the streetlamps, with one or two
middle-aged girls on each arm, singing ballistic snatches from
"The Little Shirt My Mother Made for Me" or "Sweeney Todd
the Barber," his behaviour, after all the drink, considered by the
general neighbourhood not so much objectionable as courtly,
though it periodically cost him those not always enviable few
minutes just later when, unable to exorcise himself of the disconsolate and unbearable immediate, he fell prey to the singularly
virulent *malocchio* drilling him in silence from across the darkened bedroom. But sovereignty was re-established as apologies
were made, insisted upon, sworn, repeated, sworn again, and
more than one potentially fistic evening passed away forever in a
loud duet of snores, one set markedly louder, almost triumphant,
poignantly female. What the deuce, he had often said, say la vee.
He had given Mrs. Proby a fairly full life: judicious, non-ad-
jectival, sometimes cranky, but almost always full. He was in
plastics; then he retired comfortably, took the little woman and
Weenie to Woodford Wells where they bought a modest little
house, trimmed a hedge or two, and tried as best they could to
make the rough places plain. Then, three years ago, after a nice
meal of fresh crab cakes, Cornish pasties, and a bottle or two of
brown ale, Mr. Proby took a jaunt into Epping Forest and
dropped dead—ironically, during the loveliest hour of the English year: seven o'clock on Midsummer Eve. The sudden shock
of it all caused in Mrs. Proby a diarrheal disease called sprue, an
agnail on her right toe as large as a doorknob, and, she claimed,
twinges in the area of Rosenmüller's Organ. In any case, Mrs.
Proby waked him, buried him in a spot near the Bunhill Fields,
packed her things (a lovely collection of Royal Doulton, her
woolwork slippers, a zipper Bible, a morocco-bound account of

the Anglo-Nicaraguan wars of '46, a boa she had kept from the celebration of her wooden wedding, etc.), and moved to a little street near South Kensington, where she had grown up as a girl, because she could not stand to be too far from the nicer part of London, the very quarter in which—oh, it seemed years ago, she often pointed out—Bernard (Mr. Proby) courted her, with a full crop of bushy coal-black hair, pointed shoes, and the banjo eyes she'd grown to love. In those days, England had a voice in the world, people could understand the lyrics of songs, and there were no Chinese. Changes, however, had come about and had created in her a compulsion for the *laudator temporis acti* reminiscence, which excluded, perforce, the total existence of both a certain Chinaman and any capacity in him that might try to prove otherwise. Mrs. Proby became hermetic not *per accidens* but by predilection.

A tight national budget coupled with the small personal account Mr. Proby left her kept Mrs. Proby's eye on the shilling. And except for a chance Saturday at Portobello Road (for thermal underwear, wholesale tins of quinine toothpowder, or general white elephant), a dash to a museum exhibit, or a quick afternoon at the pictures, she restricted herself to the quiet deliberation and firmitude of soul found in the English matron: a recipe available to few but the sore-footed and antique wise. Mrs. Proby bought her flat right out, dusted, put sachet lavender in the drawers, scrubbed, put up new flowered wallpaper, Hoovered the rugs, religiously scrubbed lye into her porcelain, and draped the windows in percale. Until she met Mrs. Cullinane she spent most of her time munching from a can of Fortt's Original Bath Olivers or sucking winegums, slouched lugubriously by the wireless, following episode after episode of "The Archers," listening on the BBC to Sidney Torch's dated musical extravaganzae—and of course she was, as she was always ready to add, "all for the telly," in front of which she often sat making penwipes of flannel in the shape of carnations for the old soldiers on Royal Hospital Road in Chelsea. Her teas were grim; even Weenie was no help there.

"How's your cup?" Mrs. Proby asked.

"I'm doing nicely, thank you," answered Mrs. Cullinane, whose character was basically that of blotting paper: passive, receptive, and ready for the strangest of Rohrshachs, notwithstanding those patterns of peculiarity soaked up by the thrust and imposition of Mrs. Proby's iron will and irrevocable opinion.

"These teacakes want jam," Mrs. Proby said.

"Mine are fine."

"You're having your teacake, then?"

"Oh yes, I merely put it aside."

"I noticed you did. I wondered why you did."

"I had a scone."

"But not a teacake." Mrs. Proby looked away.

"I thought I'd have it in a minute."

"Have it now."

Mrs. Cullinane bit into the cake trimly. "It's delicious."

"It wants jam."

Mrs. Proby, the recent terror of the unpropitiously topical film fast and irksome in her mind, suddenly bolted from the sofa, threw open the door of the living room, and, pointing to her pursed lips as a quick sign for secrecy and immediate silence, scuttled to the keyhole of the main entrance-hall door. She squatted, applied her ear, and peeped through, her right hand raised as a flat warning to a bewildered Mrs. Cullinane who followed her in soft, querulous hops, sucking a finger in fright. Glances were exchanged. Nothing. They mooned back into the room for a second cup. Mrs. Proby poured: "You're white."

"Lovely, and, I think, a twinkle of milk." Mrs. Cullinane,

mouse-mannered and votively appreciative, watched the sacrament and took her cup and saucer as the last word in the way of viaticum.

"Spoons?"

"Two, dear."

"Level or heaped?"

"Heaped."

"Then one."

"One?"

One, Mrs. Proby mouthed, silently pronouncing the word as she nodded once, conveying, as she fully intended, the readily identifiable world-weariness of Authority Taxed. Her eyes shut with a little snap.

Mrs. Cullinane's Lucullan urges were an embarrassment to herself. She blushed for being such a hog and looked away absent-mindedly at a fuchsia marinescape of the pebble beaches at Rottingdean crookedly hung on a far wall.

"I don't mind telling you," Mrs. Proby continued, smoothing her round, lacteal figure, "he scares me right out of my naturals, and, mind you, he's been acting strange for quite some time now. He lights incense sticks at night, worships the devil, I think. I don't know if he's grinding tea or muttering A-rab chants, I don't, but I turn my wireless up so as not to hear, you see. What I'm driving at, Mrs. Cullinane, is this: some morning Mrs. Proby's going to turn back the covers, take off her hairnet, and find she'd shoulder-to-shin with the Yellow Peril, she is.

"The Yellow Peril?"

"You might have read about it, all those little cities near San Francisco, America, are up in arms over it, catching it as fast as nightingales and flopping down with writhe all over their mouths from it, poor things."

Mrs. Cullinane was heartbroken. "Honestly, with all the riots here and space trips there, then the whole African mess, you wonder if people have left their heads home."

"Oh, it's all monkey-see, monkey-do, isn't it?" Mrs. Proby said, sipping her tea and swallowing in the middle of an important thought. "Mmmm," she quickly recovered, "the point is, when I look around me to see who's there, I don't want to see yellows or browns or purples. I want mine."

A wistful smile passed over Mrs. Cullinane's face and she patted Mrs. Proby's wrist with earnest compassion, adding with sincere force and a cross between a prophetic stare and a wink, "You'll get yours." She closed her eyes and nodded confidently.

The ladies understood each other, in the careful way that ladies do once they understand each other. They were rather a pair than a couple, supporting each other from day to day, rather a set of utile, if ill-matched, bookends between which stood the opinion and idea in the metaphorical volumes that both connected them and kept them ever apart. Mrs. Proby and Mrs. Cullinane met each other as the result of a coincidence which proved their similarity, perhaps even to a perfection or symmetry we would never be ready to accord even to types. The meeting took place in the lending library branch at Balls Green: both ladies, waiting at the "request desk," had asked the librarian—almost in unison—for a copy of *The Sinister Monk* by Raoul Carrambo. Laughter, embarrassment, and that became for them the point of departure for a parallel life-style they had cherished for a long while now. But the relationship was greatly strengthened in the two when, after a few off-hand discussions over tea and during walks, they began to realize they held common beliefs in politics, entertainment, and the public weal. Neither could understand why Mrs. Shoe, a third party (initially a friend of Mrs. Cullinane, Mrs. Proby often felt the need to make clear) who worked as a saleslady selling velveteen at

D. H. Evans in Oxford Street, was so unwilling to abhor the immigration problem. Voluntary Repatriation was the answer. One had to be purblind not to see that.

Mrs. Proby never *could* come to terms with the fact that Indians, Chinese, or Blacks even bothered to get on boats and travel thousands and thousands of miles to England—eating only peas and peppercorn or playing mah-jongg or jacks in steerage with all the chickens—when they should have known that the day would certainly come when people would be jumping off into the ocean for want of room, run screaming off into the Highlands for a gulp of air, or begin selling their hair just to keep alive. This was why Mrs. Proby always met Mrs. Cullinane at the door, saying, "Cor, good to see a human face."

Then, there chanced to happen the fully reported melee at the Chinese Embassy, with blow-up photographs in the *Daily Mail* of hissing, spitting ambassadors armed with cricket bats, flat-irons, and pinking shears, while the British police were left with only dust-bin covers to protect themselves. It was only a matter of time, as matters go, therefore, that Mrs. Proby began to notice many Chinese on the streets: hunched, shuffling, dry-mannered, and recondite in that carapax of the inaccessible and unproven. Mrs. Proby immediately bought a screw and lock for her door.

"So I got all fired up and carried away," Mrs. Proby said, plucking a tea leaf off the tip of her tongue, "when I saw this absolutely perverse Chinee with a hat like a black upside-down cup with a nipple on it and a moustache like two long pieces of dirty licorice hanging from his nose. I thought of Mr. Yunnum Fun, so help me dearie. And you would have done, too."

"Was it all blood and gore?"

"Who stayed for the end to watch, me? Not likely. I suppose I should have, strange to say, then I could have told you the whole give and take, you see." A pause: Mrs. Cullinane pulled the lobe of her ear, reflected.

"Mr. Yunnum Fun doesn't have a moustache."

"He has white hairs growing out of his ears, like artichokes. It sounds to me like you're defending him."

Mrs. Cullinane swerved her shoulders in nonchalance. "He walks around in slippers."

"He wears pajamas, too."

"But he doesn't wear a Chinese hat."

"So you defend him."

"I'm not defending him."

"It sounds to me like you're defending him. What does it sound like to you?"

What is a pair, it seemed proven only once again, is not who is a couple.

Mrs. Proby assumed the pain-of-the-unseen-wound expression, stood up, took a cigarette from her pack, and tapped it on her knuckle. She mentally envisioned a piece of black cardboard from which she sharply cut a cruel profile of Yunnum Fun, thinking of his petty insults and bumptious insularity. She puffed out circles of smoke and let loose, between the blue swirls, a not-uncommon antagonism, syncopated with hot flashes: part bigotry, part haptic bias.

"I suppose it's perfectly normal for the Chinese to come over here without so much as shoe flap, go on National Health, have babies for a song, buy spectacles for less than cost, get free teeth, and then just because everything's not all cozy and done up like a nice package from Father Christmas, frills and froo-froo and all, go out into the street and kick those handsome policemen in the kneecaps. And all the while our own have to make do with bits and pieces. Who wouldn't have bad dreams? It raises my hump, Mrs. Cullinane. It should raise yours."

"It raises my hump," Mrs. Cullinane apologized.

"*When?*"

"Just now, dear."

"You're just saying that because it raised my hump," said Mrs. Proby, an avocadine hue rising into her ample neck. Mrs. Cullinane turned cinnabar red. The colours clashed.

"I mean, let's face it, we should take care of our own first, shouldn't we? Give us a few years and we'll have books that you have to read backwards, and our children will have to write with nails manufactured in China and make those peculiar words with wings and splinters and god knows what, won't we?" asked Mrs. Proby, who, unbeknownst to her, had one of the grouts from the bottom of the teacup on the tip of her nose. "If you don't find that peculiar, Mrs. Cullinane, you're off your rails, spade to spade."

Mrs. Cullinane clucked, sipped the last of her tea, and placed the thin, blue-striped cup on the saucer in her lap, dabbed her lips daintily with a napkin, and drew her finger down each side of her open mouth which she smacked as an indication that tea for her was now over. She placed the sacramentals on the server, stood up, adjusted the jacket of her herringbone suit. "Lovely, dear. Just tickety-boo."

"Have yourself another teacake."

"Godfrey," said Mrs. Cullinane, making a clown face. "I'm full up."

"Tomorrow night, then, for the ham."

Mrs. Cullinane, head inclined and little hands joined, was smiling vacantly at her little buttoned feet. She looked like Squirrel Nutkin. She might have been asleep. Then she looked up slowly, depositing her eyes into Mrs. Proby's and quickly bumping out of her reverie. "Tomorrow night, then, for the . . . ?" She grew pursy, flutterful.

"Ham." Mrs. Proby sniffed. "My ham supper."

Mrs. Cullinane formed her hand into a pistol and aimed a finger at her temple; she crossed her eyes, lolled her tongue, and displayed, with jangling arms and a dizzy expression, her silly lapse of memory. Forgetfulness for her was a merciful narcotic. "Of course, dear." she burbled.

"Dumplings, as well."

"Lovely, dear. And so thoughtful. You see, you remembered. I can't *eat* apples as they come from the tree; the crunch goes right through me. I have a thin windpipe. You see, the pips are murder and . . ."

"I don't core my apples," Mrs. Proby interrupted. "I won't have it. Pips impart a delicious flavour to dumplings. I thought you knew that." Cored apples not only made a mock of the natural apple, they made a mock of Mrs. Proby who never fixed them that way. "You want to think about your kitchen, Mrs. Cullinane."

Mrs. Cullinane was thinking about her windpipe.

Mrs. Proby was not given to "adventurous cooking." True, ten years ago, in a mad fit of what then seemed an unquenchable obsession with experiment, she *did* once pull her bread for a cheese lunch. But cooking, especially in England, was not a question of miracles. And even if she hated eyeing potatoes and making béchamel, she knew what work meant. One does not just throw a bun up in the air, as she often rather realistically pointed out, and expect it to come down pig-in-the-blanket. Good English dishes, sweet and short! And there was an end to it. All the so-called snappy puddings, camel meat, weevily flour, cut-and-come-again cheeses, expensive chocolates, and powdered soup-and-fish preparations all shot up with additives sunk into one's stomach like a bump in a trash bin and insured hardening of the arteries, for one thing, and squammes, for another. She loved a steaming joint, a bowl of fresh cock-a-leekie soup, and especially liked her brussel sprouts hard, where they stood up and came green in a minute, after which, of course, a few spoonfuls of figgy pudding to top it all off. She was, after all, an islander. Islanders *had* to know what to eat, because any minute

the Communists, those hoof-footed dongs from the primeval
wastes who live only on smudgy black aerated bread and com-
plaints, would be swimming around the whole nation with
corking and nets in their mouths, sealing Great Britain off from
the rest of the world, and forcing everyone into a diet of cowpats,
the lesser sage, and ounces of mastick. As if life were all clover!
Islanders, also, knew about fish, and Mrs. Proby often found
herself, in the midst of a somnambulistic stroll in the middle of
the night, voraciously gripping the door of the fridge with both
hands, a volcanic lust in her mind for a nice hake, turbot, brill,
some whiting, or, best of all, a slice of John Dory, which had her
favourite piece on the cheek. And then, if she was knocked in,
maybe a nice little Pimm's Cup—just before Bedfordshire—to
ease the rheumatics and start her off again on her beauty slum-
ber. Beauty, she often reminded herself, was important as well.
You never knew.

Curatical in her bugled wool, Mrs. Proby bore regally a large
teapot toward her small kitchen. Mrs. Cullinane champed down
on a napkin to see a trace of lipstick, fixed her hair in a wall
mirror, and fidgeted into her fur-tipped seal boots. She turned
toward the kitchen. "May I pluck a rose?"

Wringing her arms of water, Mrs. Proby came back into the
room in the midst of a monologue which she had begun with
her dog in the kitchen. ". . . featherbedded and all. If it was up
to me, I'd throw out the whole ruddy lot. Sorry?"

"I have to spend a penny."

"The bottom of the hall. You know." She paused, coddling the
stanchion of her left breast from heartburn. "The bathroom sta-
tionery is in the cabinet, with a rubber around it. The bugs were
ruining the t.p. That's why you will smell pepper in the con-
venience, Mrs. Cullinane. Don't let it stop you from your business. I sprinkle pepper there, for the bugs." She snorted out with
a cruel little chuckle. "They hate it." She indicated an unlighted

passageway off the living room, through which Mrs. Cullinane poked, feeling the walls for surety. Mrs. Proby splayed herself in a chair, stretched her feet wide apart, and pinched lovingly the wattles of her dog, both staring into space. The identifiable sound of a loud gurgle and splash pulled her from her revery. Mrs. Cullinane re-entered smiling.

"You remember, of course, the la-de-da in the Victoria and Albert Museum, Mrs. Cullinane. A fine figger for the children here and about, wasn't it?" Mrs. Proby sucked a tooth.

"Oh yes," Mrs. Cullinane said dryly. "That Chinaman."

"I thought you forgot."

"How could I forget?"

"I thought you forgot."

"How could I forget?"

"After I just reminded you, you couldn't, Mrs. Cullinane; there's no point in fibbing."

The reference here was to an unfortunate incident that took place about a fortnight before the confrontation at the Chinese Embassy and which prompted Mrs. Proby, despite Mrs. Cullinane's protestations that the man in question might have been Japanese, to write to Downing Street a singularly outraged letter, notable, perhaps, most of all for its insinuation that an insidious collaboration was taking place, known to few but the initiated and politically aware, between the British Civil Service and Red China. "Watch the feathers fly," Mrs. Proby prophesied.

Mrs. Proby and Mrs. Cullinane took advantage of the English year and its rosary of annual events: the Annual Spital Sermon, Oak-Apple Day, Swan Upping, the Shrove Tuesday Pancake Greaze, and the Presentation of the Knolly Rose. And Mrs. Proby and Mrs. Cullinane loved to go to museums as well. They loved tapestries, the century-old costumes, and delicate bone china. Mrs. Cullinane could never get over the intricacy of the Eye-talian designs which she herself could never hope to dupli-

cate in a thousand million years, she said. Mrs. Proby said it
took her mind off herself. It was on Egg Saturday one lovely
afternoon in spring and a fresh rain had left the streets clean
and the air bright for a good walk to the Victoria and Albert.
But no sooner had they passed the Jones Collection and were
making their way through to the tapestries, with determined and
mechanical clockwork steps, they happened to pass a chunky
man (a Thai) huddled in a greasy overcoat, sitting on a small
bench before the elongated, sensual sculpture called "Reclining
Nymph." His hands were fumbling in his lap (a rubbing friction
to restore warmth). Mrs. Proby, biting her lip and inquisitorial,
nudged Mrs. Cullinane, dragged her away behind some eigh-
teenth-century French busts in a corner, and, her back to the
room, squinted past Mrs. Cullinane's shoulders while gesturing
with her thumb over her own, in the direction of the man. They
bustled over to the room guard and explained in euphemistically
vague but excited terms that a Chinaman in that same room was
drooling and manipulating himself, and, by way of footnote,
they stood around and painted a few word-pictures which included various suppositions, not the least of which was that it
was the Queen Mother's favourite room and that, *horresco
referens,* the Archbishop of Canterbury might be coming into
the museum any minute.

It was getting dark outside. Mrs. Cullinane stopped at the door
and smiled sweetly. She squeezed Mrs. Proby's elbow and turned
her head to one side in compassion. She started down the stairs,
turned on the landing, and spoke. "Keep your pecker up, dear."

There came a pause.

"Remember."

"Yes?"

"When the going gets tough, the tough get going."

The door slammed. Mrs. Proby relocked the door, popped a
valium tablet into her mouth, and washed the cups and saucers,

having pulled on some long pink rubber gloves lined in yellow. She thought of Fu Manchu's fingernails. She paused, her hands quiet in the water, and looked behind her. Then she shambled into the living room and stretched herself out in a crumpled way on the sofa. The dog shifted. Mrs. Proby blinked in the dark room, unhappy and on edge for the yellow cross-hatched illusions and patterns thrown on the ceiling by the passing autos outside.

II

Came morning. The shade was cranked up slowly in the main window of Mr. Yunnum Fun's market and revealed, there on the doited and chewed shelves, merchandise that had been around for years: boxes of Keemun black tea, Shatto rice sticks, Ma Ling loquats, cans of Fish-Ball soup, shrimp paste, Panax Ginseng bars, swatches of dried silver fish strung together like tobacco leaves, Lychee nuts, Chun Lee ham, bottles and packets of herbs, bean curd, Cantonese sea slugs, ropes of onions, and rolled fig. A small red sign, painted in the Chinese hand, with letters formed of sharp shapes and slivers, hung on a jar filled with a mixed array of back scratchers and joss sticks. A faded print of the embalmed Sun Yat-Sen leaned against the jar, together with a yellowed photograph, edged in black, of an old Chinese man leaning on a cane and staring directly into the camera that had caught for eternity his ancient, platelike face and the white hair on his chin, which grew thin and sparse and long, like wisps on the penis of a goat. It was dated, in crayon, Peking 1903.

Mr. Fun appeared, swept the doorway, and withdrew.

The proximity of store-to-dwelling places and neighbor-to-neighbor never really bothered Yunnum Fun, for composed within easy reach of his memory—a memory decidedly acute—was the village of Fowping, southeast of Peking, within the Shansi Province, in Inner Mongolia, from which he had emigrated some thirty-five years before. The small village was a diffused but heavily populated nest of boxes, in one of which Yunnum Fun's father worked as a tailor; houses collapsed onto each other, fluted with bamboo and sandalwood, a jumble of misapplied and colorless boards designated by the ineluctable press of destitution as living quarters.

Soon after the 1922 Civil War broke out between the rival Tuchuns, Yunnum Fun hiked, biked, and less often rode the thousands of miles through the provinces of Honan, Hupeh, Hunan, and Kwang-tung into Hong Kong. Those days were difficult, merciless. Before the long journey had been made, a domestic tragedy had exerted itself but which became, of necessity, secondary to the pain of travel, where the speed of rush and change delimited the possibilities of chronic remorse. Yunnum Fun's father got tired of his wife one day and hit her square on the head with the stave of a wheel, fatally despatching her in an instant. They were packed and ready for the trip that afternoon, during which trip Yunnum Fun was tutored in the lessons his father had generously and wisely passed along to him, notwithstanding the first and most important lesson: that women are simply different means to the same end. The boy had listened.

Once in Hong Kong, Yunnum Fun's father walked his son to the crowded dock, handed him a yellow felt sack of coins and a letter, and pointed off toward a rusty steamship, toward the sea, toward England and the West. He added the bit of advice that became his last words: "Your how is not necessarily my how, nor is ours theirs."

Mrs. Proby Gets Hers

At the very minute he walked onto the boat, Yunnum Fun scampered down into the steerage toilet, peeped about to make certain he was alone, and opened his father's letter of instructions. It read as follows:

Obstructions for You

At the water edge, notice all look-alikes who mong fish, own porkshop, and will do you mercilessly foot-kicks. These are George.

May you deign never to be purveyingly twitched aside by George and his festive brickbats. Fearsome, you hear me?, is the grunting cow who lies in weight to piss on you head under his characterless island moon which rains on his hair and even on Illustrious Bearer of The Royal Umbrella. His wood is fill of thief's, who will twist your cobblers just for comedy.

You are illegible bachelor. So do write and never wrong. In forty ways does a Woming Object accost a man; bewife none and wise up. It is only to recall Mother Shandilee and Her Bargain.

Queen of George is Elizabun.

Not stealing is a wisely compromise, my hopeless son who flings himself beyond correspondence and my one lantern. Soho is a filthy rotten shame who will pouch your money.

Whether; forgy is always

Worship his stray cat as he does; trust him and you impute doghood to a goat. Pummel your unworthy self who pongs because of bad breath before this Woming Object who is Queen of George on the grass and give mouth-warning: 'O Boy, O Boy!' She is aweful.

To thine own self be true, or your little ass will fall off.

Don't oblige noblesse same as jackals. Last was he who laughed with the other side of his face. An evil word are shits, hoor, peepee, titties, and up yours. Impinge that passport on wretched ankle or on fat of leg, to never let go even when bitten.

His Rothman cigarette, Est. 1890, is yum-yum.

A golden earring dance below your dirty ear.

Then he ate it.

The young Yunnum Fun eventually arrived in England, and, simple and steady as a plumb bob, he applied himself steadfastly and directly to the job at hand, cutting cloth, hemstitching, and sewing in the small tailor shop which he had rented in Crouch End, an enterprise remarkable, people thought, for its ability to survive, since, upon entering the shop, one was struck by the meagre components in evidence that kept the operation a going concern: a wire, headless dummy, a flatiron, and one bolt of gabardine. As the years passed, he saved his money, avoided ridicule, dodged flung objects, and watched. Yunnum Fun always watched. But, as has been pointed out, the situation which finds the human race incommodiously jammed cheek-to-jowl, shack-to-shingle, bothered no one less than the small ageless merchant, émigré, exile.

War came and the shop closed down. It had been sold, in point of fact, to a chinless, fat-legged whore with a brain quotient lower than a Gobi rainfall and lemur-like eyes that seemed interested solely in that not uncommon syzygy of money and barbarities, and, though she claimed she was going to redo the shop as a flat-cum-study—in pursuit of a college degree (physiology, doubtless)—that very night she painted the doorbell a mandarin-red and slipped a card underneath, which read: *Dana, Model, Interested in Driving Post.* In any case, Yunnum Fun disappeared. Rumour had it that he had been shuffled aboard an airliner to the Shanghai-Bund, that he was working as a ponce on Old Compton Street, that he was trafficking in opium and spying for the Chinese Reds. It was assumed he had passed into insolvency, if not oblivion, leaving neither an address nor a successor. The opening of a new market proved he was not insolvent. He had money. But he had no successor. He had never married. Mr. Yunnum Fun would *never* marry.

Though the methods of abuse are often different, abuse itself is not. Yunnum Fun was quite inured to the fact that a goodly number of Englishmen ("thrice-wretched blighters," he silently agreed to himself) resented him; however, he was resigned generally to that strict ontology which makes of all Chinese in a foreign country a simple cartoon of one dimension. Occasionally, teenagers from the East End, sitting opposite him in the Underground, would push alternate arms into alternate sleeves, buck their teeth, and say "whoosh, whoosh." Often, couples and customers would come into the store and, to amuse each other, would intentionally confuse, muffling a giggle, the letters L and R. And others would pass him in the street, mime a shuffle and toss off a remark or two, so that after a period of years Yunnum Fun found that he was easily able to combine and permute a series of about two hundred laundry jokes, none of which he found comic, all of which he heard. The solution to all these problems, on the other hand, was not beyond him: he would wipe away these people as a dishwasher, drying a dish, wipes it and turns it upside-down.

Undemonstrative, long-suffering, silent, Yunnum Fun recapitulated the patience of the unwanted and little-cared-for expatriate in a strange land, a patience, however, canalized through insignificance and not through virtue. The acts of the patiently insignificant are not necessarily the gifts of the virtuously patient. Yunnum Fun's patience, if not virtuous, was neither infinite. A normal can be changed into a hysterical individual, for example, simply by tiring him, and Mrs. Proby had tired Yunnum Fun for three long years now. And because of her, for three long years, Yunnum Fun often found himself bumping around his shop in the dark late at night, drooling, shouting, and almost blind from the powerful bottles of samshoo he had drunk as a refuge from his tribulations. Yunnum Fun loathed the English, and he intensely disliked women. But Mrs. Proby was for him a special case, a thing that made a difference, the one exception: for Mrs. Proby he abhorred. This was his sole dissipation.

At odd unpredictable moments, the pressure of his miseries, released, sent him hurling in long comic bounces from wall to wall, Yunnum Fun all the while hissing like a mattoid: cross-eyed, lunatic, and occasionally spitting jets of water or pitching spoons through the cobwebs. He repeatedly kicked the stuffings from his sofa. He delivered thundering ritualistic blows at imaginary objects. And more than once he drew huge dirigible-like faces of Mrs. Proby on wide sheets of rice paper, charcoaling each line with infinite care, and then, clipping each sheet to a wire strung out for the purpose, he repeatedly drove his mop handle crashing through it to the accompaniment of blood-curdling, almost insane screeches and wild charges. Yunnum Fun saw the ultimate battlefield as the earth, the two opposing armies male and female. It had been predicted, he believed, that sometime, perhaps in the Year of the Limping Cassowary, the whole complex of secretive and mutually warring human bureaucracies—in which marriage was only a necessarily incomplete and pathetic localized attempt to negotiate truces—would give way to an open declaration of full-scale attack, and the two sexes would separately but simultaneously marshall together a planet-wide schema to rid the world of each other, no longer now filthy little satraps biting each other's hands for inconsequential reasons, as had been the case all the way from post-diluvian history down to the incorrigible present, but vast monosexual armies creeping through each other's ribs and making inroads into each other's hearts to detonate explosions there that would fill the sea with a blood that would seep right down to the very abyssal benthic ooze until eternity rolled over. Yunnum Fun knew precisely where he would fight, whom he would fight, and why.

The market this morning was, as was its proprietor, quiet. For one thing, business had been off these last weeks; for another, this was a business mercurial at best. The urge for Chinese food is always unpredictable: famous for no occasion, standard fare for no holiday, and the constant as to demand is either whim, the needy plebiscite of instantly famished drunks, or pregnancy. Any supply–demand ratio, borne of such flux, could do nothing but annoy and create, even in the genetically silent, a hysteria etched in and bordered by a quietude that could only be termed pathological. Too, Yunnum Fun had enjoyed little or no sleep the night previous, kept awake until the wee hours by a general thumping around from the flat above and the sporadic but frequent nasal preparations, bellowed in the name of song, of a repetitious and cacophonic "God Save the Queen." Then, later, there came the screams. Periodically during the night, Yunnum Fun was ripped from his sleep by sharp, piercing sounds and ravenings which simulated the anomaly of a high dog whistle crossed with a sonic boom, culminating each time in a sinusoidal shriek at a range of about C''''; paradoxically enough, however, Yunnum Fun took malicious pleasure in Mrs. Proby's distress, even at the cost of a night's sleep, for onto her he had telescoped a revenge informed by years and years of scorn and obloquy. Mr. Fun lay on his mattress of stuffed dry cornshucks, his face pointed due north, and snorted with glee and disgust. But he was tired in the morning. And the morning was grey.

The door of the little market jumped open to the sound of a dull clack from a thick copper bell attached by a string to the top. Mrs. Proby, breasts high, strode in in a tableau somewhat reminiscent of Napoleon crossing the Beresina. She stopped before the counter. They exchanged quick glances: half stare, half glower. Yunnum Fun moaned inaudibly and dug his fist into a barrel of raw oatmeal. Mrs. Proby lighted a cigarette and tapped her foot.

"Runner beans," she announced. "A pound and a half, if you please." She raised her eyebrows and drilled the R.

"No runner beans," Mr. Fun beamed. "Only rima beans today." He was delighted and his eyes glinted warfare over the barbican of his cheeks.

"Ducky," Mrs. Proby offered. She huffed, spat out a ball of smoke, and shifted position.

"No, only rima beans," Yunnum Fun joyfully repeated in antiphonal fashion. His mouth was hanging open as if to suggest imbecility, but there was a touch of the demoniacal grin as his tongue rested pointlessly on his lower lip. A proper twit, Mrs. Proby thought to herself. She opened her handbag.

"Very well then. I need some herbs." She took out a small scrap of paper and read aloud in a proclamatory way but with a pronunciation one might use when talking to a four-year-old. "I want ravensleek, dwarfdwostle, pennyroyal, and marjoram." She coughed and added, "In your elevenpence ha'penny tins." She handed him the paper with a swipe of her hand.

"Enveropes." He bowed patronizingly.

"*Envelopes,* then," she snapped, waved her arm, and looked at the ceiling. Yunnum Fun stood still for a moment and shook some refuse from his ear with a little finger. Mrs. Proby stamped her foot; a hum of urgency in her throat ceased with a long draw of the cigarette. She tapped off an ash into an empty Chinese bowl of blue cloisonné enamel at her elbow. Yunnum Fun saw her. She saw Yunnum Fun see her. Yunnum Fun saw her see him see her.

Tish, tish, deario, thought Mrs. Proby, tish, tish.

Mr. Fun shuffled toward the basement door, threw an amused three-quarter profile at Mrs. Proby, and disappeared downstairs. Mrs. Proby ran her thumb disdainfully over the glass counter and grimaced. She scanned the shelves of dried Lang Yen nuts, jars of dried chicken, cucumber soup, glue rice, grilled eels, plum sauce, mashed and red beans, sesame oil, sugar, snap bars, lotus seeds, and Chinese pumpkin. She peered at curious labels. She picked up a dented and nigrescent tin of soybean oil. "Dogfood," she said. Then she focused on a small glass frame behind the counter, within which sat, evidently as a keepsake or some sort of commemoration, a small brown yuan—a coin with a square hole directly in its center. As quickly as she had seen it, she suffered a sudden *gestalt*: what if it had been her ear? The queasy thought unnerved her. What if he tried to jam a chopstick into her tympanum like Fu Manchu did to that poor old lady in the film? Who would know? Mrs. Cullinane? How? Who would really care? All very well to say Mrs. Cullinane, Mrs. Proby thought; she shivered and stared vacantly out of the fly-specked window. She puffed her cigarette, twice, three times. It tasted sour. And why wouldn't it, she thought, as she looked at the tip of red ash; she had smoked almost two packs all night, fretting, worrying, alive to the horrific, if self-induced, revelation that Mr. Yunnum Fun might have at any moment crept upstairs and clapped his mousy hands on her neck, snapped a clothespin on her nostrils, or tried to pull out her tongue. She had heard that the Chinese were notorious for stealing cats and dogs, sewing them up in sacks, and then serving them up as delicacies in posh nightspots around Frith Street and Leicester Square. Maybe they did the same thing to human beings, she considered. Her leg jumped. She threw the door open, snapped the butt of the cigarette into the street, and slammed the door again; the bell clacked twice. Mrs. Proby turned only to see Yunnum Fun, breathless from having just pounced up from downstairs, peeping querulously over a pile of soda crackers. "Bloody wog," Mrs. Proby muttered to herself, splitting a gingerstick between her fingers.

She felt that was him all over: ducking about, slipping around, and generally smooth as oil. It had become a patriotism, part of her war, a very sense of duty, that she make clear to him he would never intimidate her or take advantage of her native wherewithal. The cost was high: worry and nerve ends exposed. But in such cases she reflected on Nelson, Churchill, or the Duke of Wellington. Her outrage took precedence over worry and fought misalliance; homogeneity determined her crusade— at once, a life-style and a sore-point, a hobby-horse and golden rule. A subtle Asiatic, she could never forget, was a horse of a different colour, a Greek bearing gifts, a fly in the ointment, and an ill wind that blows nobody any good. Scratch a coloured man, she often told Mrs. Cullinane, and find a pickthanks. "My bubble's not for bursting," she said aloud.

Mr. Yunnum Fun shuffled upstairs and spread before him on the counter four envelopes covered with odd inscriptions like marks on a Tarot pack. He looked at Mrs. Proby with nunlike calm. "Herbs here: ravensreek, marjolam, dwarfdwostre, and pennyloyal. Erevenpence ha'penny, each, each. Three bob ten in altogether, thank you, please, very." Mrs. Proby reached into her handbag, flipped open her purse, and pulled out a ten-shilling note, thrusting it across the counter. She took her change, turned aside, and counted it, adding, "Spices go for tenpence ha'penny at the Tesco."

It would have been the Inn of the Seventh Paradise of Dragons, he thought, to flay her alive with his rattan cane until the Carp of the English Ocean tipped over the raincloud with its tail for the last time. Yunnum Fun wanted to take her English coins and notes and pack them one after the other into her craven mouth until she was fat as a goose. He remembered his father had told him, once, of the rascally Wong chieftain who had fleeced the people from Pui'pui of all their money and how, as a punishment, he had been tied into a chair and force-fed diced pearls, gold leaf, and hundreds of coins, until he dropped doomed, heavy, expensive.

The merchant spot-checked the shop. He shrugged. "Tesco is big. Yunnum Fun is small."

"You get a nice glazed ham at the Tesco, do better. A good full ham, less dear, more lean, and far and away better than those poor things." She gestured to three fist-sized hams on the tray to her left. "Good chops, veal, ribs, too."

"Ham is costly, very so."

"Well, yours cost a packet, don't they?"

"Man say in China: what melts the butter, hardens the egg."

"You won't hear that in London. They don't talk like that here. They'd think you were potty if you went around talking like that in England, which, may I add, is where we are. Me, anyway."

Yunnum Fun snatched up a piece of paper and stridently blew his nose in it. It sounded like a quack. Mrs. Proby winced and sourly turned away with her eyes wrinkled shut. He looked up, smiled. Quickly, she stuffed her purchases into a straw satchel, her jaw set firm. She pointed to a row of glass jars. "How much are those Huanese nuts, or however they're pronounced?"

"About twelve bob."

"What do you mean *about* twelve bob? Either they are twelve bob or they are not twelve bob."

"Up or down according."

They faced each other, rivetted in a unity of hatred; both knew what the other thought, each thought what the other knew. Mrs. Proby regarded him with the pity that tries to indict, but also which includes the mask of dismay that implies it is a pity uselessly, if wisely, given. She knew his teeth were smiling perpetually behind his lips.

"We've been speaking the King's English here since Adam and Eve, and I haven't seen it hurt anybody, yet, by the way." She threw her shoulders back, majestically. Yunnum Fun shrugged and made the sound of a pip. "But if people want to get on with it and skip about like St. Anthony's Pig, oinking

and what-have-you, it's jolly well good enough with me." It was
not jolly well good enough with her.

Yunnum Fun watched her through the gun-hole slits of his
eyes as he tickled up in his mind all her lies, protestations, moral
thieveries. She was like a mad dentist trying to extract his every
dying nerve. His father had been correct. Then, Yunnum Fun's
eyes twinkled philosophically. He had a lesson for her. He folded
his hands into his sleeves, bowed, and began:

> A great lady of Ping was. At meal of fowl say she, with bullying to
> servant which had arrived at treacheries, what undergoes here here?
> Is stuffing of this my fowl forever gone of hognuts always? Fowl
> uncapable in taste when gone of hognut. Woeful personage of
> servant make abruptions in sowow and him drag in dinky monkey
> who smile six thumbs wide. That, say servant who want to whip it.
> It dip into you hognut, of two pounds on the button. Lady of
> Ping, wise as great, on balances weighted dinky monkey, and here
> it smile much much with great deal. It weight one an half pound—
> and no more, any. Neither now is woeful personage of servant.

Yunnum Fun, again, bowed.

"I've never heard such tripe in my life."

"We indeed, too, say in China: speak is not so good as do."

"I've never heard that."

"They say in China."

"Christianity's good enough for me, thank you."

Yunnum Fun fought a crucial impulse to broadjump the
counter and bite her. Instead, he watched. Mrs. Proby walked
to the door, opened it, and turned. She clutched the satchel like
a football under a right arm healthily michaelangelesque, the
humerus within empirically the size of a Westphalia ham. Her
face twitched.

"You see," she fumed, "we were always taught that if people
go mucking about and foraging around with yellows, blacks, or
any another cribbage-faced nit who steps here and about as free

as Dick's hatband *in a country not his,* well then, the country won't be worth tuppence." Her full face was wide, flapping, incarnadine. "And don't you think for one iota we're going to become another Shanghai with all its cheap cloth and jerry-made cameras, because you've got another thing coming, dearie. We've had the war. Once burned, twice shy, they say. Mark me well, we know what you're about, too, and you are not, you heard me just say *not,* pulling the wool over anybody's sheep's clothing. Certainly not mine, least of all." Her womb was smoking with wrath. And then the exit line came. "Rice or no rice," she said, "if I was a Chinaman I'd flap right back where I flew from."

Mrs. Proby breezed out the door, her popliteal fat winking in several places just before she disappeared, and the bell clacked its weak reprisal. It was then that Yunnum Fun decided to kill her.

III

The magnificence of a sun hidden made the afternoon English, the sun typical, and magnificence a word highly subjective. Shoppers, transients, and businessmen hurried through streets stamped along for years. Small and large shops that lined the Brompton Road spilled forth customers, in heavy coats and mufflers, who emerged diffident, obtuse, and ready for a snack. The sky above was the color of pewter: toward it no one looked, for it no one cared. The utter impossibility of alteration, determined through centuries of unquizzical resignation and fortified by a trust in the fancy of a capable God, makes of the grey day in London an inexorability that translates into the accepted gratitude of a traditional pain known to an untraditional pleasure not. Enthusiasm, then, is modified by habit; habit is reinforced by schedule; and the schedule which excludes a hearty drink at the local is not only unimaginable, but irregular—the very situation that finds in a bright sun an afternoon foreign and the word magnificence absurdly objective. The pubs were crowded.

A short, fat girl in a pale blue workcoat came over to the snug and, with her hands on her hips, asked for the orders of three women who sat with their hands folded, worshipfully, like a tripartite version of a female Balthazar, Caspar, and Melchior grown thirsty.

Mrs. Cullinane wrinkled her nose and smiled coquettishly. "A nice Dubonnet." She held her thumb and index finger a straw apart.

"Oh me. My turn. I think I'll be a devil and have a Baby-cham." She hugged herself, for Mrs. Shoe on few occasions was used to neither deviltry nor drink. A nondescript somewhat ibis-headed English lady, she was prone to hypochondria and wore a sort of reed-woven culotte, adorned with a sprig of ceramic cherries, but, in her favour, she freely beamed from a face as bright as the Colenso diamond. She was rather tall and unlovely and had a sore throat. Her eyes sparkled at the thought of a good glass. "One finds one needs it in the nippy cold."

"A pint of Guinness," Mrs. Proby bit off the words. They all looked at Mrs. Proby. "I've been shopping," she excused herself.

"Eating?" The waitress leaned on her left foot. Mrs. Proby looked at Mrs. Cullinane. Mrs. Cullinane looked at Mrs. Shoe. Mrs. Shoe looked at Mrs. Proby. The waitress walked away.

The Bunch of Grapes was an old pub rebuilt in the nineteenth century but evocative of Dickensian solidarity and cheer: wooden beams, smoked windows cut fine with curling designs, red walls, rubbed brass rails, and a long bar in the shape of a rhomboid upon which sat a phalanx of clotted saucebottles, plates of fresh sandwiches, toad-in-the-hole, and hot sausages stuck through with toothpicks. The long gilt mirror that reached around the bar reflected men in dark suits, gathered in whispers and loud laughter, each one with one hand in a pocket, one foot resting on an ankle-high pipe just above a red and yellow carpeted floor. Three or four old men sat buckled on a bench in their cigar smoke and newspapers as they read the horses over glasses of bitter.

Mrs. Proby's feet hurt. A doctor had recently diagnosed it as Talipes Plantaris and told her to use her head about these matters, but when Mrs. Cullinane suggested the damp, Mrs. Proby said she blamed no one but herself ("In my day, you see, we were not afraid of a walk"). Otherwise she felt fairly comfortable: her ham was ready for the oven; the salad was diced up and mixed and wanted only dressing; then she would bake her potatoes, for she liked them crisp in their jackets. She wanted a green, but runner beans were out, the Chinaman saw to that, the little pig, so she would make do without. She had done in the war and could do it again. Meantime, she had promised herself an afternoon at the pictures; the matinee would guarantee that she would, consequently, arrive home for any last details by way of preparation for her nice dinner. She would take her sweet time. Decisions had been made: the girls, as was usual, met together in the pub for what they called a "hello" but what was, in fact, a masterful if somewhat dirty *coup de jarnac* which squeaked out platitudes and shibboleths and made the day the day.

Mrs. Cullinane flapped her collar up and held it to her neck in a prissy, fragile pose. "There's a filthy wind shushing through that door," she said.

"Gnf," said Mrs. Proby, her mouth bulging wet and full with stout.

"My doctor is too busy for my throat," whined Mrs. Shoe, picking a nut from a dish. "I went to see him Friday last as hoarse as ten crows, but would he write me up a chit for the chemist? Not if two Sundays came together in a row, he wouldn't. He told me to go off and suck a mint humbug, hello and goodbye."

"A mint humbug?" Mrs. Cullinane's face turned sour.

"Your five-penny sucker," Mrs. Proby added. "One of those after-dinner lozenges. Imagine." She lighted a cigarette.

"A pastille."

"A lozenge."

"A pastille," Mrs. Shoe assured them.

"*A lozenge!*" shot Mrs. Proby, jumping up like a gigged frog. "I ought to *know* a lozenge when I *take* one."

Mrs. Shoe looked at Mrs. Cullinane. Mrs. Cullinane, smiling nervously, looked away and began to hum "I'm Shy, Mary Ann, I'm Shy." A few uneasy minutes passed. The triquetrum sulked.

"Tiny premium, if you ask me," Mrs. Cullinane eventually said, adding a deep sigh. "About your doctor, I mean, Mrs. Shoe."

Mrs. Proby had now cooled off and renewed everyone with a newscast. "I hear the doctors in America won't operate unless a patient has eaten money," she said. "They play golf, and all their wives bob their noses."

"My doctor never plays golf," said Mrs. Shoe.

"What is your doctor's name, The Cripple Hermit of Malvern?"

"Crapman. Dr. Irving."

"His Noseship? A bobbed nose there, the wife *and* him," snickered Mrs. Proby with fruitful incivility and leaned forward in a kind of grim hunker. Suddenly she grew serious. "They'd nick the wallet off Good Father Hodge, you give them a chance. They eat cardboard. Their mothers use paper underwear, to save." Mrs. Proby leaned forward again in a revealing gesture of semi-secrecy, balancing her cigarette, as she did, on an ashtray of fat white ceramic advertising Watney's Red Barrel. The ladies came together in what looked like a rugby scrum. "I say," she continued in a low voice, "I say send those devilish awful Hebrew Jewish People from Israel right back where they live, with those beards and pained expressions and stovepipe hats, like the pictures in the Bible, even if it *was* written there, is what I think. They're into the woodwork, never you mind Threadneedle Street, and false as dicers' oaths, milking us white, and, let me tell you, sooner than you think we'll be burying every poor dead Englishman, pudd'nhead though he may be, in nothing but potted-meat tins and lowering him into bogwater on the Isle of Dogs without so much as a three-day deacon on hand to say ta-da." Mrs. Proby puffed her cheeks, fighting, as she was, a bulb of rising gas. It passed away in a rumble.

The fat waitress bustled over to the snug with three drinks on a tray, set it down on the table, and mumbled a perfunctory, "Seven and three, then." Each dropped her coins into the girl's hand.

"I'm the Guinness," Mrs. Proby said. The other ladies cooed and eased their drinks from the tray. The waitress paused a bit, rubbed her nose, and coughed. Nothing happened; she slid the tray away with a slight hiss and walked back to the bar, with seven shillings and three old pennies. The ladies each raised her glass an inch.

"Shillings in your sock," said Mrs. Cullinane.

"Love and a kiss/and a man for a tryst," Mrs. Shoe giggled, blushed, and her lips formed into a red bow.

"Elizabeth Alexandra Mary of Windsor and our own," said Mrs. Proby. "Full stop." They clinked glasses and drank. "Tasty, this," said Mrs. Cullinane. "I find Dubonnet can often get rather fruity. Whereas, you see, I like a happy medium: *dry* but with a grape feeling in it, too. I won't touch it if there is shaved ice in it, however. They flit through me like fish. I don't know what I'm trying to say." Mrs. Proby, having glugged two fast mouthfuls, wheezed, coughed, and her tongue flew out. She slapped at her neck. "Is it your liver, dear?" Mrs. Cullinane asked, a winsome expression on her face, her lips pursed worriedly above her m-shaped chin.

"Not a word. My liver's as right as the mail," Mrs. Proby managed to say; then she swiveled her head and barked until her eyes watered. "Only a furball in the throat," she sputtered in the midst of the spasm, her face the colour of ox-blood. She looked like the Dong with the Luminous Nose.

"Lord love a duck," said Mrs. Cullinane.

"My doctor is too busy for my throat," repeated Mrs. Shoe.

"You'll want to watch that throat," said Mrs. Cullinane.

"I tried. He told me to suck a mint humbug."

"I meant Mrs. Proby."

"Oh."

Mrs. Shoe smiled sadly.

The door of the saloon side of the pub opened, and a large sandy-haired Irishman punched through to the wooden bar in his gum boots; he wore a paddy cap, and a folded newspaper was stuffed into the right pocket of his mouse-grey trousers, partially evident through a stained, flapping mac. Mrs. Proby registered an obvious disesteem with a slug of Guinness and, through an eructation that spattered several drops of foam, grumbled, "Stinks of the bog." Mrs. Cullinane held her glass to the light and addressed it quietly, "I've seen a hundred faces like that lying in the puddles in Camden Town every Saturday night."

"Smarmy cheapjacks," said Mrs. Proby. "Mr. Proby used to say there's no bank on earth with thicker doors than an Irish head."

"They eat sandwiches they take out of their trouser pockets," said Mrs. Cullinane.

"They have no work over there," said Mrs. Shoe. "The Labour

Government says they're good with a shovel. And so they pack up, tummy and tosspot, and breeze right over here from Seven Dials to Hornsey Rise just to find, well, *ditches,* don't they? I mean, I suppose I'd be right along with them were I good with a shovel."

"Oh, but don't you find they just out and buy everything on Hire Purchase, become general lay-abouts and all?" Mrs. Cullinane ran a finger around the rim of her glass. "They're cute, say what you will."

"Shuttlecocks," said Mrs. Proby, rapping the table, "of course they're cute. Cunning as bissets would be more like it, wouldn't it? It shakes my goddam foot, forgive me. And it will be on good St. Geoffrey's Day in the Land of Never before we see an end to all those grog-blossomed faces disembarking on the Liverpool docks with their fiddler's money and forty-eleven youngsters, nappies, and plans, I fancy, for eight dozen more, all to be had, mind you, for a common thrupenny bit." It makes me faint—*ill*—WRETCHED—**MAD!**"

"You'd think people would have enough of—" Mrs. Cullinane went dramatically silent.

"That? You bet your life," Mrs. Proby pronounced. "Our sow has pigged with a vengeance."

"It's all to do with this *fertility thing,*" said Mrs. Shoe. Mrs. Cullinane paused, scanned the room, and nodded.

"Well, the bed, isn't it?" Mrs. Cullinane allowed herself to be frank. She was among friends. "I mean, don't children and fertility *really* go back to the bed?" She was zeroing in.

"Irish whist, they call it," Mrs. Proby hocked out a crooked laugh and stopped short with a sober thought. "Well, you see, there you have your Catholic: mud on the hocks and an egg in the nest, say no more. The poor ignorant things can't be out of bed ten minutes before the Pope rings them up and says, 'Get on with it, hear!' so what happens is, they're back on the kip producing at full belt and hot as a tinker's monkeys, without giving so much as a farthing's worth of thought to ripping out the bally telephone. What do they think a woman is, for mercy's sakes, a bloomin' *valve?*" Mrs. Proby blew down her snout a blast of exasperation. She lighted the middle of her cigarette.

"The blacks are the ones that bother me," said Mrs. Cullinane, "lazy as doorknobs and ne'er-do-wells on the Queen's dole, without so much as a by-your-leave. All jumped-up and eating nothing but bread-and-drippins and kittycat meat as well, I hear."

"They're furious in their pursuit of women," said Mrs. Proby, watching the black smear on the cigarette. "A remark, I think, which explains itself."

"Awful, awful, awful, awful, awful, awful," said Mrs. Cullinane. "Really, it's awful."

"Asians eat hemp," Mrs. Shoe joined in.

"Pardon me, they pinch their wives," Mrs. Proby warned, "and hit them on the bubbies with perfumed sticks. I think we can call that peculiar if we're going to call it anything, can't we?"

Mrs. Shoe agreed here. "Look at the children. That's how one tells, you look in their eyes: all filmy and yellow as wet hay from the first day of spring to Boxing Day. Thin as sticks, to boot. You want to go up to these Asian youngsters in the street and say, 'What have you been eating, *crayons?*' I saw one last week down to Ickenham, small as a cod. The children: that's how you tell.

"You're dead right," added Mrs. Proby, reinforcing her friend with the écart of a lifetime's observation.

"That they eat hemp?" Mrs. Cullinane wiped some wine from her nose.

Mrs. Shoe was not sure. "Well no, really, I suppose that they're hungry. You know what they say: Want Not and You Won't Be Found Wanting. Isn't that in the Hymnal or something, Mrs. Proby?"

"Rubbish, Mrs. Shoe." A diapason broke through the *vox humana*. Mrs. Proby sat bolt upright. "We've been the world's breadbasket since time began. Keep that up and we'll have to turn Parliament into a bakery, and there'll be a soup queue into Whitehall as long as the Burma Road. I think it's a frost and a disgrace." She drained her glass to prove it and ran her tongue in a circle through her mouth.

"Awful," said Mrs. Cullinane.

Touching a finger to her chin, Mrs. Cullinane pondered the frightening aspects of seeing a bread line five miles long filled with beggars, schinocephalic pygmies, gypsies, old men in tatters, imported grobians teetering on the edge of some evolutionary mishap, and Negroes with eyepatches and their bronze-age cutlery, stropped, blood red and as long as broom handles, all marching with their ferocious wives and polydactylic offspring into Buckingham Palace where, in a stroke, they would chew past the carpets, do the buttery, weasel into the state bins and wardrobe, and devour everything in sight, up to and including the Queen's Candles. She came to a quick decision and sat back quickly. "Well, why throw the helve after the hatchet? Give them mince and they want quince," she said, sadly shaking her head.

"Honest," said Mrs. Cullinane.

"And truly," Mrs. Shoe sighed. "I don't know why we just don't build pens for them."

"You can't get the wood nowadays," said Mrs. Proby, her face as crooked as a pastry wheel. "What, somebody told you you could get the wood? You just can't get the *wood*."

"Still," replied Mrs. Shoe, "it'd be much better than tenting out, as I'm told they do, with all the foxes and midges up there in the Pennine Crags. There'd be an odour coming up, I should think, that would turn the world around. And then some."

"It's like catching wind in a cabbage net."

"Aye, there's where the shoe pinches," muttered Mrs. Shoe as she sloshed an inch of Babycham to and fro in her glass and watched the motion, without much reaction. She was coming around.

Mrs. Proby slapped the table with take-charge force. "And so say all of us, Mrs. Shoe. I've pinched a shoe or two this morning," said Mrs. Proby, captious and wreathed with simpers. "I've tightened the screws proper to the Chinee on my ground floor, and it will be a blue Thursday in Cornwall before he gets my business again, the bleeder."

Mrs. Shoe finished her Babycham and looked at Mrs. Proby with chagrin. "No, I suppose you're right. One can't mix leaves with grass and come up with a forest." It was something she remembered she read, she thought, in Samuel Smiles' *Self-Help* or possibly Eliza Cook's *I'm Afloat*. Mrs. Shoe suddenly felt a grip on her wrist and Mrs. Cullinane's face an inch from her own.

"There you are, dear, it's all a question of a different crawl of *life*, and that's why Mrs. Proby and I are absolutely shocked to see you princessing through every highroad in and about London as open and carefree as ten vicars. Leave that for the American tourists and the Jews."

"Safety?" asked Mrs. Proby. "It's a kicking shame, that word."

"I believe in safety. And liberty, I think," said Mrs. Shoe.

"Fair words butter no parsnips, I'm afraid," said Mrs. Cullinane.

Disconnected, mutually irrelevant sentences crackled along the communications, post to post.

"Life," replied Mrs. Shoe thinking of the Middle Ages, "is different than before, it really is."

"Well, that's the bone of contention, isn't it? Different. Say the word, it *sounds* different. And if things are different, how can they be the same, see? Do you see? Now we have a good sitdown, watch at the telly, smoke us a cigarette, and once a fortnight press a call," said Mrs. Proby, her forehead corrugated with the worry that the world was not oriented the same way.

"Because this is what we like to do, see?" Mrs. Cullinane felt better. She crossed her hands. "When the going gets tough . . ."

"But what," Mrs. Proby gruffly interrupted, "the Quashees and Pygmies or whatever is tossed your way, they're not only different, they smell like the Freemasons and their queachy back-to-backs. You take a whiff of their gardens sometime. Pee, Yoo: Pew—and I don't mean maybe." Mrs. Proby held her hands out, palms upward, and slapped them down hard. "God strike me pink, we're in for it, this country. I mean, we are *in* for it."

"They think it's the fashion."

"Fashion, shmashion," growled Mrs. Proby. Her corns were shooting. "They eat queer dishes, write upside down, and what-not. Peddler's French on the one hand, St. Gile's Greek on the other. They say they can't even swear an oath on the Good Lord's Bible in the courts; they have to blow out candles or break saucers so people will believe they're not lying, the sneaks. Now, you see, who gains?" Mrs. Proby knocked a tattoo on the table and said: "I'm off to the movies."

Canikins clinked one final time.

Mrs. Shoe was leaning forward as Mrs. Proby rose. "So you told the Chinaman where to get off?"

Mrs. Proby winked like the sly fox. "If I didn't," she said, her eyes half-lidded with the tracelet of a smile in them like the seductress Phryne's, "may I turn into a titmouse and go live in a teacup in South Wales, which," she added, "God forbid."

"Very trotty of you, dear," said Mrs. Cullinane, pulling the pub door open. The cold air and dark sky held. A fog now hung over the streets like a nimbus, so thick one could have stuck a broomstick in it and it would not have fallen down.

"Think so?" asked Mrs. Shoe.

"Thought so," Mrs. Proby proudly confessed.

"Think so?"

"Thought so."

Mrs. Proby reminded the ladies of the ham dinner, pecked each of them with a kiss in an open space above the shoulder, roughly near the cheek, and bustled like a Christmas turkey across Mossop Street, up Pont Street, and toward the bus stop near the Cadogan Hotel.

IV

In the dim shaft of a doorway, set off in a mews past which Mrs. Proby swiftly moved, a small figure stood in the shadows, a dirty grey hat pulled down like a filthy bowl on his head, his hands in his pockets, and tucked beneath his right arm a black oblong box. He was as inconspicuous as the urine stains, used condoms, and gnawed cigarette butts which brought to the doorway more stink than notice: Mr. Yunnum Fun watched.

The tall metal arch on the corner where people queued up for buses was virtually empty, except for a very pretty girl with black boots and wearing a sort of black Victorian cape, around which was wrapped a multicoloured collegiate muffler thrown over her shoulder. She wore a miniskirt and was pencilling marginal notes in a green paperback book. A large red double-decker bus with No. 22 on its screen swung around the corner and lurched to a stop with a thin screech. Mrs. Proby lifted her coat, grabbed the support bar, and stepped aboard, moving slow as an eggwife's trot down the aisle of the bus. She sat down by a window and smacked her lips. The girl skipped up the rubber stairs. As the bus began to depart, the small man dodged from the doorway onto the bus and scuttled up the stairs like a dark, angry crab. The girl instinctively, her pencil in the air, turned to see who was sitting behind her, especially since she felt a hot, fetid snuff of air ruffle her hair several quick times. The small man sat rigid as a screw; two eyes glinted menacingly from a face that looked like a pan of failed cornbread. The girl stood up and went down the steps and took a seat opposite a fat lady whose arms were crossed sort of triumphantly and who was smacking her lips.

Anybody sitting on the benches near Hyde Park Corner or stepping about the foot of the Wellington Arch would never have noticed, so familiar it was, the rushing bus that wound its way through the teeming colony of cabs, scooters, and traffic, into Piccadilly; nor would have anything of the extraordinary been found in the passengers aboard: the heavy white-pink face of an English lady flat against the window on the lower tier, a dirty hat pulled over a greyish-yellow face pressed like a mat on a pane seven feet directly above her on the upper.

Mrs. Proby snapped open her purse, took out a sixpence, and paid the conductor, an Indian with a small goatee and a bright white smile set in perfect harmony against his smooth brown skin. "Tivepence," Mrs. Proby snuffled. The conductor cranked out her receipt, wrapped it in a penny, and handed her both. "Wery vell," the Indian smiled as he lurched toward the back of the bus. "Very well, my fanny," said Mrs. Proby with a scratch of annoyance. It was then that Mrs. Proby noticed in her handbag the movie ticket returned to her the afternoon before. A happy synapse took place in her mind: she suddenly decided that she would go back to the cinema, sit on throughout the whole film, to the end this time. "My bubble's not for bursting," she repeated to herself in a loud voice. The girl sitting across the aisle sat straight up and appeared nervously disgusted; she slammed her book shut and watched the buildings zipping by.

Fine, Mrs. Proby thought to herself, there was time for the matinee, a quick bus back home to cook the ham, and the added glory—in her own eyes, in Mrs. Cullinane's, in the world's—of English stick-to-it-iveness by dint of further proof in the face of fear. England expects, Mrs. Proby recalled Nelson had said, every man to do his duty. That applied to women, she reminded herself, for who that fought at Trafalgar had not been born of woman? "*You?*" Mrs. Proby angrily asked the girl sitting opposite her as she surveyed the exposure of her legs. The girl peacefully stood up and, making an obscene gesture under her cape, walked haughtily and undismayed to the front of the bus. Mrs. Proby chuckled crazily. Everything was perfect. She stepped off the bus.

On the street a pale, hollow-cheeked young man with afflicted eyes—an evangelist who looked like a pair of pliers—handed Mrs. Proby a throwaway, a single sheet which headlined in large type: "Where Will You Spend Eternity?" Mrs. Proby snorted and sent the sheet into the wind. "I'll take it right here, duckie. And a thousand pounds to a gooseberry that that is just where it *will* be."

A thin soot of rain had begun to fall. Mrs. Proby whipped over her grey hair a transparent plastic headcover and, with a halting gait of jerks and starts and fury, beat it over to a nearby tobacconist for two packs of tipped Players, a box of matches, and the sweet narcotic of three Cadbury's Fruit-and-Nut Bars: the innutritious artillery of the easily appeased. A dirty grey hat, invisible to Mrs. Proby, bobbed up and then down behind a posting box not ten feet away. She scampered into the theatre.

The theatre, with its smell of weak lilac and cheap caporal, was the perfect hush in soft red lights that Mrs. Proby loved: funereal, anonymous, the nethermost retreat where the tired, amorous, and lonesome could sleep or fondle or expatiate in ones or twos or threes, far from the madding crowd and unbothered in the reliquary of pure imagination. Mrs. Proby walked past a short arcade over the top of which a sign read "Mind Your Head" and, following the direct line of the usherette's beam, padded down the soft carpet and into her seat, where, after stuffing her plastic headcover into her coat, she rearranged herself with one fat leg tucked under her bottom and the other dangling in a manner which indicated mitral regurgitation.

Mrs. Proby bit into her first sweet in the middle of a highly coloured, animated cartoon: a black silly-looking duck, with a collar of white feathers, was standing on a bathroom sink and whistling a tune while lathering his reflection in the mirror. Then, stropping a straight razor, the duck proceeded to shave the mirror with delicacy, oohs and aahs, and the increasing relief and sense of freshness of the newly shaven clean. Suddenly, a huge humanoid body, visible from the shoulders down, lumbered onto the screen and stood behind the duck who happily continued his shaving, humming and whistling. The arms of the body crossed in the patience that is a danger sign. The duck, seeing the humanoid reflected in the mirror, did a double take, and, as a light bulb appeared and flashed over its head, smirked and pointed to the half-shaven reflection in the mirror. The arms fell and a massive fist crashed into the mirror, shattering the glass, and a loud human howl followed. A red circle closed in on the screen and zeroed in on the duck doubled up with laughter and malicious quacks. The cartoon ended to random applause. Mrs. Proby slapped her hands together twice in amusement, but a question intruded: why, she wondered, did they never show the *heads* of human beings in the cartoons? It was not the first time it had occurred to her. Mrs. Proby was now into her second sweet. I'm delighted, she thought.

The balcony, high above, swooped into a dark ellipsis to where the eye of the camera sent out a widening cone, filled with

47

smoke, of jumping prismatic combinations and riddled the screen with colour and movement. No one was about. Mr. Yunnum Fun stepped cautiously down each carpeted step to the front row, running along in front of which a much-thumbed bronze rail passed the whole length of the balcony. He inched forward slowly, peered down, and spanned the audience with a kind of mathematical radar, in concentric semicircles: children directly below; two men on the right, coats in their laps; a group of teenage girls far to the left, all tucking into ice-cream sandwiches; an older boy with long hair, his feet hung over the seat in front of him. It was dark, very dark. Mr. Yunnum Fun blinked. He watched patiently. His small head moved slowly and confidently from row to row, from seat to seat, just as if, in tracing along a continuous rope of pearls, one should be startled by the discovery of a bead so base that one would wonder how it could possibly have escaped detection. There: the bead was found. Yunnum Fun sat down devoid of emotion, wiped his hands on his coat, and placed the oblong box in his lap. He watched.

The movie had begun: a full screen, stained in a deep jelly red, began to drip away in vertical collops and slow ooze, and, to the accompaniment of atonal wooden clacks and the ping-pang of Oriental drums and strings, was revealed, in the distorted size of wide-view, the enormous, menacing face of Fu Manchu. A blue mist of cloud curled around the head, his eyes shut, and, with the crash of a shattering gong, the hint of a cruel smile played around his mouth. The eyes slowly opened. Mrs. Proby slid her leg out from beneath her bottom and grabbed for a cigarette. Her third match lighted it.

There was to be no funny business: Fu Manchu, from his throne of gold inlay, ordered right off with an incomprehensible monosyllable and a pointed finger three bald Mongols to abduct a rich old English lady (hyphenated surname, photographs in close-up) and bring her back to him. The finger curved and indicated, in the fashion of a vermilion-tipped dowsing rod, the spot directly in front of him. He tapped the spot with an embroidered slipper. A sloe-eyed Chinese girl, her skirt split to her third rib, purred up to Fu Manchu's elbow. He kicked her onto the floor, but she loved him for it, she loved him for it. The camera quickly moved in on the skirt, over the legs. Then Fu Manchu clapped his hands and a bulb-headed Chinese servant entered bearing a tray, upon which sat two pieces of hewn ibex horn. Fu Manchu grabbed the two objects and jammed them together, making a pipe, which the servant speedily lighted, bowing awkwardly, because backwardly, out of the room right afterwards. As Fu Manchu puffed, a pensive evil expression spread over his countenance, and a poetic haze was simulated on the screen by means of a semi-opaque camera lens of purple, green, and sepia. Images flattened, distorted, distended. The ping-pangs were now hysterical, as was one wild boom of thunder.

"Opium," Mrs. Proby blurted out in unmusical reflex.

"Oh for chrissakes," said a man two rows in front of her who had turned around and glared.

"Go pee in your knickers," Mrs. Proby yelled.

The close dark of the balcony had no effect on the immaculate precision with which Yunnum Fun unlocked his black box. He dropped the key into his pocket and carefully lifted two black ivory tubes out of the green velvet interior, closed the box, and placed it quietly on the floor directly between his two small feet. Then, with surgical delicacy, he neatly screwed the two pieces of black tubing together, making of the conjunction a sort of long, hollow wand. He glanced to either side of him, lifted it, and peeped through the open space at the end like a rangefinder, where on a certain point below came into focus, just above a thick ring of smoke, a blocky, cuboidal head. Yunnum Fun then dipped into an inner pocket of his coat and withdrew a tiny sack

from which he preciously lifted a small pellet: a corrosive
sublimate of letharge, orpiment, and stramonium, hardened into
a microscopic ball, touched with a drop of aconite, and shaped
to a pin. He clasped it in his hand. He watched. He waited.

Mrs. Proby wondered, at this point, if she were in any shape
for her ham.

Fu Manchu, his finger supporting his cheekbone, leaned back
onto his throne like a bored king. A gong, three kowtows: and
the bald Mongols entered, carrying over their right shoulders a
large Oriental carpet rolled into a cylinder like an enormous
anchovy. All the while, in the role of a kind of town crier, a
slant-eyed attendant lord, in silver pajamas covered with mini-
ature pagodas done in spangles, recited from a scroll of rice paper the lady's proscription (a dossier of her crimes, doubtless),
an *afflatus* breathed through with unintelligible but flowery
Chinese subjunctives. It sounded, Mrs. Proby tried to tell herself, like her letters of complaint to the dry cleaner. She spat, for
she had just at that moment fired the wrong end of a filter-tip
cigarette. The burnt smell of synthetic toast or galoshes in
flame sickened her. Mrs. Proby had begun to perspire for some
time now. The ham was off, for sure.

The homily, jagged with invective, ended. Fu Manchu again
clapped his hands: in perfect sequence, the three bald accessories
stepped a shade to the left, simultaneously dropped the rug to
the level of their six large extended hands, and, then, threw it
with a heave and a grunt flapping toward the center of the
throne, where, after completely unravelling, it deposited in a
squat and rubbery heap a blue-haired old English lady, bound,
muffled, spavined. The woman struggled. Fu Manchu rose and
tore from her throat a diamond-studded, collarwide necklace,
dangling it from his fingers over her nose, over her navel. The
girl beamed like a lotus. The servants folded their arms.

Mrs. Proby Gets Hers

Mrs. Proby stiffened, gripped the armrests of her seat. Her jaw moved.

From the folds of his silk cowl, Fu Manchu slipped out a chopstick and drew it across his hands. The sloe-eyed girl salivated. The English lady gnawed hysterically at her gag, her eyes blazing like zircons, her little feet kicking the floor rapidly like a metronome gone insane. Fu Manchu moved closer to her, one slim eyebrow crooking into a perfect caret in his no-nonsense, veridical way as he examined the circuit in the shell of the fashionable lady's ear, pinched it, pulled it as wide as a small flag. He gripped the chopstick like a dagger, and his face shook like a wobbling blanc-mange. Mrs. Proby, ready for murder, opened her mouth wider and wider. Her face was washed of all colour, and an involuntary leverage was lifting her slowly from her seat.

Quickly, Yunnum Fun slid the small pellet into the opening of the ivory tube, and it rolled like a pea down into the chute until it hit the flat of his thumb, plugging the other end. The brass rail in front of him steadied and made firm the weapon on a ruled line now trained with geometric trim on the closed point of the angle between side and diagonal in the plane through which passed, one hundred feet below, the wretched vertices that were ranged in on, for the final time, the one perfect spot in the fatty tissues of Mrs. Proby's neck.

Fu Manchu drove the chopstick into the ear of the English lady, like a good door closes: clean. Yunnum Fun took aim and blew hard.

An instant: Mrs. Proby was full on her feet: hypotrophied, an automaton saturated in her oils and perspiration and galvanized into the ready suck of a howl, an imperative bellow cut and formed into her throat but buffered by an eightieth of a second. She never said a word. The pin caught her silently and neatly one inch below the lobe of her right ear and artfully sliced into the web of medial, cutaneous nerves and the intercostal veins of the cervical vertebrae. Her eyes squinted, bulged the colour of white fishbone, and squinted again.

Mrs. Proby sat down dead.

A smooth calm and imperturbability made itself felt in the dark; Yunnum Fun sat in the silence, very still. A pale light shone from his eyes. He was tired, but he had been tired for years. The many mysteries hidden from the world and concealed from the often self-deceived had, so too, kept him hidden from the very world in which he found himself, too old to ask its secret, too tired to deceive, and so he smiled at the irony that mystery plays on itself and the mystery of that irony. Defeat? Defeat *is* before it was, yes, but surely never to be acknowledged either by useless remembrance or howls for quarter. Life was short; hope, long; opportunity, fugitive; experiment, delusive; judgement, difficult; and, especially, was outrage vain. Another smile crossed his face as a thought crossed his mind: my how is not necessarily their how, nor is theirs mine.

Mr. Yunnum Fun unscrewed the black ivory tubes, replaced the pieces into the slots of green felt, and shut the box. The Anglicide was over. He locked the box, slipped it under his arm, and shuffled out of the theatre into the cool, inexorable rain. He threw his theatre ticket stub into the wind. Then he pulled on his dirty grey hat and waited under the tall metal arch where people queued for buses. He waited. He watched. "Simple," said Yunnum Fun as he sat on the No. 22 bus which took him back to the Brompton Road roundabout, where he lived. It was his neighbourhood.

CHILDE ROLAND

*Montes parturient; nascetur
ridiculus mus.*

—Horace

2

I

Once upon a time, in the
heroic days when Harold Harefoot ruled
the island, it was all a dark, pathless wood: trees shot
up like towers from the beige expanses of forest marsh once zigzagged like the cardiogram of a bad heart by freshets, green din-
gles, and small bights of slub and oozing mud. Now, a stitchlike
ramble of shortcuts was required through that densely populated
section of London stretching in crooked, accidental streets all the
way from Houndsditch to Hyde Park—but Roland McGuffey
finally arrived. At the extremity of the park, he looked an odd
child in all that space, and he came to a halt in a dirty shadow,
swept his eyes up toward Marble Arch, entrance to nowhere, and
immediately blew a blast of hot air through his stacked fists. It
was a cold dark Sunday.

"This goddam weather," he grumbled, squinting up through
his hair. It was a strange remark. Roland was not given to reflection.

A handchime, presage of ice cream, sounded in a ripple of
metallic pips. The jolly funstop, a Mr. Whippy van buffed cream
and pink, was residentially pulled alongside the kerb. Whence
the familiar tocsin. A little snuff-coloured man, a Pakistani,
pencil-thin and lost in a stiff white service uniform, stood gazing
into space and rocking abstractly in his frayed plimsolls which
quite openly failed to shelter his toes, thrusting out, as they did,
like fat yellow slugs from the mouseholes and chipped rubber.
He wore a black plastic bow tie. A white leather captain's hat
swam oversize on his trapezoidal head which sprouted out of his
thin neck like a wood cep. He came to recognizable life only
when he tried to catch the attention of the immediate world,

which he did, occasionally, with a mechanical and soullessly un-reflective shake of his bells, a tinnitus of frightfully unmelodic and leaden binks that resembled, more than anything else, the dead rattle of sea shingle. Suddenly, a far more ominous noise split the air, for Roland, rounding the side of the van, had sent his hand slamming flatly against its tin side with all his might.

"*A Winkie!*" he hooted.

The attendant, gasping for a breath of scream, shot into mid-air and juddered to the ground, twitching and tightly gripping his ear. He swallowed, his heart having bulged to his mouth from the merciless jolt, and ran a cachexic finger down a painted sign that listed the available treats.

"Jolly Jellies, Choc Ice, Squeezie Cups," the Pakistani managed, "Cornish Splits, Ripple Sticks, or Fruities, please."

"The Winkie."

"We are not having the Winkie." A hand-washing motion followed in silence. "Such are consumed."

Roland, with thumb and forefinger, pinched his eyes tight with weary impatience, and immobile, crotchety, poised there like a griffin, he spoke from under his hand.

"Give us the Winkie."

"Otherwise," rejoined the little man with sterling control, "Cornets or Wafers only."

"I hate Cornets or Wafers."

"Leave it or take it, sir."

"I'll take it, dearie," snapped Roland.

"Whom, the Cornet?"

Roland McGuffey leaned into the Pakistani's vision and drop-ped out two words, incinerated as soon as pronounced. "The Winkie."

"Impossible."

"*You*—" The imprecation held. Roland looked away, then back to the Pakistani, appraising him through an exercised slit at the edge of his right eye and coyly advancing a question, as he did, with the subtlety of roundabout surmise. "You, ah, Mr. Whippy, then?"

"The attendant of," the little man sighed.

Repetition, among other things, is predictable, and this kind of thing went on all the time, though, to be sure, it was usually a question put forth in the windy innocence and naïve lisps of babyfaced pre-pubescents in rompers, their eyes as wide and bright as beryls, who infallibly saw the driver as captain of The Good Ship Lollipop or, turnabout, Mr. Whippy. The name was legend, of course—the motto, "Yippee, It's Mr. Whippy," stained in perfect assonance on a waving pennant above the van and gleefully echoed just as it was written by those for whom, miraculously enough, the alphabet itself was as yet incomprehensible. In any case, the Pakistani, his unaffected pluck hidden by his deceptively submissive deadpan, wisely desisted from playing the game—or, better, he played it to perfection. His answer satisfied both the fantasy and fact. No ambiguity, it simply chalked a conclusion to a syllogism not his in the first place. He jiggled his change nervously and looked away. He had had one look at Roland. Two were not required.

Roland's was a sharp young English face: peaky, unamiable, suspicious. There was no shine to the cheek. It had a sallow appearance, drawn, spotted by a rash of comedones near the mouth which was hardly improved by a rather savage case of asymmetrical dentition. A pair of gooseberry-coloured eyes (one disfigured by a squint) were framed by two large, not overly clean, ears— somewhat elongated, elfin—and, quite like Pinocchio, out pointed a long white nose. His body looked one continuous bone, instead of flesh, exhaling, as it did, however, a smell damp and unsubdued: the unaromatic, at best quasi-camphoraceous, whiff of one who was a trifle heterodox in the matter of clean linen, smoked compulsively, and frequently handled strong eyewatering disinfectants and utilitarian soaps, disagreeably tangential, this last, to a painful year-round dose of scrotitis against which, so far, a whole pharmacological armoury had proven sadly ineffectual. Succinctly, Roland looked like a cruel broom.

Bad luck dogged him, like the foolish song that has been, with its irreverent chicane, tripping through one's head since infancy. Roland more or less always showed himself down at the socks, perhaps for want of mothercare or some kind of agnatic pressure, living, as he did, on that limited but rather elastic income, his wits. He lived alone. In his sixteenth year, his parents had divorced each other, simultaneously of course themselves, and, *sequitur*, Roland, and then (*post hoc ergo propter hoc?*) met tragic ends: his mother took to female wrestling, was blinded by a flying chip at the Penywern Arena, and later disappeared—that regrettable but certainly logical correlative that inevitably attends upon those who grope—somewhere in the Laxative Islands; his father died on holiday in Blackpool (picnic, kipper bone). Roland then took a single room. But he managed, he managed.

"Have I failed to mention Drum Tubs," the Pakistani piped up in the awful silence that was characterized by a thematically abusive stare, "which we have in abundance?" Roland made no answer. The Pakistani, nervously rubbing his hands over his arms now turning from brown to whitish-smalt in the cool air, flashed as best he could the exorable smile he hoped might be taken for either stupidity or goodness or naïveté—anything devoid of possible implication would do. "My, my, how I could tell you how very many people are satisfied by the Drum Tub. I have received letters on it."

"Wow," said Roland dryly, bringing up and discharging past his shoulder a jetlike flume of mucus. Then he pointed to a cone with a knob of chocolate twirlie painted triple-size on the side of the van. He wanted it. He patted into place a lock of hair he had just combed in the fly-window and then took the cone. He halved it in a bite.

A pale transparent, almost eastern light occasionally slivered the clouds and played in winks over the distance of the park which looked like a garment of diverse cut, torn here and there by boulders and ripped by gravel paths, as if along its threads.

"Thruppence, right?" he asked as he shoved the other half away, garbling his words through a gob of thick ice cream and flapping some uningested goo from his thumb as he backed away from the movement.

"Sixpence."

"Thrups, you said!"

"The charge, sir, is sixpence. It is not otherwise." The law of Excluded Middle was a comfort.

Roland bore at him through his smirched eyes. Seconds passed, long as an afternoon. It was a case of brinkmanship. There was now an imperceptible grimace on the little man's face, but the inborn civility, it seemed, of thousands of years of tribulation held it firmly as a mask against which the chipping fury of vicissitude could not make so much as a dent or even the least furrow of scoring rage. The silence held, held.

"My friend, sir," the attendant offered wistfully, moving a bit closer and pulling demonstratively at his thin cotton sleeve, "it is my duty to make one's both ends meet, do you not understand? Is it or is it delicately not a question of financial money, please?"

Roland wiped his hand across his face and smirked. A sudden bolting swerve of his shoulders seemed that dangerous idiotic prelude if not to the immediate frenzy of jactation before a spin-fit or conniption, then to one's charging off on the run without paying. But the little man feared worse, grabbed out immediately for his wafers, and hunched cruciform, with ever-widening arms, over a pan of vitrescent toffy apples arranged there on a

low shelf of the van. "These bothers," he blurted out, his eyeballs
agonizing skyward, "I don't want all these bothers, my goodness,
dammit."

"Thruppence, you say?"

"Six"—he took a breath—"pennies."

The dissective enunciation was infuriating. Roland bit his lip
white, reached deep into the flue of his pocket, yanked out a
coin, and with a single thrust pitched it on a line directly
through the tiny freezer door: "*Have it your own way!*"

The Pakistani dove for the coin.

"Have it your own farking way," Roland snarled through a
mouth which looked like a rip in the side of a bag. "This time!"

Houndsditch was another country. The area, old brickfields
once, had not changed, at least not transubstantially, for at sometime or other in the past, three or four totally forgettable days in
history—history, perhaps, merely the composite of such days—the
bricks had been hastily thrown together, sloppily limed, and sent
up one upon the other in dreary red blocks, probably in the
vague, long ago days of the pre-unification King Offa, possibly
when grief-laden Edwy walked the earth, or during the redoubtable archonship of Harpocration in the year of the bangle. It was all now a crumbling and smoke-grimed necropolis
in boarded windows, mummified everywhere by old railings,
stagnant air, and cobwebs, where draughty hallways reek with
the smell of stale cabbage, Blakean children weep soot, and
merchants patter with Mammon and make God evanescent. The
mercantile week thereabouts was busy, rather like the First Circle: from Eastcheap to Shoreditch, axeheaded harridans went
slogging by in their hush-puppies, and old ladies like draggled
ducks, with rush baskets and carrier sacks, nosed, bargain-wise,
into the markets of Stepney for hukkabuk, Spitalfields for
bruised vegetables, and into the arcades of Smithfield for low-

priced, if purpureal, cuts of meat. It was like bush-fighting, and for the women it was soldiership they knew well. Every weekday morning as the steam of the world burnt away, their pertussic selves were revealed hobbling across gutters and crouching busily forward into the pushcarts of fabrics, produce, or fowl, with a relish for the contentious and a determination nothing if not evangelical. But on Sunday everybody had disappeared. The moving people hustle, as it were, and once having hustled move on. (That this has been said of fingers is only a synecdoche proving quite the same point.) Silence hung over everything like a nimbus. Sunday—notable especially within the creepy back-narrows spoking out of Houndsditch—was unendurable. It made limbo seem positively Neronian. Roland *had* to get away.

It was part of his Sunday, his walk: prefatory, that is, to his nightly job, a necessary, if perhaps tertiary, contribution to the British labour force, which not overwhelmingly involved hosing down and scrubbing up the coaches and buses in a subterranean garage at Victoria Station, duties he performed with ill-camouflaged scorn and a minimum sense of art. Hyde Park was an alternative to that day of eerie, pestilential calm which threw cold and mystifying personality changes on him and fated, if Sunday be regular, the regular walk—a radical unwind inevitably visited upon him whenever he remained, uneventfully, in the grip of a certain devil, Restlessness. Perhaps it was curiosity. Perhaps it was the result of that arbitrary, furiously ill-defined goad which higgledy-piggledy sent the Dutchman flying, the Jew wandering, the Mariner riming. Or perhaps he was subtly hijacked by some grey, spliced-tongued little daemon lurking within the folds of his cerebellum and suggesting some kind of horrible search and subsequent malediction—a parallel, say, to that obsessive-compulsive moment alone in the crib when the child, whispering darkly to itself, wildly cracks open the rattle and, filled with the thrill that comes only on the edge of disgrace, stares with bugging eyes and cruel joy at the small bead found inside. "It all remains to be seen," Roland had often said in contexts as many and as varied, "as the baboon said when he shat in the sugar bowl." Roland kept joke books in his room.

Comparatively, the stews of Houndsditch the night previous seemed a veritable Shangri-la, for a Saturday night at *The Drum and Monkey*, a cellar pub in a nearby black sunless mews, localized an erratically cheerful, if flinty, compensation to any who marched down the steps bellowing for succour, chiefly patrons, however subalternate or unparticular, who were just this side of being capsized by the working week, an importunate thirst, or the crucial urgencies of a not-as-yet thoroughly articulated libido. This was Roland's pub. It was always dark inside, quaking with a 4/4 beat, and fogged through with the cumulative but hardly integrated smells of calcined sausages, overheated bodies, and what seemed like a trace of fowlpest. The room, spread over in photoposters and mushy daubs of psychedelic paint, reverberated in pockets of applause, throbbing music, pulmonic laughter, and the general buzzing of East End scat, a monoglot in refained twists of speech very like the chewing of rope.

The pub boasted The Longest Bar in the World—one of the few hundred. A string of pomaded young men with loose jaws and vulpine faces, wearing just-about-serviceable black suits shiny at the sleeves and revers and vividly smelling of naphtha, sat rivetted to their tables, gravely sucking bitter and popping salted nuts. Off in a snug, three or four semi-defectives, with skin the colour of ship-biscuit and wearing aluminum idents on their wrists, took swipes at and hooted imprecations upon the flashing pinball machines that spread out before them in rainbows of glass, thumb-smudged and stippled with oily smears, each fracas followed by a renewal of deep absorption when, reaccumulating, they would again cramp together in a weird pinch of fellowship, jussling the flippers to the crepitant snaps of chewing gum and common profanities. A chimera of universal appeal was the dartboard, and, in a far corner of the hot low-ceilinged room, a drift of "skinheads" with the phrenological structure of spadoons disagreeably sniped at each other as they clomped around in their cherry-reds, collecting their darts from among the orts and metrics of dirty cigarette butts there on the floor, only to swing around and saunter back to the firing line where, aimless as loons and whistling snatches of "My Old Dutch," they continued to prong the board with rapid gunshot flurries, usually with grins indicative of what seemed hopeless *morbus castrensis*.

The place had remained a club of "Rockers" for years, spinning out, as the jukebox did, the old 45 records (*detto*: "the clutchers and huggers"), each one a pandect of incontrovertible yammer and windsong, that sang, generally, of utopias (ring, dance, moon, you), of existential recusants in leather jackets, and of the wild surmises that always diligently refused to synchronize pain with love, or compromise idealism with reason, all to momentarily swab away from the teenager that bile always so identifiable, those tears the overflow of such hearts, such hearts. And while the music played, enriching motives, the young men would lark about, bumping into poles and barking their shins as they pursued girls in that darkness which so effectively, doubtless for Adam's Fall, retarded a process charity alone forces one to term mating. That managed, dancing followed: a biological interlude spent groping for kisses and vacantly shuffling to and fro in the dirt which burst out like fire in the heat of woodash from the floorboards, at which juncture, it being showtime—for there was a show, a wee exode, a revue —blasts of scorching notes poured over the room like hot magma, roughly in the form of a song shrieked out by the songstress there billed as "Capri"—a nasty little piece of work with a bosom that looked too extensive to be comfortable, sequined ligatures, and a carrot fall which spread out, Medusa-like, in fiery points. She raked the room with a jumping hard-rock number, periodically swinging the microphone through her legs and kicking out lasciviously at the shabby, perforated amplifiers that seemed literally plugged into the four or five pale musicians in snake-skin jackets and bushes of long hair, who accompanied her on their heliotrope guitars. "Soopah! Soopah!" people yelled, "just soopah!" "Gorjus," they howled, "absolutely gorjus!" "Maaaarvelous," they hollered, drooling on their shoes, leaping up, and lurching about like red-eyed poppets to ferret out the toilet, secure a refill, or grab a handful of what one day, though it did not seem imminent, might possibly become an infinite source of nourishment to the infants of a softeyed, motherly dear who on that occasion might be breathing lullabies and answering sooner to the appellation Mother than the pseudonym "Capri." But it seemed bootless to speak of the future. It was Now. It was Saturday night. It was the peak of *divertissement.* And that Sunday followed reinforced only once again that first of first principles which proved mutability constant.

Sunday—how say it?—dawned, the only invincibility it seemed to possess. From its broken tenements, lonely streets, and empty squares had all emotions ebbed, and Houndsditch seemed a limit gone beyond, a kind of stone leprosarium of gutted doors through which the metaphorical inmates, as if suppurating with the afflictive screwworm or helminthiasis, willingly decamped in crawls, belled, as it were, to the nether of their dungeons where, in a sickly and zombie-like *lacher prise* from the weekly obligations that beat them down, they could spoon away their Sunday dinners, suck their dirty pipes, doze half-naked slumped into the sofa, or, without the slightest expectation, stare down silently through old thread-bare curtains with tired gull-like eyes to the streets below which sheered off abruptly at corners and in turn closed off pretty much of their world. Everyone had withdrawn, it seemed, so as not to be intimidated by the intimidating click that snapped them away like the catch of a cheap lock, shut fast and buried hopelessly within those monstrous building projects, tall as the Cities of the Plain, being everywhere winched toward the sky, where each building, disfigured, hulks higher and higher, its shit-coloured self rising into space like a cement Kraken out of the inattentive and varicose earth. It was like a surrealistic dream, as if all the buildings were actually cardboard and, if but tapped, would hurtle down in a spray of dust and scaffolding, revealing a vast desert of grey which reached to the fag-end of infinity.

Roland stood at the crossing, a striped walkover that led to the park itself. Cars zoomed by. A little boy was playing on the pavement nearby. From all appearances, the game he was engaged in involved remonstrating with a small stone in front of him, impugning it, and offering it little nips from a lump of edible frozen water (tinted) on a stick—an example, presumably, of that *faiblesse* whereby under-fives convert inanimate objects into boon companions. The stone, however, did not seem terribly hungry for it, and the little boy continued sucking, making a lapping sound like a bunny.

Thuk! Roland ducked, faked out the goalie on a run, swung left, and it was a sweet right foot long into the nets for the equalizer. He thought he heard the stadium go wild.

"Yoiiieeeeeeeeee!" the little boy wailed, jumping in sudden fright and indignation, for Roland had just punted away—and presumably killed—the stone that for some time now had been incarnated as a turtle.

"Belt up."

The child shook into hysteria now. "Wreeeaaaooooo!"

"Belt up, you dink."

Suddenly, a huge woman appeared with an outsized waist of about sixty, a hair-studded cheek, and a handbag the size of the Goodyear Blimp. It was the child's mother, possibly the turtle's. She pulled the boy to her side and scraped his wet cheeks with a face tissue baptized in motherly spittle, all the while glowering in white stabs at Roland. She fixed her hat, shook her dewlaps, and marched away, her mouth a punt-gun of suppressed obscenities as she passed Roland, while the little boy yanked against her hand, screeching dreadfully from a wet, prune-like face. Roland followed her with eyes lit by neither the shim nor shadow of contrition. He threw back his shoulders and sucked a tooth. "Wicked old brass," he said. Then he farted.

What sanctuary was found from the empty Sunday, for Roland, began in the early morning. The early morning began with the cardinal, rather than ordinal, preoccupation of securing the football results from the sports page which could be quietly slipped, if he was on the street early and unobserved, from the heavy editions tied and humped in the corner doorway of Stoney Lane. It most frequently fell out that Roland was late and was ever grudgingly forced to pay the fat newsboy there, a stuttering half-wit with a mien best described as zoological, who was always pottering around with fistfuls of string and trying to read the Latin inscriptions on the pennies. Upon payment, he always looked up stupidly in acknowledgment from his crazy sockets, while his black grubby mittens, reaching only to the knuckle, slowly wrapped around the coin. Commerce, as ever, raced along in Great Britain.

A long, unsparing hour followed, further sanctuary, in the walk-down toilet (dubbed "the shot tower"), a cold cast-iron street shelter marked "Gentlemen," into which Roland disappeared, and, flashing pages on the stool above his rising smell, he sat and digested the match summaries with approval if he ticked the sheets, or, otherwise, with a disgust that was indicated by vicious spurts of rheum hacked fruitily up the glottis and spat through the open cabinet often missing by a mere windle-straw, and often not, the snuffling bums gathered there, smelling of old petrol, sleeping in circles like partridges, rolling fitful in their rags and urine, and secretly being eaten away by meth, nicotine fumes, and various unnamed diseases. They clapped their chops, sputtered over their crumb-strewn shirts. They barked in the cold from cracked raw faces, scratched against spider-bite, and semiconsciously shoved newspapers further down into their groins to buffer out the damping chill. Finished, Roland would slap his paper into the hopper, take the stairs two at a time, and make for the park, heading west down Cornhill, singing—no, not singing—rather snorting, roughly to a familiar Rugby tune, a tin sing-song:

> Why should we be pore?
> My bruvver 'awks 'is brahn;
> Why should we be pore?
> My sister walks the tahn;
> Farver's a bit of a tea-leaf,
> Muvver's a west-end 'ore
> An' I'm a bit of a ponce meself,
> Why should we be pore?

His was the lyrical mode.

The trip to the park was usually rapid. Once into Cheapside, Roland would quickly produce a small half of a white loaf from his inside jacket; he would turn over toward Ludgate Hill, past St. Paul's Cathedral, munching yeasty wads which he tore off with rude authority, then rolling bits of excrescent dough into sprout-sized pellets, and, dropping them to his feet, he would then trace them off with wild sweeping dead-ball kicks for the Tottenham Hotspurs to the indescribable delight of cheering, but imaginary, crowds. He tacked over the vacant streets that led down to Blackfriars with their foxy smells and putrefactive odours of sludge and cheap meat, and ducked along the long, gummed, beaten upon, and quaquaversal thoroughfares perpendicular to the dark lanes and alleys that rollercoasted down to the brown flowing Thames, sluicing with offal, and gave him the occasional glimpse, through the slits between begrimed warehouses, of the docks where the East End there is webbed with rigging and towered over by gawky, mile-high cranes. And all the way through Fleet Street dropped the bread, a fast cross to the near post, bang!—into the nets.

Into the Strand Roland rambled, punting and heading his soft little footballs, ruthlessly blocking off and feignting at telephone poles wraiths he termed rival halfbacks, and, occasionally, with a thudding heel, sending old barrels (which presumably threatened to break free on a rip into midfield) jouncing expeditiously into the gutter, falling completely upended and spilling in their wake a klaxon of tins, squishy dreck, and indistinguishable rubbish—all done, this, with a savage sense of sport which included weedy, imitative growls for his opponents, huge monocular Welsh cretins, he decided, running around with the stupidity ascribed to giants and salivating in leek-coloured uniforms, each one of whom he bashed with elbows into gibbering moans and easy compliance everytime he passed the reflecting glass of a shop front. Footstalls were closed; the streets were empty of traffic and shouts, pedestrians and taxis, constables, lorries, and bicycles and buses. There was, however, one man who could always be seen: the old hoary cripple, with a nose like the scranlet of a plough and the bulging eyes of a pill bug, who sat on an apple crate in front of Charing Cross Station. He always nodded to Roland, never said a word, but simply pointed off toward the west like a beaked weathervane. But it was of no account. For Roland, it was a solo run to open field, directly to goal—now something less than a mile away.

The twitter of starlings, as he reached Cockspur Street, drew one's attention high above the locked stores and bleak buildings which gave off a sensation of murkiness and grotesque desertion; the ghostly closure seemed the site of petty, merciless secrets and, as well, seemed to prophesy, along with the swift approach of worse weather, the invisible but peccant setting for the hatching of some evil plot such as is generated when no human eye is looking.

Further passage confirmed it all. The subsequent descent into the pedestrian subway, a dark tunnel that beehived with exits to various new viametric directions of the city—and directed Roland toward his last lap—revealed a corollary to that atmospheric malevolence by dint of private and public messages scratched hastily on the walls in weird, almost oghamic print and quasi-literate handscrawl by those for whom the urge to express oneself on a public urinal or any other fertile location was paramount.

An underground wall is invariably the Rosetta Stone of the troglodyte. Roland skated his eyes over the surface of the wall which was scored with calligraphies barbed and illiterate. It was as full as the Personal Page in the *London Times:* pan-sexual suggestions (telephone numbers, trysts, preferences); a sprightly, if vile, series of anatomical studies done in indelible lipstick; single familiar verbs (nouns? adjectives?) spaced out alone; an omeletted reproduction of the Union Jack; the vivid declaration by Edwin of eternal affection for Angelina crossed out to question mark, crossed out to what read like the entire male population from Giggleswick to the lower Americas; unmetrical limericks; lavatorial allusions accompanied with hieroglyphs, predominantly tumescent; lovers' names ballooned in asymmetrical hearts pierced through with shaky arrows; and, finally, in bright chalks, the socio-political proclamations of the chthonic historian burdened with unscrolling his views on immigration and ethnic balance, which tripped in large, semi-uncial slants through descending letters to frantic exclamation: "Down With The Tongs!" "Baboons Out, Now!" "Keep Britain White!"

On this particular morning, Roland quickly slid out the key to his wash locker, spit into his palms, and with both hands diligently bore into the wall, with flaring cuts, shapes that suddenly spelled out:

"Wogs, pack it off!"

Hyde Park, that popular *rus in urbe* escape, where people hied to the world of trees and hopfrogs, spread out its wide acreage in tints impressionist green and whole wheat—a beautiful foliage of lungs for the respiration of all the natural children who, despite the autumn nip, came singing the praises of Pan. A commons, the elms, maples, and old gnarled oaks rose majestic and swaying over the bush grottoes, glades, and planes of dark, bright grass, which, all together, seemed to stabilize the worst of fractured episodes and enfold in the felicitous twits of birdsong and high leafy screens every man to the last: the indigent, curious, incurably peripatetic, or any another who, filled with little absorptions, chose of a Sunday to waffle away the hours in peace.

On the pavement, chestnut sellers stoked their coals, while, nearby, purveyors were selling from large boards neck-chains, souvenir nail files, bangles, wide tenpenny ties, whoopee cushions, and fat little pincushions stitched and stuffed to the shape of Beefeaters. Bitterns cheeped. Bleating children skipped after each other in silly circles, all sticky from pink bouquets of candy floss. A young couple, sharing fig pinwheels and angel fingers from squares of waxed paper, sat under a sycamore, earnestly engaged in a discussion that was obviously a complicated affair of the heart. *Artistes* ambled along, wearing leghorn hats and tapping their walking-sticks. Unmarriageable sisters, arm-in-arm, paraded stiffly up and down The Carriage Road and past the severe flowerbeds, with perfect custody of the eyes, while, across the park, large families, benched along the Serpentine, wolfed down banana and chive sandwiches a half-meter in length and sipped cydrax from paper cups while their siblings splashed nearby, rude juvenescents who zapped their plastic dreadnoughts through the water with noisy roils and hisses. Along the expanse of water, sailboats drifted. And, romping with their nannies, little girls, who looked to a one like Tenniel's hydrocephalic Alice in her white apron, chased their fluffy cats with squeals in silver octaves and hands high in surprise.

The leaves soughed. Down a wide dustpath ran Rotten Row (the *route de roi* of George II): the once fashionable promenade where Nell Gwynn prammed her royal bastards and, later, a walk where prostitutes, so rouged and incarnadine they looked like cherry bombs, ambled slowly along in their Adelaide boots and solicited under the garish gaslight. Now, riders cantered their horses there in the cool early morning. The willing copulatrix, however, could still be found—here, there, in every quoin of the park. The Great Chain of Being went from the advanced voluptuary to the plain "fire-ship," from the broom-riding old tart to teenie girls in glossie paraphernalia, just one step away from menarche, all the way down to the most gruesome of gruesome frigstresses. Foremost in that generic subculture of the titled were the Royal Tarts, then the Bankside Ladies, the Fulham Virgins, and not least—well, perhaps—the accurately, if rather uncharitably, termed "scrubber," the two-bob hop or tupenny upright—neither eponym, however, really suggestive of discrimination, nor, in point of fact, the possibilities of high fortune.

Roland dodged traffic over to the northwest part of The Ring and immediately noticed on his right—perched all alone on a bench, with a half-bottle of woodpecker cider and a plastic transistor radio the size of a lozenge, playing quite loudly—a plump, whey-faced girl, arms folded, and her legs crossed in a short rusty black skirt which fully revealed the iceblue thighs of a majorette, the one mobile foot raised and enticingly waving a figure eight in the wand of a tiny shoe. Spice, as it were, made a living thing. Her hair, teased into a chemical blond nest, wisped down into sparse, uneven bangs which blurred her heavily made-up eyes, arched, obviously, with a piece of rare coal and which, upon closer inspection, revealed the open moonlike face of the pert agitatrix, part obduracy, part infantile cunning: *in nuce,* a Rubens on the way to becoming a Braque. She snapped her chewing gum, and, with a downward smile and sidelong glance toward Roland, blew out a thin pink trifle like the rising bubble through a slice of rubber tyre. It popped. She placed a finger to her mouth in coy surprise. There was no question about it, he knew, her motor was running. Roland turned his head, spat over a cluster of phlox, and walked toward the girl. He made of the hello the hunting call it was.

"You Gert?"

"Rose."

"Not Gert, then, lives in The Cut, over in Waterloo?"

"Rosamund, actually."

"I thought I knew you. I heard the music. I thought I knew you."

The girl shook her head, partly as an indication that she did not *think* he knew her and partly as a bopping accompaniment to the beat through the radio. It seemed a glutinously indefinite mind.

"Little Jimmy and the Tokays," she said, raising the transistor to her ear and bouncing rhythmically to the song. "Flippin' well marvelous, they are. You fancy them?"

"Cor!" Roland snapped his thumb and finger, once. A revelation of some sort was about to be born. "He's a good friend of mine, Little Jimmy there!" He held high an oathful hand.

"Straight as a pound of candles. Comes out to the *Drum*, him, the local. Well, night club, really. We're like *that*." He shot two fingers together. The girl might be from the farmlands. One never knew.

"You havin' me one?"

"Not bloody likely, Gert. I have his albums. Where else would I get them?"

"Rose," she corrected him. "Rosamund, actually."

There you are, thought Roland, a bloody hog-scrubber from Yorkshire or somewhere, noticing, as he did, the cruelly appointed marriage of adenoidal tendencies on top of a North Riding accent. She seemed the type who always moved her lips while reading the agony column. Roland quickly looked her over: not really Snow White, he thought, but that was all right; you don't look at the mantel piece when you're poking the fire, as he often said. Through the process of genetic drift, or simply a backstairs conception of elemental hygiene—clearly the problem was not detergent build-up—she revealed in close-up, skin the offensive colour of toilet porcelain, a slight hydrophobia, a small bust, and spatulate fingernails, raw and black from chronic nail-biting, aligned, probably, to the attendant worries of budget squeeze, pimples, a hateful roommate, and, doubtless, long months of waitressing.

"You a waitress?"

"Was." And long months of waitressing.

Roland then gestured hopefully to the half-empty bottle sitting next to her; she passed it to him. Without pausing, he swung high the bottle of cider and pushed it vertical against his nose as he drained it, wheezed out the carbonation, and flung it into the bushes.

"Made by Japs, aren't they?" He burped. "The Nips?"

"What?"

"Them." Roland pointed to the transistor radio.

"Dunno," she answered. "Never looked really."

"The Jappos, fiendish really, up at all hours of the night and working until crow-pee under their filthy little microscopes, making those piss-sized paper transistors no bigger than a bimp."

The girl tapped the mesh of the little speaker. "Don't work good in the park, this. Gets all buzzy it does. Blinky." She tuned it up. It sputtered.

Her breasts, thought Roland. Flat as a warming pan.

"They could care. They shoot the moon back to Tokyo in Japan there with a nice little pocketful of good English bunce, yours and mine, luv. No sooner that happens, they come back here walking around in their bushy slippers so you can't hear them and begin grinding out a billion more. Look around you. We're rotten for Jappos. You don't *see* them?" Roland snapped, with a gesture that swept the horizon. "All over the shop now."

"Don't bother me none," she replied, delicately plucking a loose eyelash from her conjunctiva, "he got it on the whisper, anyway. Hire purchase and all that."

"Glad and sorry system, eh?" Roland gave out with a dry noiseless laugh, the kind with no lungs behind it, like the chuffing of ashes. Then came a pause. "Who's he, then?"

"He?"

"Him," Roland winked, "the one what give you the radio."

"Well, he's"—she hesitated—"my uncle."

Uncle! Here's Harriet the Chariot, Roland thought, sitting in mid-air, sharking around alone, as wide open as the Birmingham motorway, and with this supposed *uncle* of hers? Tell that to the bleeding Bishop of Ballytrunion when he's out on a toot in June, was what he thought, though when Roland asked her why she had come to Hyde Park she simply fluttered her eyes closed and said she was waiting about for the train to Pidley and was not exactly cruising around if that's what he was implying, she thanked him very much.

At that moment, two grinning Sikhs strolled by, both with cameras slung around their necks. Probably from the Punjab, they passed by the bench, showing a native zeal for an un-checked but healthy self-esteem. The Indian's was always a marked walk: one hand gripped in the trouser pocket, usually the left, they swung along, eyes rather vacant, their right arms also swinging with the regularity of piston rods, all giving the impression that they are wound to a tight spring, like a key clock, and set into motion in lovely, precise tickings. Both of these men wore plaited beards and turbans, one in a suit with a magenta waistcoat, the other the typical mode of Indian dress —a long Russian-collared tunic over white cotton jodhpurs crushed into wrinkles around the ankles into open sandals. Roland followed them with his eyes, staring glacially.

"Look at that. Indian coons, you see them? Right over from Monkey Island in bagsy trousers, proper winkle-pickers, and not a sixpence to scratch their asses with. It sends me up a pole." Roland continued in a rather odd way, for his interest in the world rarely involved the reflections that might change things, which is to say, either his interest or the world. "Thing that gets me is, the law protects them. You hit a nigger, he dies on pur-pose to spite you."

Racial misrule, for Roland, was far and away the worst of the many and world-besotted, inconceivable dooms. His was a reve-lation of England, gastronomically, as an infected cake or rancid pie shoved through with poisoned raisins, rotting currants, and split with dark, suspicious mould.

"Got marvelous rhythm." The girl snapped her gum. "I'll give them that."

"More squeak than bloody wool, I'd say. Bugger them all."

The girl suddenly stopped short, this side of an incipient bubble, and went slack in the mouth. "What about Little Jimmy?"
"Who?"
"And the Tokays. Your friends. They're niggers. They *sound* like niggers."
It was a fissure. Roland threw out his hand matter-of-factly. "Sort of, I guess. What, he autographed a photo for me mate once. Anyway," he added, shifting abruptly on the bench, "that was way back when Pontius was pilot, so who cares."
"*I* don't know, I'm sure," the girl answered, her face as vacant as an empty plate. She snapped open her purse and pulled out a tube of purple lipstick, a bullet-shaped phallus called "Loveshine," and began rubbing it over her lips. "They got a smashing beat. Groovy and sort of African-like. Mysterious, really. I like a mystery. It's not like you *know* everything when there's something you don't know. I don't know, I like a mystery."
"That's because," Roland snorted, "that's because they're all Bolshies is why. Pinks, you see? You think they make those records over in ruddy Sopewell, for chrissakes? Or over in Wormwood Scrubs? They make them in Moscow in Russia is where they make them. The Bolshies what are niggers are worst. Try to touch one of them up for a cup of tea, a kip, or an excuse-me, and it's cheery-bye for you, darling, and I don't mean maybe. They keep microphones underneath their tongues and carry swords in their brollies, the bastards. See, so if you was to give them a jostle, say to nick a couple of needy bob for the night, then—shooooop!—in goes the sharp-o so you don't even feel it, man, and next day you're pissing out of your shoulder blades, you can count on that, don't think you can't. Look, don't tell me, sister. I see them everyday, duffing around down in Hackney Wick or down in the Fruit Exchange, over with the kikes."
Down the walk, then, passed a little Indian in a white suit;

he was carrying a tennis racquet and a valise and moved with an obvious sense of mission.

"The Pansy Patrol," Roland murmured drily.

"Who?"

"Him. A good bashing'd do him up proper. Comb him out." Roland jammed his heel into the pavement and laughed crookedly. "Me mate once did a Chelsea pensioner who give him some lip in a shot-tower on Beak Street. Put the old fart's nose right into parentheses, he did, and better he is for it, I've a mind. Them Indians, you have to watch out, they'll razor you up just for your brass buttons. They're taught that at school. They get rewards for it. They sleep with their mothers."

"I always watch out, anyway," she said with a high muffled giggle.

Roland sat back unimpressed. "Do your level best, do you?"

The girl folded her arms and turned to him. "Now, what's *that* supposed to mean?" Rosamund wasn't born yesterday.

Goddam, thought Roland, real north country: one of those wimps who know nothing from a titfer, and just enough to suds a sink, brown the bread, and scald the grapes or apples in their wretched pies. Or, Roland wondered, is she just fiddling in the woods here? After all, she smelled like a barman's apron, looked like Mother Midnight, and showed no more interest in getting away than the Lady of the Limp.

"Those blokes will go after anything that stands still," Roland explained. "That's what I meant."

"Well," the girl offered mathematically, "it's one thing to watch out, twice another to kick about with them."

"Kick—!" The aposiopesis signified horror. Roland fiddled for words. "Look, back in 1960 or something, I think, I *think*, I seen one of the Tokays in a crapper in Shoreditch? So what am I to do, burst into bloody flames?"

The question hung in the air.

An old man, pulled on a leash by his infirm canine companion
—a tiny Sealyham, which looked like a kidney covered with hair
—zigzagged by, both looking as if they moved on power-induced
artificial limbs. He hobbled shaggily along in screwy directions
and, at intervals, peered for the sun. The sky, a dull gold with
cool tones in middle afternoon and solid as a hammerbeam roof,
now seemed breaking up, broken, and all was now smoked in a
mottled light, a gunmetal wash. Refractory little boys, now
everywhere, were dragging tearfully on their mothers' hands,
bored, tearful, blubbering. Fathers, in various areas, stared dis-
consolately at ruined kites. The afternoon was passing.

"I want to go to the Dilly Bar, and dance," she implied.

"Can't."

"Why not?" She masticated the gum quickly, gnashed a
bubble.

Roland shrugged, sniffed. "Not a tusheroon on me."

In the natural order of things, an effect followed hard upon a
cause. The girl slipped her radio into her handbag and looked
vaguely in the mood to set off.

"Show you the Round Pond, though," Roland asserted,
rakishly straightening out a loose strand of her hair which felt
like a piece of dental floss. He patted her thigh. She didn't flinch.
The compass read bedward.

"Bold as a miller's shirt, aren't we?" she said, looking at him
with her eyes shut. Now was his chance. Roland smiled; he had
held on for the long run, drew the goalie out, and would soon
be in like a ferret, pulling the ball wide of the net with his right
foot, then, whap!—into goal with his left. An unstoppable shot.
Roland, very bucked, turned toward her.

"Come on, time for a Dutch red and a glass."

"Can't."

Came an hiatus.

"Why not?" Roland stood up. Roland sat down. "Now why the hell not?"

"Meeting my uncle."

"Why get angry? Can't hurt by asking, they say, huh?" Roland asked, hurt and angry and speaking suddenly in a low, menacing tone. "That it?" He burned. "Stuff your bloomin' uncle." It was an alternative.

"Uh-uh." She disagreed—and stood up, balancing on her little heels. She headed away, flapping a hand somewhere behind her. Roland was on his feet.

"Rosie the Rivetter," he yelled. *"Rosie the grubbing, bleeding Rivetter, that right?"* She turned and with a sweetly icy face nodded once.

"Rosamund, actually, thank *you*."

Uncle! All bloody flap that was, and Roland knew that within a brace of shakes she'd be all hands to the pump in some cul-de-sac in the Edgeware Road, with those two drum-eared jungle bunnies who walked by, just begging for it. That, for Roland, was the *osculum infame*, roughly, "kissing the devil's fundament." The brain-racking insouciance with which he generally met the world here stung Roland into a cold fury, a splenetic grudge which ripened into a bouncing loath specifically for those smut crazed piratical Asians, roasting with satyriasis and ready with their poison juices to roger anything warm and horizontal, only to send pullulating over the indiscriminate bedsteads of Christendom a witless, sponge-headed progeny of biological variants, all with three breasts and minds like silly putty, conceived to a one in a perfect *Walpürgisnacht* of pithecanthropic howls, reechy innuendo, and drools.

His resentment burrowed in bitterness the geometrical, if underground, trenches of philosophical Patriotism from which, when the whistle blew its warning, he would burst, plumed and armiferous, into the irrepressible English ozone, splintering the air with war cries like sprays of dynamite to call to the barricades, into the fight, all who would outface, and must, this Zulu, this Asian, with his endless streaming hordes, those dark plumed beings of the Middle Air, and buttress all his wrath against that flood which was spilling over the tidemark of the world like an endless tidal wave of paint and staining all an excremental brown. Love Thou Thy Land! *Dieu et Mon Droit!* Into the Valley of Death Rode the Six Hundred!

A howl suddenly tore the sky!

"Speaker's Corner," a side show of hammering hands and spitting rhetoric, had thundered alive. Shrieks jerked everyone into crazy attention and brought people running over each other with furious abandon. This particular area was like a bunch in the fabric of the park, where it seemed all the irregularities in the universe were detectable, thus leaving the useable portion spread wide, unrumpled, relatively pacific. Tourists hopped up and snapped photos in blitzes and sudden pops. Men and women seethed through each other, wrenched into position, blent like muffin mix. So crowded was it that someone might easily have blown another's nose and easily escaped detection. They swayed, fell down, got up, leaped, yelled, and dizzily sang out retorts, insults, and repartee in the yaps and hoots they proudly felt were dialectic. But it was the speakers, the metal of Old England, who simply amazed, for it was singularly this vision-haunted (occasionally beer-irrigated) array of nobodies, filled with the arrogance of disenchanted insight, who, in the war between order and entropy, ran scratching hand-over-hand high into their makeshift boxes, and, flying into diatribes and mighty gusts of Homeric wrath against God, Devil, or anything else that bent their wick, they cast—on a Sunday of rain, on a Sunday of snow—imitation pearls before genuine swine. Roland punched and fought to the front of the wide, shifting assembly.

Woe betide you, as Jeremiah once said, you idiotic bastards! ['Same to you, old boy, with knots on!'] All you so-called yoomans, glimps, toads, half-wits, and rushers-about in society out there looking up at me, why don't you all go out, give yourselves a treat, and get your heads sharpened? ['We use pencils, you nut!'] Why am I up here on this here thingummy, amongst all you pathetic twits, and not down in the Albie Hall with the swells where I should be? To talk to you is why: not about drainage, not about the Chelsea flower show, not about the price of mouse-shit in the Isle of Wight—but about *wogs*!! ['Hogs, you say?'] I have something to say to you about blinkin' wogs! I make no distinctions: chocolate, black, brown, yellow, red, and, if you like, West Indian aquamarine—all the colours in God Almighty's rainbow, in fact, who stink! And what do I have to say, you're going to ask. Well, don't bother asking. I asked. I'll answer, that fair? I say it's bloody high time we go right ahead and tell every one of them to bung off!, to bung right thee hell off! . . .

The invective, a delivery somewhat unprepossessingly short of being Marcoaurelian, was all one man's. He was waving his arms like a tic-tac man, trying to show, presumably, that the homologue on everything was writ large. A scullion of low breed, his face was swollen with erisypelas, blue jowls, and hair, and the collar of his open shirt hung askew, below two dysplastic ears, like a limp ferrule circumscribing a head three-fourth's neck, in which a single hole, the width of a peg, beeped out a flitter of dirty bleats—mutations bred from the shotgun wedding of half-baked ideas and free speech, fraught, to be sure, with statistical pitfalls, but which always seemed to squeeze into one major annoyance: *"Beelzebub Agragat!"*

. . . Go ahead and laugh, you pinheads! ['Aw, piss off!'] The escapee from Bedlam who just yelled that is a very sick chap. Now, listen: Look over at Whitechapel! Look at Brick Lane! It's the wogs as is killing us and sending England, Home, and Beauty right up the bleedin' spout, air mail, the filthy beggars. We're humming with them, for chrissakes! We have an annual inflow of 50,000 dependants parachuting down like locusts, floating down hereabouts like Tinkerbelle. ['He's a fairy!'] Who isn't, *you*? In fifteen or twenty years we'll have three and a half million immigrants just from the Commonwealth alone seeping in here, spading up your gardens, and grunting around next to your nearest and dearest. Commonwealth, did I say *Commonwealth*? A catch-fart, I meant the barmy house! Consider, now: in the year 2000 there'll be five to seven million of these devils in here sucking up your air, peeing in your parks, sticking their horny feet under your mahogany, and putting the boots to your women, see? So where, may I ask you, does it all end? ['When your missus gets a bun in her oven?'] Belt up, you creep! There's always one, isn't there? Now see what I mean? A million every twenty years—legally, you twits, legally, and as easy as kiss my thumb. And it's we've got to pay for it! It's rank carelessness is what! We've *already* gone and kicked it through the uprights, haven't we? Give over, now, haven't we? It's hardly worth the flippin' candle for us what *owns* the place anymore, is it? Well, is it? . . .

Furibund, the speaker thought he sniffed a whiff of complacent jackass. Not for him the pasteurized euphemism; he ranted, accused the crowd of bestial acts, peculiar preoccupations, and being interested in nothing more than a lifetime of French games. Then he leaned forward and surveyed his audience for just a bit of complicity, and in spite of—perhaps because of—the shower of spittle that sprayed down from the shaky podium, Roland, looking about him, began to lead a cheer of loud hurroos, while thumping and drumming a paradiddle of agreement on the foot of the box like a weird little apostle.

The Corner looked like the Battersea Fair, and like the Battersea Fair it had a variety of entertainments: ratty escape artists rolling out of multi-padlocked bags; goosecap fools shaking bells; albinos with dowsing rods; cripples dancing the hornpipe;

toothless buskers duck-squatting through everyone, playing the spoons, twanging ukeleles, or singing "Knees Up, Mother Brown"; and gymnosophists jumping up and down under umbrellas, like geysers.

Some had names, reputations established. An undeodorized little woman named Mrs. Budget had been to the Corner, she said, for 103 years, playing the foot-trombone.

Then, of some notoriety, was bespectacled Paul the Pseudoplutarch, American oligosyllabicist, ᾽ανθρωπάρεσκος, and poet laureate of rural Malawi, who scuttled around in his pants of beaten wool and round cap, waving copies of his own *Velocity: The Key to Writing,* (o.p.) a vade mecum for gerundmongers and the sourcebook of his widely cited, narrowly appreciated, long-held theory that one's literary output should cease only when one ran out of possible dedications—and that remained, not a family, but a world away. A certain Mr. Sheekey, demanding his throne, claimed to be the disinherited bastard dauphin of France, and, since bastardy purges itself in the third generation, he insisted upon not only a massive triumphal march into Paris but also an immediate and costly coronation.

And, dear to the hearts of all, was the Italian midget named Mario—author of the bibliothecal rarity, his first and only manumission in the mysteries of hierodulic logic, *Mother Mario's Gnostrums, or A Demonstration of Just How the Holy Spirit has Two Right Wings, Wherein is Contained, Beside the Pleasantness and Sweetness of the Stile, A Letter penned in Shorthand in which is incontestably and logically Proved, among Many Sage Things, that the Aureola of the heresiarch St. Onan was Really a Donut.* (8 vo., in white tortoise-shell boards, with juvenile "pop-ups" included)—who claimed to have been ordained a priest, but was, in fact, a paradoxically credulous atheist whose thesis was that he believed anything *not* found in the Bible; he also asserted that friars should copulate to generate new virgins *ad majoram Dei gloriam;* that indiscriminate fucking by Christians will defeat the fast-growing Communists; that he himself had been taught to read directly by St. Simon Stock; and that bed-wetting in children—the major sign that the infamous Beast 666 was roaming abroad seeking the ruin of souls—could be easily cured by the habitual wearing of a sterilized, papally blessed rubber snood, appended to the weenie by an elastic band, a totally effective device, he claimed, and which he sold for £5 each from the trayful of them that hung around his sacerdotal neck in place of the pectoral cross he insisted he once owned but had dutifully melted down for Mussolini to hasten the destruction of the heathen Ethiopians in 1935.

Meanwhile, the blue-jowled orator hulked forward, gripped the sides of the podium with what looked like two non-opposable thumbs, and held forth, scowling darkly, like the Christian-hating Emperor, Maximinius Thrax:

. . . Shift them out, shift them out! Into the drink with them all, I say! Else we'll all be over flogging apples in Corned Beef Island, won't we, twitching with the jerks, dodging the shitstorms ['Manners! Language!'], or stoking bloody furnaces next to them Eyeties from Italy with beards and shoe sizes about 43-80, with no more respect due them than a thruppenny packet of bum fodder! Laugh, go ahead! ['Ha, ha!'] You see laws being passed everyday, don't you, stuffed into us like pork pies by Mrs. Windsor over there, don't you, and by that overpaid, under-rehearsed vaudeville show over in St. Margaret Street, don't you, slow as a wet week and not a one of them who can tell his arse from an umbrella! ['Ahh, rats to you, you peckerhead!'] Buzz off, you stupid queer! Now, where was I? Oh, yes! Now, while these so-called legisla-tors of British yoomanity are trying to argue the leg off an iron pot, we're pouring good English money down the grid, as if, mind you, as if each one of us was all like them big, gravy-slopped American-born stooges crapping all over us with their greasy dollars, spitting their dirty money all over the world! ['Throw them out!'] Pre-cisely, mate!

Because what we ain't no longer is an Empire! A fact. No tricks. But we'll soon be a dead spit for them Americans, you don't think so?? This is only a little island, dearies, made of coal, surrounded by fish, and small as Rutland—so small, in fact, if we bent over, a pigeon could pick a pea out of our arses! You heard me! Our cools! And what we *have* no room for is room for a bunch of Pygmies clipping rings in their noses, wearing bits of sacking for underwear, and riding camels into the traffic jams in the Victoria Embankment. Who said that? A racialist? A common, boozed-up, bumph-minded yobbo of a *racialist*?? Sweet Fanny Adams it was! It was a Citizen! . . .

Typically, he did not speak, he announced. No microphones were allowed into the park, but it did not seem to matter. The noise threshhold seemed infinite. Metaphors flew about like loose tiles. Each speaker seemed only interested in firing off squibs, like bananas, to disconcert the gravity of the orthodox, implicitly asking, as all did, that profound, if essentially poetic, question: into the nosebag of unbiased recapitulation can we accuse what historian of putting his snout? Speakers everywhere shot up high on their stands, amid the crowd, like foghorns blasting war news—an eristic jawing of bottomless fart-gas, messianic rant, bilk, and boozy guffaws, wherein guesses became prophecies; whim, dogma; and candour, far more frightful than caricature.

Nostrum peddlers, compulsive system-builders, and nature mystics gathered here in earnest and rewrote history, drew up plans, read stars, planned attacks, and gave warnings. Solutions far exceeded problems. It was, indeed, a Mecca: Ranters; Forest Saints; Expectants, with leaflets; Those With Not Just a Pretty Face; needle-workers; Atomists, who lived to tell; Anthroposophists; flat-carthists; Icthyophages; anarcho-syndicalists; Behemists; Lords of Misrule; dog-lovers; Druidicals, with scrip and staff; those who resented salads; Socialists; mispronouncers; Shaking Quakers, who shook; Unbelievers (who shook their heads); Millenaries; banana sahibs; dog-haters; Rechabites;

Theobotanists; Futilitarians, yawning; Just Plain Workers, announcing new victories of Labour over Capital; victorious Capitalists, with wives in labour; Recent Reincarnations, in whom the dybbuk of past antagonists had recently, if inarticulately, entered; and, *nisi quod potius,* those not unpredictably epiphanizing the keenest of keen senses of community—the Communists.

. . . Communalism? Keeping bloody cute, sneaky, and together is what that means. Anglo-Indian, Indo-Anglian, Afro-British, blah, blah, blah. It's the same song everybody tries to whistle, but nobody knows the tune! And where does it all *end,* huh? Huh? ['In the grave?'] The comedian in the front row here can go home. We're all laughing at you, you silly fart! Off the track now . . . what happens is, they come over here for a slice of Resurrection Pie, and then, *then!,* when they're set up on the doorstep, living on cat scrunch and budgie food, next they start trying to creep their mothers in here, then the grandfather, then Uncle Max, and then the whole family tree comes over the Channel at night in a rubber life-raft, eating chapatis and singing 'Merrily We Bloody Roll Along' as if they were going to an ice show at the Winter Garden in Clapham! ['Why don't you go and get stuffed!'] You in the back there, shut your hole! Shift out the whole lot of them, you hear? Into the dustbins with them! That's my theory, sweeties! . . .

Theory was to "Speaker's Corner" what the chain-pull was to the Crapper Flushing System: a valve was pulled, the pipes flew fast into siphonic action, out emptied the cistern, and all was sent cascading down the flush pipe in a downrush of water that splashed into the pan, ringing like a peal of bells. Everybody had a theory. Advanced, notably, were: that bees hummed the one hundredth Psalm on Christmas Eve; that *Shakespeare* was a play written by Sir Francis Bacon's Italian half sister Ameletta (*Anglice:* Hamlet!); that, at this minute!, an umbrella was being invented for retarding a ship when driving into a storm; that the elbow was the most beautiful part of the body; that the dichromatic game of the Persians, popularly known as chess, was a racist pastime; that licking the stamp rather than the envelope was the single source of cancer; that over in Woking a man had invented a pill that will grow leather on the footsole to do away with shoes; that God was a Mechanic and His screwdriver was coincidence; that the circular flow of money was the cause of all disease; that an Estonian gownsman named Tiit Priks had revolutionized travel when he fashioned a pair of three-foot-long canoe-shaped shoes out of wood and walked thirty-three miles down the Thames; that the two greatest of all books were, respectively, Walter Curtain's *Prelude to Aftermath* and, then, the Bible; and, finally, that all invalids were selfish, dwarves mean, congenital diabetics petulant, and, of course, that the entire Capoid race was each, to a man, the living and demonstrable *point d'appui* of native recalcitrance to hard work.

. . . A coloured bloke over with me down at the job . . . ['The rag trade?'] I'll forget that, the chap's clearly a nut. Um, yuh, this bloke down at the job, as I was trying to say, who'd nick the pennies right off your eyes, is unable to see a ruddy hole through a ladder, browns off every time it clouds over, and is taking home *twice* what I am! Twice, goddamit! ['What's that, tuppenny ha'penny?'] The potty half-wit who just asked that had an American accent. Go home, you filthy little mouse. Anyway, twice, *twice* me, see? Cushy, man? Let me tell you. Bone-idle! And what really gives me the pip are these Indian thuggies pushing their bags of grunge, so you've heard, through little old lady's letter-boxes. Oh, don't pretend you've heard this for the first time, you cringing yahoos and swivets! Not only little old ladies, either! Little old ladies whose sons won fifteen or twenty bronze clusters fighting the Hun, some the George Medal, just so you all can freely take your tikes up to the zoo and not have to stop every two minutes and scream, 'Wha' whazzat?' or 'They're bombing again, Alice!' or 'Hit the farking dirt!' No, you look around. Them monkeys and terrapins are in a *cage*, not some plastic sack stitched up wholesale by trained gorillas in the so-called Republic of Botswana! Am I saying it's rosy, though? You're a liar if you said I said it, you miserable gets! ['Oh, go crash your bike!'] Oh, piss off, you hopeless bastard. *Rosy?*

White tenants are quaking, for godsakes! Take the letter-boxes. Naturally, these poor souls think it's the mail, don't they? Just imagine looking around for some kind of package posted down from your favourite aunty up in Mumbles and then, instead, simply finding—well, I don't have to tell you, you can spell. ['S-h-i-t?'] The person who just spelled that is a cramped and unhappy little jobbernowl down here who's drooling all over himself. Ignore him. He's a poor basket-case with nowhere to go. But you see what it all *means*? It's all bung in your eyes is what! Didn't one of them Greek philosophers from Greece tell us, 'Life is a journey'? ['What a stupid bastard he must have been!'] Get knotted! Now, where was I? Right, life being a journey and all that. That's just what it is, a *journey*, and I say the clock hands are now pointing to zero. ['That a Greek clock, you pimp?'] Ignore him, he's mentally ill. Zero hour, yes! Journey time for the woggos! We don't want them! We never did! What, do you tell me we did? We did not!! How do I know we didn't? *They* do! Hear me now, hear it all! You shall not—*not!*—put up with this kind of horseshit anymore!

Abruptly, the speaker finished, flung a rag out, and bathed ribbons of sweat from a face radiating that kind of pride that can only come when one has established, on the spot, the Eleventh Commandment. Like a bride her garter, he threw his handkerchief into the crowd, and Roland snatched it, stuffing it into his pocket. The orator shinnied down. Eyes followed him: flat Goan and Bantu faces, Biafran and Congolese, some from Cameroon and Upper Volta, all silent, heavy-eyed, resentful, and tense with concentration.

"Bloody marvelous," shouted Roland, having experienced a feeling very similar to that which we're told follows parturition; he pumped the man's hand, crying, "That's the stuff, mate!" Then Roland shouldered his way imperiously past a small Negro wearing an Astrakhan fezlike hat and tribal marks on his cheek that looked like Hundertwasser spirals; Roland wanted to give the dithering little chap a shot to the ribs, a whack-up into the jaw, just from jubilation, but he was hungry and wanted to get to the tea shop on Chapel Street before closing time, the punctual but late-in-the-day consideration of his Sunday, when, ritually, he would have a quick supper of tinned pilchards, a few cold tea cakes, three cups of tea, and then, blotting his mouth with a trencher of bread, would be off. People drifted away. It was a diaspora of tired souls, bleary-eyed dogs, cranky children, and parents with big swollen feet. With such events do afternoons end, and this was no exception.

Roland was into Grosvenor Place, on the run.

Hyde Park engendered shadows. The dying greenery of hurt-bushes and larches, under the grey shells of clouds that now began to snap with rain, caught that feeble light in London, neither night nor day but rather that feeble compromise which, more than the presage of autumn, filled one with a sense of long-forgotten things and showed itself to be that time when vague yearnings and regrets begin to cumber the soul. Over the plains of grass burst puffs of irregular wind, sprits that spun the falling leaves, hectic, red, flapping through the wake in little side streets where, now, no one was to be seen, having long since hurried away through the silence and the telling cold. The ragged mirage of day had suicided into the cold dusk. Night fell.

Once into Victoria Station, Roland stopped and listened. There was no reflection, only shadow. No one was about. The station spread out before him. The trains, sealed shut, were pulled along-side each other until morning. Pipes dripped. He listened again. The sound of water was pouring from some sourceless spot, a broken aqueduct, perhaps, or maybe some conduit water spilling out of an ancient furrow or some lead Roman leakage of old Londinium. Roland blinked his eyes to adjust them to the dark-ness, then disappeared into a stairway like a bit of dirt into a Hoover—and stepped into the damp cellar. The cold light of tiny bulbs, blue and pennysized, strung out between eerie shadows and revealed a hushed ash-grey tomb, a cell of must, cannibalized, as if by Mulciber, into a warehouse for those who work by night—the dark, witching hours that slowly pass, soured, it always seems, by those deep and unassignable final causes that desperately remind us of our odd naked frailties and whisper to us we owe God a death. Down the width and breadth of the cellar, red and green coaches and buses, in for the night, sat dumb, heavy, humped asleep like pachyderms.

Roland shot open a door: his locker was filled with soaps, brushes, rags. He pulled his gear together, threw off his jacket, and suddenly bashed by pending work into a fiercesome frame of mind, he decided he needed a quick cup of tea. He charged upstairs, two at a time. And it was there in the waiting room that he saw, upended in the far shadows, the suitcase, tennis racquet, and, beside it all, alone on a bench and huddled into a tiny embryonic position like a small, brown croissant, a little Indian—the white collar of his shirt ironed into wings, fluttering to the rhythm of his snores—dead asleep. Roland moved no closer. He crouched, blinking in the half-shadows, and spoke once:

"What's the game?"

II

Bong! Bong! Bong!—there were eight. An old high boxed clock with a crack in its wide face smiled down a sunny morning from the waiting room in Victoria Station and tolled in a wonderland of sounds in a stately measure that serised the long night and overrode the drastic dark, keeping time known, pattern orderly, and rhythm alive. Dilip opened an eye, then two. He then sat up directly, rubbed his eyes, and clicked his tongue happily, mistily cognizant—just before he dismounted from his dream—of a sweet meditation he had had of Krishna who had been hop-footing, fecund, through his unconscious in a fountain of golden rain with his 16,000 wives and 180,000 sons in attendance, each holding up a moon-kissed rose that shone forth, in bubbles of blue dew, the Peace That Passeth All Understanding. In a mental communion, arranged by him so often over the years, he consulted his guru, Menu: "In no other ship than the barque of dreams may one ride so refreshed." Dilip had a revelation: sleep was the thin white meal one took absolutely alone. It gave one a taste for solitary pleasures. He smiled at that, for he was alone. And now he was awake.

The waiting room, he saw, as cognition followed revelation, was like any other waiting room: dark, pigeon-flecked wood, patinaed over with the colour of faded bottle-green. Newspapers were strewn about. One light bulb dangled on a cord over the room; a large radiator pinked out noises; and some travel posters to Brighton, Winderby Sluice, and Aberystwyth, which he was unable to see earlier in the night, were posted high behind a coin-operated tea machine. It was still, however, somewhat shadowy in the room. Dilip unlocked his valise, took out a box of matches, and, walking over to the timetable board, held up the match to read the schedule. Satisfied, he dropped the match.

"They don't like that."

"*Pardon?*" Dilip blurted, spinning around quickly and collapsing frightened into the wall as his heart staggered. He swivelled his eyes over the far shadows to catch the parapsychological source of the voice. Roland McGuffey slowly lowered the morning paper.

"Throwing matches on the floor. They don't like that. Chokes up the public utility."

Dilip stooped down and retrieved the match from the floor, a utility public, and transparently Britannic, only in that generation after generation, pressing on to the trains, had pounded into it its hereditary dirt: the invisible memorials of endless evacuation. Dilip continued to read and re-read and re-read the timetable, a blur now before his embarrassment and slight shock. He looked like a shiny new spoon; his bright liquid eyes sparkled like black treacle and shone peacefully from the clean brown glabrous skin of the Aryan who, more than two thousand years ago, had thundered in hoof beats through the Khyber Pass during the invasions. Groomed perfectly back was his glistening black hair, as immaculate as the almost phosphorescent white suit he sported, pressed to a line and as crisp as a folded piece of origami work, a neatness that reached right to the perfect little half-moons on the nails of his slim brown fingers that now dexterously, if quizzically, tapped the board.

Roland slapped the paper.

"I'll be stuffed," he said. "A goddam vicar just come up on the pools, a vicar, a goddam vicar, a vicar. You see what I mean, where it all goes? I've been waiting to come up on the pools, what, five years? Six, maybe. Six years beating the streets, who'd believe it? Then this satchel-arsed son-of-a-bitch goes and does it, there's his picture, tickling up the shillings to make sure they're not tin. They get their tea and three slices, what, you don't think so? Get onto yourself, for chrissakes, don't you believe it. You'll not find a sneakier lot. Perfect fiends. I see them up at the Duckery, the Stock Exchange, the Duckery. It's for the money. Churches, see, they come up once in a way, on the tote. See what I mean, just churches? Nuns. They're over at the betting office, putting around for a horse. What, *nuns?* They never stop." There was no pause. "You going to Brighton, then?"

"Indeed, yes."

"I thought so. I see you have a tennis racquet. Going to play some tennis, huh?" Roland nipped at his crow-coloured nails.

"Pardon, sir?"

"Don't have to call me sir. I ain't Lord Gussie of Fleet Street. What I said was, you're going to play some tennis."

Dilip smiled a smile of politesse. "Of course, yes."

"Down at Brighton."

"Yes."

"Thought so."

Quietly, Dilip unlatched his valise and took out a book. That settled, Roland tore from the newspaper a large sheet, threw back his sleeves, and proceeded to thoroughly scrub his arms, hands, and elbows free of the flinty powders, detergents, and imbedded grit that had aggravated his skin raw and granulated, like repson board. The night was always long, longer in the fall when all the steel rot had rusted hard and rotted cold into the deep layers of the buses in petrified stains. His clothes gave off the closet smell of sweat, sponges, lampblack, tin metallic water, and, worst of all, the strong acidic odour of the red carbolic soaps he used to scrub the filthy wheels, square bars packed tight with volcanic pumice.

The Washing of the Buses was hierarchical, a little *mandatum* all his own: first, the hosing down, a decentralized application involving suds, then into the decks to mop off the rubber floors with hand-hot, chlorinated water. After that came the windows, which he squeaked clean with swipes of the squeegie, then the sloshing of the headlamps, a quick run over the leather seats with neat's-foot oil and a shake or two of the chamois, a dashover with the broom, and, once again, a last check—the tenth was usually terminal—for Lost and Found, a little spin-off he afforded himself as Part of the Job and which had yielded, thus far, a trove of seventeen magazines (blue), countless theatre programs, three wallets, a Victorian tobacco tamper, a brass call bell, an earthenware jelly-mould, and a netsuke monkey brooch he had flogged in Petticoat Lane for eighteen shillings. Umbrellas were so common he ignored them. He worked by commission. Terms: this had been a Nine Bus Night. The worst had been a Three (Guy Fawkes night, burned thumb). The peak had been the famous Fifty-nine Bus Night, the very first night he got the job, in fact, when he had ingeniously crawled to the rafters and, with loud proclamations of "tally-ho!," dropped in Niagara-like splashes fifty-nine individual bucketfuls of steaming water onto the buses below—and almost got cashiered the next morning. On this particular morning, however, Roland realized he had lowered his average, and would not have but for the six trips to the waiting room to make certain Dilip wasn't burgling, prying at the safes in the ticket office, or having into the trains. Dilip woke six times, bought six teas, and went back to sleep six times—to prove he was not.

"Hey listen," Roland said, standing up. "You got a tanner you can see my way? Half a hog? Not that I'm flat, I'm not flat, who said I was flat, but all's I got on me are notes." Roland demonstratively unfolded from his wallet a flaking bill that looked as if it had been lined as a parchesi board. "Not so much as a Joey."

"My goodness yes, I have coin," responded Dilip running over to Roland, his little hand a hill of goodwill and change. "As well, I have not infrequently found myself with as sizable a misery."

"A pain in the ass."

"A bugbear."

"A kick in the ass," said Roland.

Roland rooted among the coins. "I'll take one of these—and one of these, thruppence twice, to pay you back as soon as that" —he snapped his fingers—"in a piffle. Hold off, you got a sixpence. Now you see what I'm doing? I'm putting back two thrupenny bits and taking the simon. That's what we call them in Houndsditch. Simon"—Roland winked—"means Jew." It was the lexicographical touch.

The tea machine took the coin; a crank, the *pock* of the cup, a splash, and Roland, once again, had his tea: a beverage for all, epidemic in its consumption and gulped wholesale, from Fork-beard the Dane to the Magic Now, to momentarily dose away the punctual *cri de coeur* that illuminated in the English the complicated neurasthenia of general complaint coupled with specific cure.

"By the way," asked Roland, "didn't I see you yesterday?"

"On the train?"

"Walking."

"Walking on the train?"

"*On the ground!*" Roland barked. "*Walking on the ground!*"

"Oh yes," Dilip said, engulfed in a whelm of embarrassment, "through the Park of Hyde."

"That's right."

"Yes, sir."

"Thought so."

Dilip saw a reddening trace high in Roland's cheek, like spinel. Oh pish on me, thought Dilip, for I have made this friend here, new as he is, waxy, something testy, and composed of some irascibility. The consulted Menu had often revealed: "A fly's worst luck it that it has never been killed before."

"You know," Roland suddenly remarked, throwing the paper aside, "I was just reading about this here graveyard they have in Surrey. The men are buried on one side, and women are buried on the other. Get it? Point being, you probably think we're all daft over here, a bit off like, and wonder why you stay here." Roland sipped his tea and immediately grabbed his tongue. "*Crikey!* They will make these things burn your ass off, won't they?"

"It tweaked your mouth?"

"Yes. I swear they make them so they'll burn your ass off. They're like that, these people"—and Roland spied past the doors of the waiting room and saw, in his mind's eye, all the venenating cooks and caterers who partially comprised the world, pouring vials of nightshade and henbane into their bowls, dishes, and goblets, just for a vicious lark. He blew the cup, shifting it from hand to hand. Dilip, meanwhile, was fluttering his handkerchief five feet from that same cup as an aid to help circulate the air.

"Anyways, as I was telling you before, there's this graveyard down in Surrey in England. The women are buried on one side, and men on the other. So you think we're bonkers for that? I can tell you do. You've as much as said it." Roland slid the paper along the bench. "Look, down there. Read it." While Dilip, nodding, ran his eyes over the article, Roland lighted a cigarette, puffed it alive, and, turning, pipped the match into the clock face.

"You see what I mean? That's a bit of marvelous what-do-you-say, en it?" Roland chuckled, puffed out smoke, and elbowed to freedom a bronchitic cough. "They probably think the dead bodies will go bezeek, get up in the middle of the night, and start the old diddling. You know? Get up and start mixing it up with each other. I mean, even though they were *dead*. Some world, huh? When they think dead bodies will start—" Roland cruelly drove his thumb into his palm. "You know?" As quickly, a dark *aliquid latens* expression clouded over his face. He squinted through its shadow. He took Dilip in through the side of his half-shut eye. "No reason, at the same time, for you to go and bitch about the country, commenting on how we've gone off our peckers, on calling us all potty. I've seen worse." He looked Dilip straight in the eye and spoke very, very slowly. "Bloody worse." Dilip's smile froze, fell off, and dashed into smithereens. With an even greater formality and reserve than before, he sat up and checked his watch.

Moods here, it seemed, shifted abruptly—with the speed and reckless alarm of flipping pages (growing plots) in children's books when, travelling across the crudely coloured page, large walleyed but trusty elephants and nice kids like mites with faces smudged like cranberries, friends all, are suddenly chased by goops, grinning from teeth as sharp as bag needles, who drop hairy and malign from a network of dirty caterpillarvic vines and, howling, flapping webfooted, trail them into caves, squat, lick their chops, and knap them up like ginger.

"You can keep the paper." Roland clapped his hands and rubbed them together. "I read it."

"Gratefully many thanks, yes, but I have book here."

"Look, you don't have to be shy," Roland said, pointing to the paper soaked in rings of wet detergent and bunched silt. "That's the morning run. I just bought it." Roland slugged down the tea and hurtled the cup over the radiator like an agile forward on a throw-in. "It was a gift."

Dear me! thought Dilip, perhaps I have burdened myself with a needless enmity in speaking so. He consulted the Menu: "To disgrace is to dyscrase." He could not help but agree.

"Please," replied Dilip, "please do not think this is disesteem, but imperatives have it that I must read book. I shall soon have," he laughed, "examination in book, and, goodness me, it is high time I should apply myself, elsewise shall I be a failed B.A."

Roland threw his head back and gave out with a tubercular wheeze. "Oh, oh, oh, *oh*, you go to *university*, that it?" He tapped the book. "Me see?"

"You shall find it distasteful," Dilip said, smothered in a self-imposing and diffident giggle. "Alas, it is book for my course study. I think very, how you say, boring?"

"*Analyses of Step-up and Step-down Transformers,*" Roland read. He looked at Dilip. "Mechanics."

"Electricity."

"Yes," Roland agreed, "mechanics of . . . ah . . ."

"No, friend. Not mechanics. Electricity. I study circuits and wiring methods."

"Oh, that it? What, you come here to learn electricity, and then you go back to . . . ah . . . Pakistan there?"

"I am from India."

"That's what I meant. Then you go back to India, right? Teach them what you learned here." Roland snaffled a page of the book. "About this stuff."

Dilip checked his watch. "Do you please have correct time?"

"Half-eight," Roland answered quickly, catching the clock, "but what I mean is, then you go back to India to tell them everything you picked up here, that right? What you had a look at, like?"

"You must be knowing, perhaps, I have no intentions of returning home just as yet," Dilip laughed a bit nervously. "For now, let it be said Brighton is sufficient."

"What, you're going to stay here? You're going to settle in."

"Temporarily."

"No, you see, but when—*when*—you go back there, when, that's what you're going to do, isn't it, tell them what we let you see, what you picked up, what you had a look at when you were over here, right? I mean, right?" Roland was an inch off Dilip's ear.

"Yes."

"Tell them everything."

"Yes."

"Thought so."

And Roland leaned back, staring at Dilip pontifically, contented in the knowledge, clearly established, of the rigid rules set up in the wide, bipartisan, but unequal world. It was the ontological brief that posited Roland a Who, Dilip a Whom: the syntactical brickbat of Fate, Nominator and Accuser, which categorized forever "the actor" and "the acted upon," whereby the Indian, among others, remained, ineluctably, that shuttlecock which must drop to the ground if its elevation is not secured, and constantly maintained, by frequent blows. Such, such was the case.

England was no final resting place. Here was involved, for Dilip, far less a matter of expatriation than a process of identification, having as its point of departure the poetic laconism of Gormata, the Digambara saint: "Perceive, do not analyze." The two years thus far spent at Cambridge, which boasted many illuminators of the age, partially extended that perception, like two gigantic klieg lights that were clicked on and, like electric flowers flowing colour, suddenly flashed out in crazy blue plops, throwing off a pure, moon-white incandescence to the farthest reaches of the Unknown in ever new moral and intellectual moulds, dips, and rushlights. It was not simply, however, that the university was either enough or idiot-proof. Dim bulbs, everywhere, proved the formally educated not necessarily the more widely informed. It was *electricity* he must know. Electricity, alone, rattled in flares through the spores of vegetable man: an ichor that pumped through him the vibrations of loving motion, up over the distant stars in phosphorized strides, and into the electric air like a torchbeam sweeping over the world and then up again, traced a thousand parsecs away into the disappearing dot of Time and Space wherein every karma was purged off from the soul until it was light enough to ascend, still further, out beyond the quasars to the peak of the universe, where, bathed in sulphur, one met one's self, finally making life seen, then life known, and then life life. He believed in life. He was a Jain.

Dum Dum was his village once, but no more. Indeed, for Dilip, there *was* no place—to re-emphasize, and run the adage widdershins—like home. Born there in the northwest reaches of Assam, of Saraswat Barhmin parents, his very first memory was of August 15, 1947, the very night of The Partition. It was a night of great rain. Suddenly, on that night, two huge men had burst into the house, Moslem goondas from a nearby enclave, who looked, both, like Hanuman, the Monkey God—speaking in strange tongues, carrying Enfield rifles, and wearing hoods which showed their eyes beads in a shiny wild glare, the drug-crazed leer of opium. Were these, Dilip had wondered, the Men of the White Poppies he so feared? His father had often pointed out to him, on their little trips to Calcutta, the distant fields of white poppies, blowing free—life; later, he was told of the opium farms of Bengal where the virginal white flowers were cut and thrown into presses, oozing out, in martyrdom, a sticky black juice which was then hardened and diced into cakes of one or two pounds, giving off a pungent, sickish odour—death.

The rain came down in sheets through it all. The men shoved Dilip and his sisters, Pushpa and Premila, into a corner, and, laughing, they sat the father and mother, terrified and humiliated, in the center of the room. From a cloth about his waist, one of them untucked a pillbox, and for hours, time passing slowly, they unrolled cubes of sticky brown opium from green leaves which were wrapped, each pellet, in newspapers the size of a lump of sugar. It was either chewed or mixed with water and swallowed whole. Then, suddenly, the men hooted and screamed and spit wrath; they spilled into a water bowl a sack of dry powder which they forced Dilip's mother to drink, at gunpoint: a compound, this was, of finely cut-up tiger's whiskers that perforated the lining of the stomach, causing the highly potent gastric acids to be released into the body, which, in turn, scorched the vitals in a spontaneous acute illness, resulting in death. "Rama," she mumbled and tumbled over lifeless into a pile of pink sari, her braid showing out like a long rat's tail on the floor. The father was led, naked, into the courtyard. There was a shot. Pushpa and Premila, after they were raped, were sent to a brothel in Hyderabad. And Dilip was left wandering in the rain.

Domestic memories paled as the years passed, but Dilip could never forget the cold lump of loneliness he had felt in the pit of his stomach (where nothing else was to be found), during these first days, when he had come into Cherrapunji: raindrops fell as big as marbles and the soaked earth swelled with mud, queer fat mushrooms, and dropsy. Monsoons left everything slippery in green slime. The Whom was predicated to the Who. He walked alone through a rabbit warren of narrow lanes and saw in the dusk, before nightfall, thin little brown men with no hips, barefoot, huddled around dingy watch-fires, swatting flies, and chanting mantras to the big dead moons. Herds of wild monkeys frightened him, pillaging and sucking voraciously from rotten melons and fruits and tossing the shells away as they went cheeping along, gibbering, past animal-faced statues. Down from Nepal, over the ultramontane Siwalik Range, had wandered Mongolian Buddhists; orange robes, long bead rosaries, and queer earflapped caps pulled down over their heads from which jutted cheekbones the size of bells. Ox-drivers railed at each other in furious Assamese exchanged in rapid shots as hands flew.

Eventually, Dilip had turned into the Jaintia Hills filled with tumid heat and the screams of goshawks, sheldrakes, parrots. He slept in weird, emerald forests, often sitting up all night, eyes open fearfully, especially when he heard in the distance the wild dogs in wet, reddish-white fur, snarling at each other or tearing at the carcasses of monkeys which they tossed like dolls. He once saw two rams fighting, their slablike foreheads crashing in spurts of blood, the noises exploding in flushes bunches of macaws from nearby bushes, and the treetops all around squirting birds into the air. Elephants trumpeted, and tigers, with diamond-hard eyes, bolted through the underbrush, hot for something's blood.

The Whom travelled on. Through the shimmering heat and into the teeming cities he came, eating rind, begging, and lost in the maze of jostling crowds that collapsed in on each other, shoving, yelling, pushing beneath the blistered bricks, high wattle-daubed flats, and cardboard shops, the colour of bleached iodine, storied, one upon the other, like a nest of warped boxes and constructed upon the principle of *communiter*:

> The union of the weak
> A powerful bully stumps;
> The hostile blizzard spares
> The shrubs that grow in clumps.

Bad, truly, was an antonym of worse. In little rooms, endogamic families grouped before their single window where their washing flew like pennants, or gathered round the floor, eating, licking curry off their elbows, and then sleeping in large numbers on string cots, while loathsome bandicoots slithered in and out underneath their houses. Up and down Calcutta's Chowringhee the tramcars clacked, and over in the markets the begging priests and sadhus rocked back and forth in loincloths: moaning, quoting the Rig-veda, palms extended, as their thin long hair, matted with filth, ashes, and cowdung, all hung in ropes about their necks like strings of brown beads. Pariahs shook their sandals for scorpions. Battered Fiats honked bumping over kerbs, beggars rapped at the car windows, and thousands of children wailed after them in looping trails of green exhaust. Dilip saw little *sabus* sprawling over the pavement under the toddy palms; ponces munching *pan* and scowling; and in the doorways harridans, nasty as spayed cats, raised their thin cotton saris and screamed, "Jig, jig?"

The stenches along the Hooghly were sickening. Into Budge-

Budge he passed, where, in the wet ditches, glebe water-cows, with faces like dugongs, sloshed in rice and looked up dopey, drooling from purple mouths, foolish with curiosity. The workers, or *sudras*, moped by, carrying pails of foul drinking water past trees filled with saucer-eyed toucans and where kraits hung like black whips flicking their tongues; and all along the roads, people, here and there, each with an arm against a tree, stood retching with cholera or heaving up in the last throes of starvation from distended bellies, their little dinghies, with hook-cut sails, in similiar states as they leaned over, useless, in clooms of the sucking mud.

Weary, dirty, unrecognizable, up toward Delhi rolled the Whom, past the mud walls of villages, which, throughout the land, were alive with frescoes of gods, demons, men, and animals executed in yellows, ochres, and umbers, all ornamented with geometric patterns etched into the dying mud by the artful fingers of a people alive with beauty, but irrevocably faced with death. In the aged flats of the country, Dilip occasionally slept in temples, his ear perked to the croak of crows and hopefully nothing worse; in one he heard a voice: an old *sennyasi,* in the midst of a long pilgrimage to bathe in the Godavari, had whispered a blessing and given him an old wooden-bound copy of the *Ramayana* of Tulsi Das, which Dilip read and forthwith memorized, thereafter, passing many a lonely but self-contained night, sitting up cool in the mountain grass, singing softly to himself in sweet notes the "Song of the Adorable One." And the days went by as over the whole country, shaken with cyclones, earthquakes, and floods, he passed into Karachi, through West Bengal, Orissa, over to Bhopal, way down to Mysore, and up as far as the Punjab.

The big cities were all alike: Mewar, Patna, Cawnpore. But he was somehow changing with the experience, being led somewhere, though precisely where he could not as yet tell. Dilip always sat in the large open squares, fractured in cracks of slate and pebbles, beating the alms bowl with his bamboo and begging for *pice*. The square was like a window to the world. He watched the Moslem *fakirs* or the men in baglike garments called *burkas* followed by their secluded women, a purdah of dark eyes beneath veils, shawls, and chintzes. Fierce, smouldering *marathas*, in turbans of rust-red and dust colour, casually puffed hashish and chewed betel and sometimes gave him an *anna* to go on errands to get one of the disshevelled *veschayas* from the brothels, where the furniture was upholstered in dirty pink rep with horsehair showing through the corners, and the dying marigolds in clay pots were as faded as the curtains in the windows where sad-eyed ladies and nautch girls, painted in *ghaza* and *hajal* mascara, slouched in the shadows of a paraffin lamp like the chromos of half-draped women and fat odalisques which hung on the walls within.

Violence, too, seemed to run through everyone's life, like the silver bar through the bank notes the British controlled them by. Indian communists sold copies of the *National Front* everywhere and shouted headlines like hysterical warnings: "*Biplab*! *Biplab*! *Biplab*!"—predictions of an imminent revolution when the poor would rise up and mercilessly cut the very eyes out of the rich they despised. Little men up from Bangalore or Darjeeling, half-mad, sang in twangs unmelodious tunes that tragicomically rehearsed the fateful stories of their lives, poverty, and crippled brains. And everywhere thousands upon thousands of the fifty million scavenger-eyed "Untouchables," whom the British *raj* euphemistically referred to as The Unscheduled Classes, went about filching into garbage cans and licking sewage from their fingers. The duck gongs they wore clanked and warned people of their proximity, for they were said to pollute India even by their shadows, and, occasionally, they were shot by indignant Hindus of high caste for growing their mustaches upwards instead of downwards, according to caste demands. Dilip often saw them chased to the bottom of filthy alleys, where they were kicked and spat upon to the cry of "*Harijan! Harijan!* And yet always, as always, even in the midst of violence, whether the culture changed, or the language, in the mountains, along the sea, over the plains, evening still crept in, night hushed its stormy brood, and the interminable dark spread over India once again, while the lonely *bhisti*, or water-carrier, appeared, sprinkled the streets, and, then sitting alongside his lampion sweating grease and oil, watched patiently as he had done from the beginning of time the last of the orange sun eaten away by the ravenous dusk. The kites sailed circles in the last of golden air and, another day or year or century shadowed over, had passed from the paper-strewn, mephitic earth.

One night, in his sixteenth year, Dilip found himself standing alone in the inner porch of Tejahpālā's temple at Dilwārā on Mt. Abu in the district of Rājputānā. It was a rock-cut temple of solid masonry, a *stupa* in a moat-girdled zone of walls, carved inside and out with the minute detail of a jewel box, a delicacy, like the effect of hoarfrost, all done in deep relief and chase; aisled and apsidal, the entire surface of arches, doors, columns, and gates was fretted, until it looked like repoussé work. It seemed an actual forest of pillars and statues, all heavily carved and painted: sandstone bulls, long elephants' trunks, stealite seals, monkeys' tails, and sacred cobras, each one fantastically exaggerated, especially the goddesses with wasp waists, voluptuous hips, and breasts as round as cricket balls.

Alarmed with beauty, Dilip stood spellbound under the hemispherical dome which mounted to a small pavilion on the summit and, rising from this, a mast bearing a symbolic umbrella. Though he had never seen them closely, he had often heard of the pacific Jains, mostly from Gujarat and Bombay, who prayed here: the stark-naked Digambaras, and the white-robed Shwetambaras—who, according to their ancient *gachchha*, never killed a single thing, always wore filtering masks, and travelled everywhere with long brooms strapped to their backs to sweep away from their path anything that might be hurt. Dilip's "perception" dated from that night, a lay co-partnership in spirituality, in which he took vows, that began in learning contemplation, purity of thought, and repentance, and ended with a sacred gift of twelve flawless Magok rubies that he might go abroad to learn, in full, the key to the Modern Birth Cycle: electricity—the lifestream of the New Universe—for that was the God-drenched will of holy Menu, the shaggy saint with eyes like anthrax, who stepped into the temple porch that very night and, with raised arms beckoning him, spoke through his respirator: "Your body and your spirit will be nourished by my moonlight." Dilip was converted on the spot. He had at last come home.

"Where's your home? You know, where you belong and all that."

"India."

"No, I knew that," said Roland, lighting another cigarette. "India. But what I mean is, where abouts from? The capitol, right?"

"Formerly, Dum Dum," Dilip smiled.

"What the hell kind of a farking name is that, Chinee?"

"This was the habitat of my parents. A go-ahead willage once, truly, sir. To date, I have confessedly been hither-thither, at one time reaching even unto Chicago."

"Now *that* ain't in India."

"That is in United States."

"That's absolutely correct," said Roland, standing up and saluting. He sat down. "Say there's money over there, in dollars; I don't know, never got around to making it over there. Say there's money over there, though. New York, Texas, Chicago.

Oh, I know." Roland hooked his thumbs into his belt. "Pahdon me, ma'am, Ahm lookin' for Big Bad John Wayne." He leaped from the bench and squatted behind an armrest, holding his hand out as a revolver. "Blam, blam, blam!" Then Roland stood up, smiling and blowing on the barrel of his finger. "Texas. All them cowboys and—" he paused—"Indians. Only they're red, you're..." Two replies followed simultaneously: "black" "brown." The latter was not Roland's. His was the former.

Dilip would not allow himself to be mured in by a wall constructed, and perfectly acceptable, by someone whose opinions were clearly, if different from his own, just as honest and possibly even wiser.

"Distant cousin of mine is technician in Chicago. He takes care of—"

"Oh, I know, I know," Roland interrupted. "A technician. He works with those . . . ah . . . laboratories . . . oh, I know. I got you." He picked up the newspaper harshly.

"You go to university?"

"Sorry?" Roland's eyes peered just over the paper.

"You go to university, my friend?"

Roland did not reflect. He deliberated.

"No time," he shrugged. "No, I don't really go, in the sense that you mean. I just have no time to go. You see what I mean?"

"Yes."

"Yes."

The cigarette was tossed into the drain. Roland smoked with a nervous energy, destroying his cigarettes as soon as possible, as if it were a duty to be finished with it in the shortest possible time.

"Funny, you know?" replied Roland. "You need *time* to go to university, if you get me." It seemed a marshmallow disguised as food for thought. "Look, I'll ask you if you got time to go,

then you ask me. Me first. Hey, mate, you got time to go to
university? Huh?" Roland waited. "Go on, answer. Have a
shy at it."

Dilip, if bewildered a bit, was always a good sport. "Yes," he
smiled.

"Now you ask me."

"Excuse me, my dear fellow," Dilip laughed good-naturedly,
"do you have time to go to university?"

"*Not. On. Your. Farking. Nelly,*" snarled Roland, his face
showing a marked feral strain. The words were ice-covered. The
sentence, broken up, was delivered slowly and clipped with precise fury, the more horrible for its control. There was not even
the trace of a smile. "It's as bloody simple as that, you."

Have I just now detected the hubble-bubble of anger in a
voice, Dilip asked himself, a sorrowing discord in a dear spirit?
But shall I then condemn only a voice? Consult the Menu:
"Learn how to separate the duck from its quack?" Dilip felt
he would try to do better.

"Fag?" Roland had a pack of cigarettes aimed at the Indian.

"Thank you, no."

"Take one."

"I do not use them."

"Do you smoke them?"

"Neither am I doing, to this age." Dilip began to read his
book.

"I'm going to have one. You have one."

"Please, sir?"

"I'm offering you one," Roland said darkly. "Take."

Dilip hesitated; he thought he detected a sharp edge on the
word, an unspoken *arrière-pensée*, buried somewhere, that
showed his new friend not as yet fully delivered of himself. Shall
I then be so uncharitable? he asked himself, taking advantage

in a small pause to consult the Menu: "A gibbous moon is no less a moon." Dilip felt better—and took the cigarette.

"Thank you, wery."

"Don't thank me. I get them half-price where I live. There's more where that come from. That's the thing about England, I mean. You can always have a fag when you want one. Not like some countries where they ration the fags, like Warsaw in Poland. Guess that's one reason why I like it here, and stay here, too. You want a fag, take one. No beating around the bloody bush. Just take one." Roland cupped a light for both cigarettes. "You speakee the English, right? Am I talking too fast?"

"No, sir," coughed Dilip, blinded by his own billowing gas of tobacco.

"It's the greatest country in the world," concluded Roland. "Just look at a map, where it's in the middle. It has the exact same shape it had when Henry the Eighth was the king, not sandwiched in with all the others like Shepherd's Pie or gone out of circulation. That's because we're an island. You look sometime. The greatest."

Noises, whistles, voices, the racking of satchels and valises, and the sounds of people running, cars hitching and coupling brought the morning to consciousness, the train station, after the long night, had now disintegrated into the full of the day and the vigourous flux of business.

"You taking the 9:07, then?"

"The half-nine, sir."

"That's what I meant."

"Yes," Dilip nodded. "I will board momentarily."

"Don't like trains much. See, I'm not waiting for a train. I'm just off the shift, the job, the shift. Well, I had some time to kill so I thought I'd pop into the waiting room here, get up on the news."

Dilip pulled his cuffs straight, secured the buckles on his valise, and smiled; he was ready to be off and away, anxious.

"I have taken trains, though," Roland continued. "Chrissakes, we've all taken trains, right? It's just that I don't like to take them. I took the two-pound ride from The Wash to Henchy once, and for the whole trip this little bugger, a little bugger, only three feet and a kick, was sitting near my back with one plastic toy, playing . . . ah . . . playing, what's that song"—Roland, puzzled, drew back his fist and squinted down to the floor, exploring it for the answer—"yes! 'Mother Redcap Wants to Know,' I think it was. Anyway, it was driving me up the bloomin' wall, he wouldn't belt up, see? So I told the little cod to shut it off. 'Shut it off,' I said. '*Shut it off, you little bastard*!'"

Roland paused. He looked up and beamed. "You know, he did?"

Goodness gracious me, Dilip reflected, this poor keen chap has his spleen on fire; full of bobbery and griefs must be his heart, thus making mine.

"The little bread-snapper was probably off to Brighton, as well. Don't like the place myself. Course, some do. You're going down. You should know," Roland said. He knew he could detect in the Indian's eyes a lingering trace of corruption, for he had often seen taken that dangerous and retrograde step where proprietary blacks, Indos, and Pakis, better whipped by slavers, recruited to their chaperonage and harems all those unsuspecting English girls with long eyelashes and beautiful names and bombed them to a rubble in seaside bedsitters with their whale-sized, extra-terrestrial devices reputed to be the length of yard-arms. This was a rapid recognition: Brighton was the rendezvous, the girl *had* to be English, and Roland would find out, he would —then collar him, nail him to a flaming post, and have the stones off of him before Jack Dashed.

"I hope I should go. The rail train appears to be late."

"You taking the Express To?"

"Exactly so."

"The Express To's late today. No one told you?" Dilip tumbled over his valise. "Delay somewhere on the track. She's leaving at, what?, eleven-ought-two, or, no, no, she's leaving at eleven-fifteen. You thought she was leaving at half-nine. I thought you knew."

"I have dozed past it?" asked Dilip from the floor.

"It's late," Roland said. "Thought you knew."

"It has gone pish-pash into a tree?"

"Laaaaaate, is all."

"Capsized unwillfully?"

"*Late, goddamit, late!*" Roland bounced to his feet and looked down: the ball sat, still; it was only a short run, moving left, in with a kick, then to ram it high with a stabbing foot and wind it away—thud! Point!

Dilip picked himself up, a motion which, unwittingly, saved him from the singular experience of having a sharp, wing-tip shoe driven summarily halfway through his rib-cage. The train would be late, now; he felt disappointed that he felt sad, sad that he felt disappointed. He consulted the Menu: "Consider, always, to what degree is pattern arbitrary." Poop, he thought, I should have known this.

Roland swung away and sat down. "Though it'd be hard to know," he said, pulling up his socks and gesturing to the schedule board, "since they didn't put the card up."

"Well," replied Dilip, with a low resigned laugh, "in India they sometimes forget the card as well."

"You have *trains* in India?"

"Oh yes, fine trains."

"Didn't know that."

"Bless me, yes."

"Didn't know that."

"You did not know that?"

"Well, I *knew* it, yes," answered Roland, "but I thought they were old. Old trains."

"They are old."

"*That's what I said, wasn't it?*" Roland stared hard at him. "*Wasn't that just what I farking said?*"

But Dilip was driven past the question in an old Indian railroad; it chugged into his memory: whistling steam up the brain stem, it rolled to the fornix, screeched to a halt in the hippocampus, and stood, hissing, spitting water, at the frontal lobes of his mind. The hot dust-powdered cars overflowed with thousands of people squatting on the roofs and hanging from the windows, all chattering in a macaronic babble of Hindi, Tamil, Sanskrit, Malayalam and many of the other 845 languages and dialects spoken throughout the country. Under the beating sun and in the unbearable heat, the cars steamed almost red-hot, while widgeons and snipes walked over the roofs, their tracks making question marks in the dust; and, throughout the trains, young Indians waved their arms wildly and cheerfully during a stopover, while the toothless old sat within, bowbent in their dhotis, sharing their corn from screws of newspaper and squatting into their soft laughter.

The train stations reproduced a carnival atmosphere, or, better, a kind of tableau like Bosch's terrifying "Last Judgement," or, best, something of both: lepers; tertiary syphilitics; St. Vitus dancers, real and bogus, spinning into the wind-sprits of a clonus; lunatics, with spittle on their chins, fluttering to a ghostly music within their own brains; others twitching for profit, while blind, maimed, and deformed children, pinched with hunger, snaffled pieces of food from the stalls of *karibat,* in front of which run-down peddlers barked: "Cups of Leepdon's dee, hot,

hot! Hot Leepdon's dee!" The quavering singsong of the vendor's chant came from everywhere, selling *burfi,* ice cream, the syrupy sweet *mitahis,* and various Indian savories. Tradesmen haggled through the open car windows, bargaining, flipping long fingers, and tossing from small wicker baskets all kinds of fruits: peppery, puckery, bitter. The Parsee merchants hopped along the cars: the Screwwallah with his cheap hardware and odd, little mongery, and the Sodawaterwallah with his bottles, shaped like begging dogs, filled with bright pink and green soda water. Bells clanged, and tin loudspeakers, announcing arrivals and departures, blared out the schedule list of towns in a chain of loose, booming squawnks. It was a network of constrictions, contractions, constructions. The platforms were a vortex of pushing, struggling shapes, especially during the times of conventions, and melas: the religious festivals that shifted all humanity toward the sacred Ganges in a wild, calamitous din, a barrikin in which pilgrims gurgled, lamented, spat, and trooped shoeless over the tracks, into the waiting rooms, eating papadom, fruit, tobacco, and glugging glasses of a murky rack that tasted like tractor fuel. Women hawked baskets of painted toys, wooden models of Hindu gods, and pottery bowls of curds, while, framed in their booths, the merchants or *Vaisyas* jingled their wares from trays of jewelry, anklet bells, bracelets, nose rings and pointed proudly to their endless displays of *khadi* and homespun. High-caste ladies, wearing white and silver saris, rattled into the stations in gaily painted *tongas,* one- or two-horse vehicles with covered tops, pulled by bullocks with brass-tipped horns and sky-blue beads around their necks, and, occasionally, a Highness elephant might be seen, covered with a cloth of gold and a network of brilliant mesh strung over its back, bright shiny rosettes of gold like tiny inverted bowls. But the poor were clearly the majority, and all the whining beggars and children, with sore eyes and pleading voices, bleating, "No papa, no mama!" and offering to perform acrobatic tricks and somersaults in the dust for a *hoon*, or a *dahm*, seemed of little consequence to the officious, high-stepping babus—their social position designated by the furled umbrella—who stepped over them with disdain and who, if buttonholed while waiting to catch one of the dilapidated victorias which infrequently passed, turned on them swiftly with an indignant bark of "*jao, jao!*"

The trains came. The trains went. And that was all: they were never really Late for that presupposed an Early, indicated an On Time—a mensuration of false and arbitrary starts that diced into occidental segments and irreligiously bisected the Cyclic Sphere of Eternal Time, compressing all *dharma,* and, further, robbed man of the sweet resignation that billowed up like *Arabia felix* percolating from the incense in the thurible of his prayer: not action, but release from action. The Indian acted on that premise. It was a paradox. It was the smile that showed the dimple in the cheek of God, a Divine joke which proved the essence of all mysticism laughter.

"Hey, you'll get a giggle out of this. One of me mates down to Ladbroke's, a bit older," Roland began, standing up like a Rhapsode reciting an epic passage, "a Welsh bloke, a right tear-away though, well, he spent a couple of years in India as a sergeant-major, I don't know how long ago, and the reason I tell you this, and remember it, you see, was the *trains!* He used to ride the trains all over that bloody country, up and down, in and out, even up in that part where they wear pajamas in the street, just to see a Rajah, like a king, a Rajah, see? This here Rajah liked me mate who used to go visit the toms down on the chi-chi street, the tarts, you see?, get a good shag, have a bit of a go for nothing more than a bloody scrope, a ram, and all that, see what I mean? Chi-chi street, he said, up in India. Anyway . . ."

Dilip lifted his eyes toward the clock with a hang-dog plea to get himself organized. "I am fearful lest I am not telephoning. My anticipations may not fructify." Roland took his wrist and turned him to attention.

"So anyway, me mate's off to see this Rajah Something or Other, I forget the name, they don't have surnames anyway, not to worry—and he goes to this shindig up there, a party in a palace with everybody walking around in pointed slippers, veils, goony knickers, those red dots on the cheek—"

"Tika," Dilip said.

"—red dots, like, curved knives, the lot. The real thing, this was. So what happens? That's right. Me mate gets pissed as a cricket, walks up to this Rajah—and, mind you, it's getting late —and he says, 'Rajah, old boy, tell me something. Do lemons have feet?' he says. Lemons, you know? Like oranges, the fruit, but lemons. 'Do lemons have feet?' he says. So this Rajah says, he says, no, you know, of course not. Then me mate, a Welsh bloke, see?—I mean, what did he know—then me mate comes right out and says, 'Oh Christ, man, I just squeezed your canary into my flippin' drink!' "

Roland socked both feet into the air and burst into a paroxysm of screaming laughter, wringing his arms with hilarity, tears starting to his eyes, and whooping out a fusillade of brackish cackles from lungs scratched black from farthing tobacco. He repeated the punch line twice.

"Peradwenture, my friend, would you do me the favour of allowing me to impose a wow?" asked Dilip.

"What's this?" Roland cut the laughter short and soberly spat a ball of grey slaver across his shoulder.

"May I impose a wow?"

"A wow? I don't know what that means. What are you say- ing, see? What are you getting at? Spit it out." He buttoned his back pocket.

"Would you consider doing me a great serwice?"

There came a pause. Roland assumed a high-profile attitude and surveyed Dilip with a gimlet eye.

"You want money."

"Indeed not, my dear friend. Simply, I am not happily circumstanced. I must only already call ahead to explain the tardiness wisited upon me due to the late-arriving train. Pray, would you be so kind enough as to observe over my goods for me? I will then, of course, hastily return and proceed with them as was my plan in the original."

"Right, right, guv-nor," Roland swept into a deep, unctuous bow. He unbuttoned his back pocket.

"Would you think me lacking in educated good taste to have required this of you?"

"Never mind all that. Telephone's down by the loo, first left, near the stairs."

"This is an eminent kindness."

Dilip zipped off.

It's the girl, Roland thought, it's the girl! The telephone call was obviously urgent, and even now the line would be jumping with his wheedling artifices, or, worse—like that movie of The Incredible Hulk—filled with evil commands whispered huskily in likerish and diabolical croaks, the brain-trepanning spells that those bottle-nosed nigs, Congoids, and Hottentots cast at midnight in pointed hats and trick coats, using corpsedust, newtliver, and toads filled with mercury as magic barometers to swallow children, blow up churches, and work love potions on those harmless but not terribly percipient English salesgirls, who were later posted off in lumpy parcels to Port Saïd or Bombay, too ashamed, of course, to go back to Chepstow or Boodle and the happy life they had known there selling lollies over the toy counter in Woolworth's or shining the torch down the stalls at the Roxy. It was clear. It was horrible even to think of someone exposed to the fleers of this lustmonger, ready to wipe his smears of shoe-polishy discharge on some poor Trilby with skin like goldenrod and hair like down, probably now bound hand and foot and stuffed like a Norfolk pheasant into some dirty old wardrobe in a Brighton hotel, where her mother didn't even know where she was, never mind her father. It was a dead give-away. But he had to have proof.

Roland was alone in the waiting room. He quickly looked about him, then again. Then he jumped like a cat to Dilip's valise, charged with the expectation that would infallibly reveal, if not a stack of hypnotic books, packets of thaumaturgic seeds, and vials of the devil's oatmeal, then at least some kind of evidence, damning and vivid. The snaps, unlocked, flew open. First came the light and faint odour of cheap talc—and then, inside, two neatly folded drip-dry shirts, a book, a pair of green tennis shorts, a comb, a little image of Ganapati, the Hindu god of good fortune, and there in the middle, brightly wrapped in a large bow, red transparent cellophane, goldleaf, and tulle fluff, a goodly sized box of chocolates. The tag read:

> *Your Diligence,*
> *Miss L. Bunn.*
> —*My Dedicatedness, Dilip*

It was the kiss of death.

III

The Jain Code held forth one rajor rubric, long-established and inviolable in its tradition: women could never reach the state of nirvana. They could dip roses in the lake and brush them across the lips of Krishna, incarnation of Vishnu. They could worship at Shiva's temple and pour melted butter on the huge iron bull, several times life-size, and watch it glisten, dripping with *ghee*. They could kiss the noble phallus, weave on the loom, pick hog-plum, use the tandoori oven, rub the soles of their feet with red powder, and like the blessed kine, high-humped and lactate, splash out a vigourous progeny of offspring and thick, sweet milk, in agony or joy, and populate the earth. A woman could flute, and sing, and moan with love in the night, or she could drench her hip-long hair in the cool, dark wells and scamper her happy life away through scarlet crotons and sheets of zinnias, four feet high—and, yet, even if she should die spread out in that idealized and hierophantic contortion, her bare feet touching Mother Earth and her hand grasping the tail of Mother Cow, it was her disconsolate lot, *horribile dictu,* to be forever excluded from a future life as a holy never-to-be-extinguished filament burning hot in the great Bulb of Eternity.

At Cambridge, however, Dilip was to meet a woman.

In the beginning, Dilip had never been assigned a tutor. Once, actually, he did speak to a don—upon the occasion of the opening-day sherry party—at which time he expressed a desire, when asked if he had one, to reach across a continent and light up all of India; the red-faced don in question, who had been swaying unsteadily, hiccuped and lurched backwards in bug-eyed shock, delivering to Dilip an on-the-spot lecture on Terminus, the god of boundaries, after which he pulled Dilip's nose and reeled away.

Dilip, eventually, began to find his feet. In pursuit of the honours degree, he signed for a three-year sandwich course and subsequently passed the C.G.L.I. exams in advanced telephony, analogue computers, and microwave radio relay systems. On his own, he burrowed like a mole into the libraries, sitting up and crunching apples in the half-light, and proceeded to master in amazing detail three-fourths of Applied Electronics; he studied crystal lattices, radar, waveforms, and transitone diodes. He got to work with the new harmonic oscillator, a laser, the interferio- metric machine, and Gunn-effect devices. Then, he wrote a monograph for the periodical, *Noise Studies,* which attracted some attention, and perhaps on the strength of that, he was ex- tended an invitation to escape to East Berlin and, as well, offered a blank cheque book from an American university to go over there and do nothing but simply allow his name to be used in the catalogue. And it soon fell out afterwards, refusing, as he did, the two money-bruised offers, that he was given permission to work in the famous laboratories off the Fen Causeway—at the specific request of a resident don there, whose reputation, among other things, reached everywhere. Though the don was English thoroughly, she was a woman just. She wanted to teach Dilip vibration and thermionic emission.

Miss Lorna Bunn, D. Sc. (elec. eng.), M.I.E.E., was 63 years old. She looked like she lived in a cottage of gingerbread and brewed toads. Her breath was as sour as endive. She walked in a slouch, boneless as a snail, and the constantly crapulous ex- pression on her face, which showed her somewhat like an un- successful Hogarth, was due partially to a skin of rather high pilosity and, along with marked epicanthic folds, an obvious case of shingles, in the eyes—all which tended to support a campus rumour that she was one of the Weird Sisters, born in a coven during the invasions of Ereenwine in the year of the big wind. Two other of the many theories, those handmaids who service enigma, were that she was luminous in the dark and that she suffered acutely from the "green sickness," the disease of maids, the medieval mind has it, occasioned by richly deserved celibacy. Some said she discovered electricity. Some said she created it. "Sexy" (her nickname) kept fifteen cats, read avidly in sci-fi, and, away from the academy, kept alive with fitful bouts of lawn

tennis. Her passion—if of passion we may speak—her passion for
tennis was superceded, however, by only one other—and it was
to him alone that she extended invitations: to go for rambling
walks along Christ's Piece (occasional) and to come for visits
at her seaside *pied-à-terre* in Brighton (open). Briefly, it was a
late fling; by definition, presumably, one has few. Dilip had always hesitated to go, but on this particular weekend she had lost
a bit of poise and begged, slipping him, as she did, a pair of
green tennis shorts, a super-annuated racquet, and the train
schedule. He had consulted the Menu: "The aged are only young
people in wrinkled costumes." It was an errand of mercy. He
then decided he would go just this once, for he had great compassion for his don. She was "Sexy" to the students, a don to
the college, Miss Bunn to the world, but for Dilip she was always *Burra Beebee*.

"I am contacted," Dilip happily announced at the end of four
jubilant strides that brought him well through the doors of the
waiting room. "Everything is understood. I circumambulated
thrice the station, seeking into what niche lay the telephone.
Forgive me my delay. I thank you profusely for tending my
goods."

"Bite?" Roland was eating a sandwich. "Probably not."

"Many thanks, no."

"Good roast beef."

"I do not take beeves."

"English cut."

"Sorry, please."

"Aitchbone. From the haunch."

"Nor eggs, nor poults, nor the feathered chicken," Dilip
smiled. "These I am not taking."

Fussy bastard, thought Roland, eyeing Dilip with a pollution
of limp assumptions. They come over here, pitch their tents on
our doorsteps, and try to prong anything in a skirt, then turn

up their noses when offered a bit of good nosh. He thought of the food *they* shovelled in: bitter saline tea; grungy vegetables, the colour of kidney; rubberized desserts; and bread that tasted like canvatex.

"I see your name is Dilip or something. Saw it on the trap there."

"Dilip, yes," he replied, extending a hand. Roland ignored it, devouring the last bit of sandwich, his cheek bulging out in a goiterlike distention.

"Roland's mine. Roland McGuffey. Easy to remember because one name is English and one is Irish. Just like the countries, right next to each other, in a manner of speaking."

"I see."

"Don't get along though, the English and the Micks. The Micks get a few under the belt and they're ready to go for you. Bethnal Green's full of them, Micks. Three or four of them always down in the doss houses or the sheds, nourishing themselves on saltines and into the bottles of cheap plonk until the day they cock up their toes. But that's what spoils it; they have a few jars and they're ready to climb onto you. Do you see what I mean? Am I talking too fast?"

"No, sir," said Dilip.

"I'm not talking too fast, am I?"

"No, it is that the Irishmen sadly drink too much and seek out someone to go punch, punch, thus generating a drubbing."

"You do get me then. No sooner he has a glass of flip in him, a glass of crowdy, then, bang!, he's going for you, for the throat. Watch." Roland suddenly grabbed Dilip's arm and began to bend it, gritting his teeth and delivering sharp little knocks on the tight, twisted elbow: "really (knock) hurts (knock) don't (knock) it (knock)?" Smiling, Roland let go. "Micks. Turn you into a doodlesack, they will."

Dilip sat pale. A flame of fear shot up in his heart but he was not afraid of fear. Fear, in fact, was a kind of violence. He recognized it but refused to accept it, primarily because of what he had been taught in that most important lesson of his life: the law of *ahimsa*. And as he then suddenly thought of non-violence, he seemed, in an epiphanic moment, to also hear the voices of people faintly speaking words that, in point of fact, had echoed down through all the years of his wandering: "*Jai, Jai, Mahatmaji!*" He saw rising in his mind a picture of a little wizened, owlish figure in a loincloth, spinning at his charka; he was bald, with a pointed nose, spindly shanks, prominent jutting ears, and eyes twinkling behind his cheap spectacles. Simultaneously, Dilip was taken back to the very first night he had spent in England when he had stood alone in the pouring rain, in the middle of Tavistock Square in London, before a bronze statue of this little fellow, a man who had fallen down in a gunshot so many years ago, but probably, from somewhere, able to have heard Dilip's soft, plaintive cry on that same night: "*Bapugi, Bapugi!*" For Dilip had always loved Gandhi, the little grocer who peddled peace.

The clock in the waiting room showed half-ten. It could be heard ticking in the void of silence that had now fallen between them, almost reverberating in the strained atmosphere. Like tension along an earth-fault, it seemed slippage would soon occur.

This dear fellow is impaled upon my silence, thought Dilip, and it is the nub of my duty to show him I bear no ill will. And he nodded pleasantly toward Roland with the *tu quoque* gesture that spells out empathy between free-speaking intimates.

"You have terminated your work this morning, sir?"

"Me? If you mean me, then yes. I'm a wiper, me. Wiping down the buses is my job, downstairs. I won't be doing it for long, just til, ah, things blow over. I'm going down to Inchy next week and get some work on the ships, well, simply because

I like to work on the ships, if you see what I'm driving at," said Roland, standing up. "You can learn a bloody lot about ships just by looking at them." Seconds passed. Dilip again had to break the silence.

"How?"

A vivid how contradicts.

"*How?*" Roland screamed. He walked to the tea machine, spun around. "*How?* It's the *shape!* What, you don't *know?* In the ship, chrissakes, you're on top of the flaming plumbing, see?, the guts! All them...pipes." Roland's eyes suddenly went vacant, glazed, and his voice slipped out of its normal tone into a strange, incredible brown study. "It's . . . all confusing. All . . . them pipes." He was soon back to life. "You see, ships don't get the hold on you. The grip, see? A mate of mine down the docks? Blimey, man, he's all afternoon down at the *Monkey,* the pub, *The Drum and Monkey,* the pub. Goes back to the job, he does, and signs on as if he was there all day," said Roland. He paused, looked straight at Dilip. "It's a night club really, not one of your caffs. So anyway, when things, ah, blow over, as I was telling you—what's your name again?"

"Dilip."

"Right, that's what you said. Well, anyway, when things turn over I won't be wiping anymore, won't be sitting around or jacking around waiting to get on with it." Roland hitched at his socks. "You probably thinking I'm jacking around all the time."

"Oh, no, sir."

"Or moping about."

"No." Dilip was crestfallen.

"It's not that I haven't anything to do. There's lots to *do,* I mean, lots to do if you've got the open mind. The Labour Government gives you that, that's one thing." Roland began to struggle into the abstract nouns of analysis, fuming for words and confirming, perhaps, the theory which asserts that the trouble with one's vocabulary reflects the trouble with one's life. Again, came a silence.

"The train shall be here soon is my presumption."

"Though the Labour Government is desperate, just desperate, when it comes to closed doors. They've been hell with me. Matter of fact, it was only through me own savvy I got to be a wiper in the first place; no one stuck in for me, don't kid yourself. But what? It's only a fourpence ha'penny worth of job anyway, face it, and then when it comes time for the pension cheque? Sweet blow-all, that's what. I was a milk-roundsman once. It's just that there's nothing in milk around here anymore," complained Roland as he stuck his two thumbs in his mouth and meditatively leaned forward. "Not a bob to be had anywhere, really. What, you're telling me the navvies are doing a bit of alright? Coo, not bloody likely. Navvies?" he said, rolling forward, then onto his feet. "Nothing there! I wouldn't touch the ships if I was on me last goddam sice!" Roland suddenly kicked the machine a furious shot and dented it.

The inconsistency registered. Dilip consulted the Menu: "When a lie is told, who is responsible, the liar or the lie itself?" It was quintessential wisdom, and Dilip's wide sympathy spread out and enfolded Roland in a total and fraternal absolution.

"Past drawbacks," offered Dilip with his own particular sense of direction, "incline to bend one around from his level best, and, instead of reverting ahead, one indeed goes down in the mouth. That is when the game is up." He shook his head. "It is wretched how you have been treated, truly."

"I'd say shitty."

Dilip swallowed. "Indeed?"

"Not that I care. I don't *care,* if that's what they thought I'd do." Roland folded his hands behind his back and began pacing up and down like a wolf. "But what if it involved *other* people?"

"Wital obligations."

"Responsibilities."

"Dependencies."

"Right, right," Roland snapped, standing still, "like my . . ."

"Your . . ." Dilip was pity-stricken.

"Well, he's"—he hesitated—"my uncle."

Uncle! Here is this keen chap, Dilip felt, who suffers grievously, trying to manage his mercies, his employments, and to seek findables for an uncle who is doubtless hungerful, wageless, and eating *doob* on his narrow pallet, while bossman tells him to go whistle on his thumb. He does not thrive. What means this shameful deed? Goodness me, thought he, it is so much poopah.

Roland reached into his pocket. He was at the tea machine. "It was the sweetheart, you see, who took it on the chin."

"Your esteemed wife needed, of course, the monies."

"Needed it, *earned* it really. Earned it and needed it both. She stuck by me when I didn't have a cripple in my pocket, not a cripple. But, like the poet says, the poor man gets screwed everywhere he turns. Only thing is, chief, she ain't . . ."

Alive, thought Dilip. He was about to hand Roland his suit on the spot, his pocketful of sweaty shillings, and mail him, express, one of the lovely Magok rubies. The Menu, consulted, had often revealed: "Write your prayer on a flag and wave it."

"Well, she ain't the wife. She's my sweetheart, lives up in Yorkshire, Rose is the name, Rosamund actually, a nice bit of crumpet, you married?"

"I am still quite unattached."

"We seen raw days and sunny ones. There's a big difference, but you takes them as you finds them." Roland slapped at his trouser pockets. "Sorry, guv, how about a sixpence for a cup? I'm crackeye without a cup in the morning. Don't think me the bummie, I just happen to have a ten-bob note and no clinkers."

"Oh, of course, yes."

"Ta."

Dilip gladly gave Roland the coin, rejoicing simultaneously in the words from "The Song of the Adorable One" that had thrummed in his head so often, now, just as it was in his odyssey through India:

> The coin that costs a hundred toils
> That men are wont to cherish
> Beyond their life will, if it be
> Not given to others, perish.

Rose, he thought, rose: a flower. The common cipher for beauty, it was a beautiful name. *That* was something to cherish beyond one's life. It happened to be the case that Dilip had had no experience with women whatsoever, even in India. But now he thought of his sisters, Pushpa and Premila: catchwords, casual as birds, that came to him smelling of attar of hibiscus and warm wind. Pushpa, too, meant flower; Premila, the odour of bougainvillaea. And for an Indian, he knew, there existed one special relationship above all others, closer than mother, father, wife, or brother; this was the sacral communion one had with one's sister. It was true all over India. And I am twice-blessed, thought Dilip, in this mystical joinery.

Once again, as if by a miracle, he harked back to a vision, a déjà vu which elevated his spirit like long-forgotten music: it was the family house at Dum Dum, covered with white tapestry, and, here and there, the rosewood tables, intricately carved, that stood gracefully on low, hard *thakats* or wooden platforms, holding Benares trays piled high with jasmines. In the courtyard, Pushpa, drawing circles in the dust with her toe, sat near the sissoo tree while Premila worked her hair: a thin braid of three to six hairs was plaited along the hairline to outline the forehead, while the rest of the hair was pulled into dozens of narrow braids and finally woven into a thick braid reaching to the waist.

Somewhere, someone was playing a sarod. The girls laughed softly, glittering in tinselled mulls and strings of jade beads. Puberty came early in the high humidity, and often, because of their beauty, his sisters were sought out by the Rajput princes, the flower of the aristocracy, and they would all sit in the court-yard that was festooned with moist vines and enjoy their meals of stuffed parathas and bowls of saffron *pilao,* delicately serving themselves with the left hand, and ritually eating with only the right. It was a beautiful, beautiful memory, stolen from him as a child—and, if the truth be told, not really in perfect congruity with the small picture now forming itself uppermost in his mind: notably, a first-draft preconception of a certain Missahib Bunn, her sweatshirt gorged with tennis balls and her old wooden racquet raised in a scold, hopping around a net in her sexagenarian bloomers and whiffling at a white rubber ball in crooked, cantankerous swipes. Tennis was termed sportive, he knew, but all hard striking and hitting motions he felt somehow useless. Contact was always a byword for lunacy.

Crack! Roland had slugged the tea machine, splintering in a rippling splat one of the slots of glass.

"Sods! Isn't that just like them? Take your last hog and send you half-cocked to Land's End." He whacked it again. *"Blast!"*

Merciful me, thought Dilip, his body has a mind of its own.

"Perhaps another coin would release the tea. Unlikely, may I surmise, it is fully out of its commission?"

"Now that may be correct, see?" Roland fished into his pockets. "But, well, how are we going to find out, you and I?" Dilip proudly produced a coin.

"Use this one."

"Ah, yes!"

"No doubt the other coin had a chip in it."

"A chip?"

"A little crink."

"What are you getting at?"

"A tick, perhaps, in the milled edge of the coin."

"A *tick*, yes," Roland agreed, nodding. "Now that's better. Yes, many a coin does have a tick in her. They make them like that, minting them, I mean. Chip? That's coming it a bit strong. Stop looking at your watch. I had a coin with a tick in her once, and it was enough to drive me out of my rubbers. Useless: tea, underground, fags—you couldn't get a thing with it." Roland looked around him, then sidled up to Dilip and whispered. "But, you know, people do make use of them; they use them"—again, he looked around—"for *slugs*!"

"Slugs?"

"Dicky coins," said Roland. "Blacks use them. Sorryaboutthat. Anyway—"

"No, you see, I am—"

"Listen. They shove them in, see? Sometimes they use wire and sometimes rubber gum. You just looked at your watch again. Using wire"—Roland stooped theatrically, nailing Dilip with his eye— "using wire, they tie it round the coin or, see, *or* make a hole and slip the wire through, and then they lower it into the, well, the fag machine, for instance. They dip it in s-l-o-w-l-y. Then, ripitoutquick." He snapped his fingers. "A pack of fags, as the poet says, gratis."

"Remarkable and wonderful." Dilip checked his watch.

"The rubber gum takes more—" Roland tapped his temple. "Now look: with the rubber gum, they press that onto the coin. Do you have any with you?"

"Coin?"

"Rubber gum."

"No rubber gum."

"The coin then."

Dilip gave Roland a two-shilling piece. "See? So they press the gum on the bob, see, then—ha, ha, *then*!—you press a string on the gum, underneath, tight, firm, making sure it's stuck proper, and when you're going to phone up, well, say, Shepherd's Bush, you shove the coin in and just as quickly yank it out." Roland stepped back proudly and waved his hand expansively. "And you bloody well talk to Shepherd's Bush that day, dearie, rest assured of that fact. You did it again."

"What?"

"Looked at your watch. It gets me up."

"My train shall arrive *soon?*"

"It will, it will. And it will have you in Brighton in ten bleeding shakes. But you're going to get me up, you keep looking at the watch, see? So don't." Roland pocketed the two shillings as a perquisite and dropped the sixpence into the slot. He waited.

"*That coin didn't fetch me tea, either!*" The observation, anyone's, was followed by three consecutive lacerating kicks, Roland's. "*Goddam it all, now!*"

"Yes, it failed!" Roland brayed. "What else do you think it did? Right up the ruddy spout!" He dove to the back of the machine and, *ferro flammaque,* furiously pulled at the wires; the flex was ripped from the plug in a shower of sparks and a puff of smoke. The machine went dead.

"The machine went dead."

"*Perished utterly?*"

"*Dead, boy, dead!*"

Dilip held a finger to the tip of his nose.

"Perhaps I could apply myself," Dilip offered magnanimously and took off his suit jacket. He crawled behind the machine and once there, breech presentation, he mumbled happily in his work. "I do believe this machine is controlled by a series circuit. The box here should properly be transcalent, and if I unplugged it in order to—leep! it is hot as a trotter!—let me see, if I gain access . . ."

"Goddam thievery. My last six."

"...then, with lady luck, there might be found an open or a broken circuit, forbidding the path of the current which may be overloading. Wait! We must examine the series resonance where the maximum current in the circuit has its capacitance and inductance in series. Such is the crisis we are facing."

"Pirates."

"And yet possibly, however," said Dilip, fumbling, his little feet showing out like paramecia, "there is, touch wood, a built-in circuit breaker automatically interrupting the flow of current when, indeed, the very current of which I speak becomes disconcertingly excessive. No! That is hubbub and bangle! This is a parallel circuit, as I first suspected. The positive poles or terminals are connected in one conductor, perhaps outside of the train station, and if that is of course the case—sorry, sir, may I trouble you and ask if you are possessing a knife?"

"A knife? What do you mean?"

"Zip, zip."

"Oh, in other words, a knife. No, now that's something, isn't it? Oh, I know I should have, but I just do not have a knife on me."

"That is acceptable anyway, sir. Any digging tool will suffice. I will employ the clasp of my tie, so as to"—Dilip draped himself full, almost overturned, behind the machine, gritting his teeth—"so as to wrench around a screw that should make the machine yield the tea you initially wanted." The sound of little pecks were heard. Suddenly, the machine jumped into a smooth hum.

"Do you hear those noises?"

"Those noises?"

Dilip peeped out, his nose smudged. "These noises."

"Ah, *these* noises! Now, that's a different story. I hear them very well. Perfectly, in fact."

Quickly, Dilip disappeared again. "The breakthrough should

be made," came a muffled voice. "Place a coin in when I tell you to do so, if you would be so kind."

"Well, that's just it, I haven't..."

"Now, sir!" The voice again. "Dip it!"

"I don't have...I don't..."

"*Now!*"

The goddam fool, thought Roland. "*I don't have a bleeding hog to do it with!*"

A pindrop silence.

Slowly, two eyes were to be perceived from the side of the machine; a face followed, blushing like a red winegum. "Goodness me, I thought formerly you enjoyed a shilling, or a sixpence. No?"

"None!"

"Even a bitty one?"

"*Never none!*" screeched Roland, a wildly indignant mode of exculpation in which grammar was sacrificed to emphasis.

"Oh, I am entirely at fault," replied Dilip, reappearing. "Consequently, I have merely left you in a flurry of wishful thinking."

Dilip again scooted behind the machine. And, again, Roland flipped a shiny new coin.

"Set?" sighed Roland.

"In one blink of a moment, my friend."

A whoosh of exasperated disgust from Roland ended in a curse involving someone's mother and an unusually inventive dog.

"*Now!*"

Roland slapped it in. The coin clinked, down flipped the cup, and an uberous flow of tea splashed down smoothly, on perfect cue, filling it to the brim in whorls of smoke.

"Ha, ha," proclaimed Roland, with the ratiocinative wink of Dupin, "then it was the, ah..." He wiggled his little finger.

"Parallel circuit, yes it was."

"That's what I thought, but it's a damn shame we have to knock our arses off just to get a cuppa. They should manage these things a sight better if they expect my business, the bleeders." Dilip put on his coat.

Roland then sat down on the bench and slurped an inch of tea from the cup, his satisfaction affected in clucks and sips—an onomatopoeia of digestive noises indicative of a renovation attributable solely to that sweet, warm brew, the absence of which, in England, is a synonym for death in the popular mind and the potential de-fuelization of an entire island. That Roland had three-fourths of the cup in his mouth struck Dilip as curious, for in India the Hindu never drank directly from his vessel; instead, he tilted his head back and simply poured away. Similarly, in smoking the hookah: his father, he remembered, had always curved his fingers themselves into a tube and drew the smoke up through his hand. England, India—two abstract nouns, really. Countries, Dilip thought, should be named for, called by, and defined as verbs. Verbs alone not only classify, but indicate behaviour, and it was the behaviour of people, and of countries, that made them different. He consulted the Menu: "The legume at home is always a nut abroad." It was so wery, wery true.

"Tea," Roland smacked his lips, leaned back and yawned, "was invented here. England. It's the leaves, you know. Home-grown. Did you know that?"

"Actually," said Dilip, smiling, "it is carted over from Orient. Importedly."

Roland sat around. "What?"

"Tea plant is mailed here."

"I was thinking of coffee." Roland fished for a crumb in his tooth.

"Ah," Dilip replied again, "in the century of the eighteenth *grabb* after *grabb* from Andhra Pradesh in India sailed to here loaded to their wery teeth in most pungent of coffees.

"It don't matter, does it? It don't matter. Don't try to get the argue, lovey. My point was, we need a good drink here, for the rain. It puts you right, see? We have more rain here than anywhere else in the world is why. We love it, rain."

It was a game. Dilip could see that.

"Assam," Dilip giggled, prepared with his little prank, "is wettest place in whole world—420 inches a year, to London's 26." He bounced with free fun.

It was a shoulder-charge; Roland back-pedalled only to be ungraciously bumped upside down inside the penalty area. Fans were leaving. The shirty bastard, thought Roland.

"Rain," sneered Roland. "Or sun. Where's the real difference? The *real* difference."

"Three and one-half hours of sunlight, daily awerage in Great Britain."

" 'Sright, mate. Which is bloody huge, goes right up to Scotland. Mountains. Seas."

O glee! thought Dilip. He loved the academic gavotte. "You must be knowing, India is eighteen times larger than Britain. We are one-fifth of world population. Mountains. Seas. *And deserts!*"

Advantage interviewee; interviewer to serve.

"Shakespeare."

"Kalidasa."

Roland's nose whitened. "God Save the Queen!" he shouted. It was a periodic rather than competitive remark of Roland's and there, he felt, was an end to it. He lighted a cigarette. But Dilip, mistakenly, thought the game continued and named *his* national anthem. "*Jana, Mana, Gana,*" he said, clicking his heels with delight. Now, Roland's face grew dark as the Doncaster pits.

"Buckingham Palace!"

"Taj Mahal!"

Dilip, his voice raised in naïve, bubbly excitement, actually hated to be so correct. But it was always the best of his humble replies, he thought with innocent joy, for the entire world, surely, was in total agreement about the beauty of the Taj: marble lace walls gracefully curving up into perfect onion-shaped peaks in luminous soapstone, carnelian, and jade mosaics, all rising beyond a reflecting pool trimmed about with perfumed grisleas, acacias, dhaks, and sals. For all its grandeur, its pomp, Dilip knew, Buckingham Palace looked like a small tuppeny loaf of rye, or a rather sad Leicester cheese. Then, all of a sudden —with absolutely no hint of a warning—Roland exploded from his seat, howling: *"Power! Battle! War!"*

Saint Menu of Rajputana! gulped Dilip, his heart withering, that is a preachment all its own, leaping irrevocably beyond my poor ability to reply or even grasp. Have I then bungled so hopelessly in this good relationship that these words of attack have found deliverance in such angers? The words cut him. Violence crushed man like pestles spice. Hate caused violence, and he almost hated himself for recognizing the violence in himself— which simply proved it all.

Dilip well knew the history of antagonisms under the British *raj* in India. It was part of the folklore. The English might seemed always the legacy of the twin tyrannies of The Will and The Wish: bedfellows both, salt as hyenas, bucking under polluted sheets in a calendar of nights that knew no end. The Will imposed, the Wish conceived—and out burst the ugly runt of Colonialism, an infant Mars swaddled in chain-mail, blowing fire, and screeching for dominion. Even as a boy, Dilip himself had been exposed to that formula of oral tradition which records, collates, and channels once again the news of long ago and weaves anew, in repertorial bric-a-brac, legends that never die: the Sepoy Mutiny; General Dyer and the Amritsar Tragedy; Curzon's "Convocation Speech" at Calcutta; Bentinck hunting down the Kali thugs; and, of course, the illustrious Clive, in red tailcoat and white breeches, leading his little columns of sepoys through the green jungles, crying defiance from the ramparts of Arcot, and waving his sword triumphantly 'mid the cannon smoke at Plassey.

All his life, he had heard the caveat against those graft-ridden little boffins, the I.C.S. officials; the carpet-bagging traders from the East India Company; and the interminable regiments of gin-soaked, mutton-chopped drubbers, many educated at Elphinstone or St. Stephens, who marched through the villages in puttees, white helmets, and uniforms imperialist red and gold, all chewing from thick rolls of compressed Cavendish tobacco and swinging swagger sticks at the poverty-hounded illiterate rustics in Kottachairy or Kerala who stood by on the roadside in a queer sort of silence, filled with dark sad stares and reproachful echoes. "If every Indian were to spit once," the radical-conservatives of the Jan Sangh party often cried, "we could drown the British for good!" *This* was a collusion in which Dilip could never participate, for, turnabout, this was *also* the indulgence of The Will and The Wish: a Scylla and Charybdis through which the spirit of love could only sail in peril! Touching on this, he had often consulted the Menu: "What receives blacking from one age should be polished in the next."

Dilip looked pleadingly at Roland, like a mouse might crawling over the horny, yellowing toenail, wide as a cornfield, of the Tyrannosaurus Rex. Was there forgiveness in his heart, he wondered, for his own unforgivable rudeness? He felt small as a penny. The *hysterica passio* in this recent intercourse, thought

Dilip, perhaps only showed a man weary of his many toils. There was nothing personal, surely.

"Say, do you mind if I put a question to you?"

"Surely," smiled Dilip, glad with a chance of contrition.

"Surely, you, ah, *mind?*"

"I do not mind, even a tweet."

"Well," Roland jiggled some wax from his ear, "I was just wondering if, ah, I was wondering if you're making it down the line, to Brighton that is, to, well, just for *holiday,* is it?"

"For weekend, yes. A short wac."

"Wac?"

"Wacation."

"You mean holiday."

"Yes."

"I thought you meant whack. A quick shag, bit of a jig. You mean holiday." Roland smiled. His teeth looked like the cromlech of Stonehenge.

"Yes."

"Thought so."

Roland picked up the newspaper, which now looked like a shred of ancient papyrus. He paused: "You, ah, you going down" —he looked behind him surreptitiously, then back again—"with anyone else?"

"I go by myself, yes."

"On your tod, is it?" Roland nodded. He chuckled. "No, um, no bird going with you, or anything? No girl, like?"

Dilip suddenly caught the gist of the conversation. He laughed brightly. "No, indeed. I shall ride down alone."

"Oh."

The ball was Roland's on a hold. It was a wall-pass, now for the dribble through the pivot, past the sweeper, and then a nice banana-shot into the money.

"You, ah, got a girl."

"Sorry?"

"I say, you *got* a girl. Haven't you? Someone to"—again Roland looked behind his shoulder, then back toward Dilip and breathing in confidence—"someone to keep your back warm, eh?"

"I know English ladies from time to time, yes, and have both rambled and interdined with my chairman several times. I find them most unselfish and never devoid of self-respect."

"They are, that."

Chairman! thought Roland. Chase me around the wash-house! Not enough he's on the razzle with half the crumpet in the British Isles, he's a bit of a Nancy to boot! He had heard that before. They did it for candy. It was part of their religion.

"But what I mean is, you don't have a girl down in *Brighton.* That's what I had in mind," Roland clarified, "when I put the question to you." Dilip now entertained a peculiar feeling and picked up his book to read. He tried to smile.

"Yes, sir. A woman is waiting for me down in Brighton."

Roland pointed beyond the waiting room. "That's, ah, who you rung up then, that it?" There was not a noise. "That it?"

"Yes, sir."

"On the telephone?"

"Yes."

"Thought so."

Roland went back to the newspaper, Dilip to his book.

The intervallic questions, quiet, created intervallic silences, loud—and filled with terrible implications. Dare I suspect connivance?, Dilip asked himself. The consulted Menu had once stated: "Look for the insomniac in every sleeper, the drudge in every queen; then, look no more." Surely, Dilip felt, the treachery is all mine. Dilip read firmly into a paragraph, to lose himself in the business of a diversion that would save himself from the form of murder called rash judgement. They were still both reading. Roland never looked up.

"English?"

Dilip lowered his book, slowly.

"Sorry?"

"I say, an *English* girl?"

"A lady."

"Ah yes, forgive me. A *lady*, I meant." Roland bowed.

"Yes."

Roland bit the inside of his cheek. "Oh."

A cruel shape suddenly seemed to stand astride them, over them, casting a shadow that lengthened along in eerie, almost nocturnal distortion—an eclipse disquieting and monstrous. Then, Roland spoke one word from behind the raised paper.

"White?"

Light flooded in: a failsoof, clearly, has asked that question, Dilip knew. I am in the presence of an aborigine Bheel, he thought, and quickly consulted the Menu: "Deception is only Perception spelled incorrectly." Oh yes, thought Dilip, it *was* a matter of perception, and he wanted, there and then, to recount for his suffering friend the ancient Jain tale he had once heard on Mt. Abu: *Mrs. Elephant and the Yowls.* Four blind men (it began), whereby to know it, hastened to describe the creature elephant. Their similar affliction caused dissimilar interpretation. So, was the elephant described: he who touched the ear saw her as a fan; he who touched the leg saw her as a pillar; he who touched the tail saw her as a whip; he who touched the trunk saw her as a dong-pull. Thus (it ended), were the men truly blind and left to wander forever in their umbrages, all the poorer. That was the story. It was a good story.

"I said, *white?*"

Roland stood up. Dilip blinked once.

"Yes, sir."

There it was: a long-range drive into the pitch, a boot-and-run on an overlap, a punch through the clogging and—chop!—gametime! Gametime!

The bell for the train rang.

A strange incident then followed as Dilip fixed his necktie and stood up. It was a pavane: Roland circled the bench. Dilip circled the bench. Roland circled the bench. Together, they halted.

"Into the sweetcake, aren't we? Bit of a spiv, aren't we? Over here having a right old knees-up, aren't we?" The voice was cast iron. "*Huh?*" Dilip jumped into himself in fright.

"I am hearing the train go 'ding,'" Dilip croaked.

"*Huh?*" screeched Roland, choking on the word, his eyes flashing fire, like the little boy, pop-eyed, who screams mercilessly when his vegetables suddenly touch each other in the plate. "*Huuuuh??*"

Wiolence, thought Dilip.

The little Indian lowered his eyes and picked up his valise. "I must embark now."

"One thing, en it, to give them a box of sweets, like a bloody ponce, maybe even a Dundee cake. Quite another to be giving one of our own the free ride and turn us into a ruddy jungle over here, a zoo, a goddam zoo, a zoo full of them secondhand mongrels and golliwogs, black as pitch, kids walking around all with a touch of the tarbrush and pointed heads, what?"

Meep! Dilip inhaled a deep, horrified breath and jumped fumbling at his valise. "Oh me, had you to poke through my personal goods, sir?"

"Awww, ease off it, guv'nor. The bloody thing flipped open because you forgot to put the yank on the lock. In a public utility, what'd you expect? This ain't the Ritz. No more than you'd do."

Wengeance, thought Dilip.

"I could not do such a thing, my friend," asked Dilip, almost inaudibly, "could I?"

"No, no," Roland growled, his jaw distorted, "you'd only be having your own peek-a-boo session down in the Brighton sands is more like it, en it?" He breathed fury into Dilip's face. *"En it?"*

"I do not understand."

The bell rang again. Roland, his head cocked at a pathological angle, now drew toe-to-toe with the little Indian, drawing a curlicue around one of his soft buttons, staring like a hawk into his eyes, and speaking thickly: "You can get crapped for that where I come from, ducky. You know that? You don't know that, do you?" he wailed. Then he spit out in disgust. "Course you know it, you sneaky bugger! You bloody sharker!"

Wiciousness, thought Dilip.

It was, however, like throwing stones at the rising sun. Dilip, with his unending versatility of intake, merely stood in the midst of the horrible echoes bathed in the bright radiance of his queer and uncommon faith, which the military and secular call bravery. Then he quietly, patiently, picked up his racquet and valise and tottered just to the doorway, wondering, all the while, only why his friend had thrown his character away, almost like a pure electrical flow sputtering out in a frayed plugless knot of snipped copper wires—and all for nothing. Dilip felt himself a failure and, furthermore, terribly, terribly concerned, for in this matter—not uncommon for him—he had often consulted the Menu: "Nullity is nothing to worry about—and we all must!"

Roland then sprung out of a sudden, like a birch-broom in a fit: *"Keep your black, bloody paws off the missies, Jack! I've got a good mind to come out there and give you the treat."* He paused, gone white, twitching. *"A damn good mind!"*

The final bell rang—just as Dilip turned to Roland, with a face shining like white samite in what looked like an almost unearthly and serene resignation, his eyes twinkling like gems. His heart was like a rubbed ciborium: year after year, beaten upon, battered, and buffered into a smooth rich gold, it now shone out in a pure silver-white lustre, in blazes, very like a flame; and from that ciborium, filled with hosts of gold, Dilip then lifted out one incredibly lovely wafer and held it out to his friend in a very, very quiet gesture of communion:

> The Buddha, being abused, was silent, pitying the folly of the man who abused him. When the man had finished his abuse, the Buddha asked him, saying: 'Son, if a man declined to accept a present made to him, to whom would it belong?' The man answered: 'In that case, it would belong to the man who offered it.'
> 'My son,' said the Buddha, 'thou hast railed at me, but I decline to accept thy abuse and request thee to keep it thyself. Will it not be a source of misery to thee? As the echo belongs to the sound, and the shadow to the substance, thus.'

And Dilip was gone.

Roland's eye darted: a quick peck, like the eye of a corncrake, through his sharp squint. His heart dripped with fury—then it drenched itself dry, grew hard, and finally it shut. The train whistle blew before he moved, his fists closed at his sides, his sharp defeated face long and gooselike. He lurched forward, then, in rapid actions: he was out of the waiting room like a whippet, down the dark stairs, and once again within the station cellar, flea-pits gunpowder grey and hollow as a cenotaph. The sound of water was still pouring from somewhere in cold splashes. Roland heard his own whickering footsteps echo to the end of a long tunnel where, in these catacombs, one bus sat alone in a kind of Scotch mist, the glassed-in sign, top front, having been rolled to show its destination: Houndsditch. Roland boarded it and sat down in the shadows, a sort of violet deathlight round his jaw.

The bus was empty. Roland, in a slump, knee on the bar, stared at the biscuit adverts, job notices, a sign from the chamber of commerce of Wiss. For some reason, then, he began experiencing a vague sense of agitation, even worse than the recent battle he fought. It was instinct, what then happened, for now suddenly unnerved—perhaps as an occupational irritation—he began levitating slowly as he caught, just beside his ear, on a wide panel that ran like a ghat to the rubber floor, a very small, inch-wide blot. It was dark, almost perfectly round. He look away, but the blot seemed waving in the cornea of his eye.

Roland flicked at it with a finger. He hitched his cuff into his hand and drew three swipes across it. Then he felt his pocket and pulled out a handkerchief. It was his souvenir: the vernicle of the Hyde Park orator. With it, he rubbed the spot again: swish, swish, swish. The blot remained. Roland turned and faced the panel; grinding his teeth, he gripped the cloth into a wretched ball and drove it furiously over the spot in sequential rubs and fast, violent tugs. He spat into the panel, spat into the handkerchief, and went at it again: nothing. He bashed it. He scratched at it. He bonked at it with the edge of his hand. Then he looked, bewildered by what seemed, but could not possibly be, a simultaneous result: the panel coming up like new, the blot remaining as it was. Roland looked again; he could not see his reflection. He lowered his head, jerked it to the left, the right, but from the polished panel came no reflection, no reflection whatsoever. There was only the shine. There was only the dot.

Suddenly an idea, slim but cogent, sprung quickly into his mind, that *apparat* of sweet craft, closet skills, and arithmetic trickeries, which revolved so fast it almost seemed to swallow itself up, very like a barber pole. Roland sat up in his seat, on the edge of a resolution instant in its appeasement: *why not simply pretend the blot was part of the bus?* Hel-lo and bloody good-bye! All was borne in on him in the swift nose-thumbing logic

Roland called his own, and inner suasion that almost formed in a bitter smile on his lips: but not yet a smile, only the slight trace of cunning flickering in the eyes, like the child who marches into the kitchen, looks about, and swiftly pockets a cookie. Why should he give a damn? Why should he give one damn? On such premises did the experienced wiper act—that is, if he was to get on into the next wash and not send the night dickering into the day. It almost made him laugh, out loud.

Roland, however, did not laugh. Out loud. Or within. What was curious, in fact, was that he did not laugh at all. The whistle of a laugh, if any formed at all, had been for some time now strangely snuffed out at the base of his windpipe, oddly stuck fast and dry like a hollow reed pinched tight by the terrible force of some inexplicable press of gravity, almost as if—through some ghastly misplaced pressure, increasingly more manifest— he saw that his entire life now rested within the grip of that single frail resolve; as if, in point of fact, it was *only* that single frail resolve, made there in the shadows, that alone could make the busride back to Houndsditch less painful, and, if to speak of perpetuity, the only possible way one might ever possibly believe he could live happily ever after.

THE WIFE OF GOD

Reverend is not a title. It is an adjective set before a proper name—and perhaps not even one all that proper.

—Alexander Theroux

3

I

The Reverend Which
Therefore sucked, then swallowed a black
jujube, one on which he could just as easily have bitten
down, he was that agitated. The ormolu clock beneath a portrait
of Lord Eldon bonged eight. He discomposed himself on the
sofa, with the relish of tragic collapse, facing the shut door of
his mother's bedroom with a frantic concern he was momentarily
unequipped to assess but which was traceable, in fact, to an
exasperation stalled only by two inner oppositions: the duty to
be civil to her who bore him, and the need to point out that
they would be late for the ballet. He thought of St. Theodylus,
patron saint of those who suffer from cruel apprehension.

"Mo-ther, *really*," Which complained, using syllabic distinction
for emphasis in a question he felt a justified simplism, "is this
like you?" But he merely heard a high silvery laugh form into
a coo, the coo into a growl, all from behind the door that
wrecked any attempt at direct confrontation.

It was getting dark. The pulled windowshades of Lady Therefore's commodious flat on Great Cumberland Place (W.1.)
filtered out the world of trade and swop, any glimpse of
smoky sky, and any intimation of the reality of the non-proper-
tied classes, and yet always somehow kept intact within the
brushed and curried elegance of the lyric past. In no way could
the furnishings and general décor of a room be more studiously
focused on that invisible point of coincidence between the dog-
gedly alive and the much-lamented-for predeceased. Here, the
nostalgia, the sting of implication, in a room through which the
swagger of a vanished age lighted up those temperaments
sympathetic to it—a mid-eighteenth century tallboy in winestain

mahogany rubbed to a manic shine; a glass boscage with a stuffed touraco and monarch butterflies on milkweed pods and panicle; and an S-shaped Louis XVI tête-à-tête of soft blue velvet, upon which sat a pack of cards spread out in an unfinished game of solo and a magazine opened to an essay, the title of which was emotionally circled in red ink: "The Osprey: World Endangered Citizen?"

Suddenly, the door flew open and through it marched a little old snailshaped lady dressed in black surrah silk, who held a small crystal pot at arm's length and, rolling her head from side to side, sprayed on her flavescent skin a heady perfume with cadenced squeezes from a grapesized syringe of lavender. A squawk of delectation. A sniff. She brushed the air and pushed her nose into it, sniffing, detective, her eyes closed. A sniff of delectation. A squawk. Two oval spots on her cheeks were rubbed the hue of prawn, one of which she mechanically turned in profile to her son, raising her neck and jutting out a very, very firm chin. The votive offering: Which bestowed upon her a dutiful kiss.

"Mmmm, there's a good boy." Quickly she recoiled, sputtering, "Eccch, your tongue's black!" Her son flinched and then, his hands flat on his hips, he paced to the other side of the only room to stare vacantly at a painting of two cows lolloping across a Constable heath.

"A comfit."

"Oh," she burbled. "Isn't that just you all over."

"This is *beastly* inconvenient, you being late, if you must know, Mother. And to actually be amused by it all." He split the infinitive deliberately.

"Ours is a nasty life," she matter-of-factly remarked to a placebo as she popped it into her mouth. She stuffed some keys and cigarettes into her handbag.

"Well, it is all rather a mess, now you mention it," Which petulantly replied and looked away.

Tidying her hat, she feigned a whimper. "Aren't *we* the stormy petrel?"

"Dash it all, Mother, I've been sitting there one *hell* of a long time." He pointed over her head.

"Were you? Were you really? Pity. When I should know specifically you much prefer I hurry off without so much as a sprig of mums on my lappet to jolly myself up." She paused; then with a glare through a cribriform veil she had just pulled over her face, she enunciated crisply, "Please however—" Which saw the danger signal of the conjunctive adverb and the load it carried coming into view. "Shut up." She looked up sweetly and smiled, then coolly arranged her bluewhitegrey hair with fluffing self-indulgent motions and, sporting the price of a few lives around her neck, ordered into trim six pieces of fur, the colour of henna: foxes, with eyes like small sepals, biting each other's tails. They decided not to take the limousine and trundled out to find his car, Which's mother moving along with a curious poultrylike flutter and refusing his assistance on the landing with a thwack of her cane. He hated this independence in her and thought of St. Genuina who always used the imperative when praying to the Holy Ghost.

"It's *Sleeping Beauty.*"

"I saw that last year."

"You're always ahead of me."

"One year to be exact."

Lady Therefore was a compulsive diarist.

The trick was now to drive as quickly as possible to Covent Garden where, rising high out of the fruit carts and stacked cases of guava, the Royal Opera House sat dead center in the sacramental universe and sent out to the world from the primeval swamps of transpontine London its nights of song, its evenings of momentary illumination. They burred off down Wigmore Street and into Oxford Street with a hook movement, Which fulminating at the wheel and his mother hanging onto the bar at the passenger's side like a dark silk mormoop.

For Lady Fanny Therefore (a Spottswood-Sheets), born of an old family from Tittinhanger in the county of Hertford—the ancient manor house, "Runcible Acres," used by Wolsey to stage rat fights after the dissolution of the religious almonries by Henry VIII, F.D., in 1536, still stood—the close relationship to her only child was paramount and shifted into the area of possession only when jeopardized, an alarming possibility, she knew, in a world now rife with alternative. She accepted her role as mediatrix of all graces to that glorious, if fading, past, down through which their good name echoed in histories, proclamations, and battle cries. The past alone mattered, an occasional rubber of Écarte—and her constitutional. Through all the civic rubbish did she walk of a morning, a starched and spotless figurine on a funereal drift, who frequently took tea at Lambeth Palace with the A.B.C., could fondly quote Castlereagh from memory, and never ceased to scoff at the new machines that clacked against her heart, a closed valve now to all the common wrangling and innovation, appropriately devalued, especially, when she summoned to memory either the resolute Elizabeth I who used to walk winglike in her jewelled dresses through her palaces on floors of straw, or thought of Queen Victoria who rocked across India on her howdah and, even if unamused, never so much as hinted for a glass of water, to say nothing of a rubber cushion. Now, was all a mess. Only last year at Wimbledon a company of Tory peeresses, with a duchess at their head, had hissed the Queen; Americans repeatedly refused to kerb their dogs in Belgravia; the sandwich had found general acceptance; and children, once loyal to their mothers, would now think absolutely nothing of pronouncing the word "exquisite" on the antepenult, grinding the salt at table, or blowing out the Christmas pudding before grace. Where now the days of Old King Cole, three-hour sermons, and the glissando of swans that mirrored the flight of young hearts, O where?

The Age of Shoddy was alive. Everything had become all that it could ever be, she felt, just about the time Rupert Brooke gave up the ghost (and poetry) in the Aegean, deluded in thinking, poor boy, that some corner in a foreign field might be England, just when all those young men who looked like Donatello turned, waved goodbye, and were gunned down in the sun and sea-shells—a time when England, *esto perpetua*, was a land of fat green pastures; policemen had walrus moustaches and hearts of gold; and handsome men in plus fours, crewelled pullovers, and boaters joshed each other goodheartedly with cricket bats and noisy love on the trimmed lawns of Swanage Bay in Dorsetshire, where Lady Therefore had been taken as a girl at the start of every season. She looked back mistily upon that age—enacted, signed, and enforced—when a large annuity meant safety, England meant civilization, Thackeray meant romance, and women piped cakes rather than slovenly made do with a rough icing.

Here, nip. There, tuck. An age of random piety this now was, slackly trained to believe that sincerity was an excuse for nearly everything. She took umbrage at the slurs against the aristocracy, for if they were in-bred and out-of-touch, as was alleged, was not this the lesson of pedigree, that a good wine needs a good bush? And to be out of touch with the modern world—the peculiarly noisome allowance of Bolsheviks; thick cups stamped with the name of the Bangkok Railway used at tea (where people never bothered to take off their gloves); and crimes as horrific as Peter the Pointer's now committed every day—well, this was more praise than indictment. But hers, she knew, was a creed outworn; her husband (an Old Blue), long dead now these past twenty-five years, was ever to point that out—that is, before she lost him in Somaliland (Br.) where, doing research on a brief history of the world (which *his* father had brought down to A.D. 17 from the Creation), he was poisoned by a tribe of hydrocephalic Pygmies, all with creased skin, wide mouthfuls of broken teeth, and fly swatters, and, being flown in a mail-shuffle back to London where he showed himself swollen to such extreme they couldn't see his eyes and no more of his nose than the tip of it which looked like a wart, he fatally succumbed—but not before he rose on one elbow, squinted over the counterpane, and proved himself the Christian everybody had hoped he had been. "Read to me of The Four Last Things, Fanny," he managed just before he drooped into Eternity.

"Blast!" sibilated the cleric as he spun the wheel through whizzing mopeds and some flimsy curricles, and, missing by inches two men wheeling a pushcart, he swerved rattling into one of those dark narrow streets within Covent Garden, where, not a century ago, rotting match girls with hollow eyes and skin the colour of paper sat huddled in the doorways, whooping, rheumy, consumptive.

"They're all out tonight, seems."

"They?"

"Fruiterers," Which shrugged. "I suppose."

"Yids." Lady Therefore peered into the outer darkness. "To a man."

"These were black chaps," her son replied. He paused. "By the way," he snapped impatiently, suddenly aware of a bitterly literal realization he had thus far managed to repress but which had been nagging at him all day, "I find out yesterday I'm to be on the *qui vive* for a new choirmaster." He honked a pedestrian leaping onto the kerb and angrily mashed the accelerator to the floor.

"Signifying?"

The answer came hard. "Cyril is leaving."

"Cyril?" Her eyebrows arched into pyrrhics. "Your nigger?"
"*Not,*" Which pushed his face an inch from his mother's, "your common garden variety, may I add?"

"Bonzo the Magnificent," said Lady Therefore with a dry spatter of croaks that might have signified laughter; Which heard the sound, but when he looked into her face he could not find even the slightest trace of amusement, only chagrin. Then she added, her mouth thin with disapproval, "One of the descendants of Cush, cut the cake as you will."

Which, zooming along, offered a bit of muddy resistance, one of earth's old fierce simplicities, as he explained a semi-carbonized people in terms of the wicked equatorial sun that had grilled the lower Africas for centuries; but his mother, beeping out in a voice of an angry peewit, pointed out in what had for some time now even exceeded her bimensual fit of pique that the rays (which Phoebus avert) could have done the same thing to England, but did not; that it had, for instance, left the good people in Lapland perfectly wax-white, God bless them; and that he had best mind his driving. Deedum, deedum, deedee, thought Which.

"He is really such an amusing fellow and says such absurd things, well, I'd have thought you'd rather adore him."

"Poppycock," she grunted.

"You know, they're not *really* foreign, not quitcish. Rather like you and me, in a way," exclaimed Which from the side of his mouth as he ducked his head out of the window in order to negotiate a parking space. There was no room. He drove on in bumps, like the conversation: systole, diastole.

"Anyway," replied Which, "that thing of darkness I acknowledge mine."

"Well," she said, shifting in her seat, "that was rather well put."

"I can't claim it."

"Who can?"

"He of Stratford-*super*-Avon."

But Lady Therefore was thinking of Cyril. "That blackamoor has the manners of Wat Tyler," she snorted, sitting up explosively as she remembered the day she had been seated across from him at one of the church buffets for the Barnardo Homes, a curious act of commensality during which time—establishing himself somewhat as an African Heliogabalus, who would eat anything that didn't crack his teeth, shriek, or make his eyes water —he had consumed an entire bag pudding, four large bowls of Gooseberry Fool, and then proceeded to attack a whole baron of beef. He had drawn the platter toward him by the tablecloth, and, smocking the joint with consecutive blows of his fork, dangled huge slices before his hidden face, at which moment, as the center concaved and disappeared, everyone sat back aghast as he slurped and chewed until the rest of the beef followed in with a loud cloacinal suction, while the juices streamed down his chin. After that he ate a few spoonfuls of butter, burped, and walked away.

"Still, in a way, he's clean," Which smiled, unable to repress an amused, if fleeting, thought of St. Bridget who was, according to legend, vouchsafed in a vision that she could, without sin, wash herself twice and even perhaps thrice a month.

"Perfectly grotty!" barked Lady Therefore, amplifying that with a sour face. "And we don't need a full-blown psychotic episode about *him*."

She pictured Cyril mythopoeically: a Dark Morlock, sloppy, smokeyed, limping through her dreams with his socks down, a salivating anthropophagus chewing khat, punching mandrils and hartebeest, and, with his thousand tribal members sitting on their haunches in the clearings, drinking strip-me-naked from wooden bowls, polishing their teeth with pieces of soft stick, and farting into the grass.

Rev. Therefore noticed his mother, her mouth locked on the

cigarette she had lighted which was half-coated in red lipstick and which she constantly yanked away to make her remarks through a smoking rictus.

"I wonder how their lot ever got into the Ark," she puffed.

"They're—what?" Which looked for a word on his trimmed nails. "Basic."

"Cuckoo Pie!" his mother protested with a frown, her little face with its high colour and wrinkles twitching like a turkey's caruncle. Which tried to explain himself, but Lady Therefore, jaw firm, held up her hand as a semaphore that nothing further would either be said or listened to. They rode on, a solved antinomy.

"Park here," she said.

He did.

Together, linked without a fumble, Which and his mother joined the enfeoffed gentry stepping grandly from without Rolls-Royces and Bentleys in front of the Opera House. A sense of métier prevailed: a flow of juristic faces, bordered in fur and spanking white collars, beamed a fugle of salutes, blown kisses, and effable recognitions. Infatuated with continental swish, Which Therefore felt at such moments that a gorgeous angel hung pendant in the sky, somewhere overhead, blowing out a silver *incipit* on his trumpet and was having, doubtless, a whacking good time himself. Ever solicitous of his mother, he now skittered at her side from group to group as she spoke to friends her vatic wisdom in backchat and tiny paragraphs: one could see them begin, gain momentum, lengthen, and snap off into quick dead ends. She moved among and remonstrated freely with old rouged dukes, M.P.s, and the Men Who Moved Affairs, embarrassing Which only on one occasion, when—purchasing her program—she peevishly confronted Lady Glendower (who was neither): "Why in hell weren't you at Mass Sunday?" Then she marched away like a ruffed bustard, confiding to her son, with alarm and indignation, that the woman in question was in fact a Christian Scientist, born of crofters in Huntingtonshire, a county not only sunken in fens and a hotcupboard of Nonconformism but which also suffered the reproach of being suburban.

The orchestra struck up. The lights dimmed to that artificial sundown that silences the chatter of voices and rustling pages; a sea of heads lifted toward the stage. Lady Therefore, who would have been much happier playing out a hand of Piquet at home, sat like Boadicea with a lorgnette. She glanced at Which who asked wasn't it wonderful, and then for the opera glasses; he sat smiling, translated to heaven, waiting for the curtain. The priest's figure lacked consequence—sex. She thought of that day at Sotheby's several years ago, when Which had worn green gloves and sipped soda and Campari through a straw all afternoon, and of the remark one of her acquaintances had made, unaware that the man in question was her son, that he looked terribly *tapette* and was he?—the answer to which a more energetic, because a slightly younger, Lady Therefore provided, umbrella foremost, in the form of a quick kung-foo shot to the ribs.

Rev. Which Therefore—an old name he thought more a Divine Wisecrack than a parental choice (though an odd, quasi-ecumenical temptation *had* suggested itself to Lady Therefore at her son's christening when, the faith aside, she seriously considered calling him after one of the beautiful names of Leo XIII's encyclicals: *Humanum genus, Aeterni patris,* or *Longinqua oceani,* all arguably better than a relative pronoun)—looked as spruce as an onion, wearing an off-white shirt of satinet with Wildean flounce at the sleeves. He had eyes the colour of clarified butter, showing a kind of flexibility and openness betrayed neither by his slight but energetic body nor his volleyballshaped head that looked like the full, round topside of an Harrovian boater. His hair was thinning somewhat, often prompting recollections, uninvidious to be sure, of St. Nichodemus of Thyatria,

patron saint of bald heads, who was circumspectly martyred by
having a goatskin nailed to his pate with a tenpenny nail. Which
welcomed the chances to go clubbing with Mother, never bruised
the gin, and believed in the importance of being earnest. He
had, in short, the soul of an interior decorator—and found dam-
nable any and all of the popular space theology so rampant in
the England of today, especially in the Blavatskyite and theo-
sophical underground. No mystagogue, he was ordained according to the Order of Melchisedech, which he considered himself
more ambassador from than representative of; nevertheless, he
occasionally surprised himself with a passion, which perhaps
exigency forces out, for amplifying the Gospels and pigeonholing
for the young at heart the vouchsafing graces of the sweet,
multifaceted, and adaptable Jesus over Whom he couldn't help
but poeticize, even during summer. He did so, however, in the
same non-precipitant and assured way that one recognizes with
specific discretion and passes along to another of worth the deep-
chested soundness of some Piebald Ten-Year-Old at Ascot or the
very place where one can find a disquietingly toothsome *poulet
de concombres* in the London area. The rest was quibble.

Religion for him did not involve the ascetic preoccupations of
wearing hair shirts, fire-walking, hanging oneself up by hooks,
avoidance of baths, or nakedness at vigil. Depressing to him
were the various ecstati and trancists howling for universal repentance from soap-boxes and then, especially dispiriting were
the Salvation Army girls in their unbecoming coal-scuttle, poke
bonnets, who gathered together on weekends passing out copies
of *War Cry*, booming away on drums, and singing out with
seamless optimism a monochrome "Jesus Is Our Baby Brother"
or, a favourite, "The Bottle's Only a Downpayment, There's No
Way of Counting the Cost." Neither could he abide the neurotic
malaise in England that spawned and sent shuttling out into the
traffic little pavid sandwichmen who gave their lives to religion

but feared to search for God (lest He somehow turn out to be a Latitudinarian) and who squeaked angry destruction from behind placards which broadcasted grim, fatalistic warnings from Isaiah and Paralipomenon, nor those odd faiths, animated contumely, which goosed thin, hawklike anythingarians, aswarm with pockmarks and spicate hair, into prooftexting the Bible to and barking for maniacal repentances from the night crowds and theatre-goers lolling around Piccadilly and Regent Street on any given night.

Which, a delicate boy, had been raised by three nannies, all of whom looked like Mrs. Danvers—bunhaired, always dressed in bombazine, weird—and one of whom, on a train to Goole one rainy weekend, hastily and for no apparent reason put aside the complete volume of the rhythmoids of Nurse Lovechild, from which she had been reading aloud, and began discussing in a fit of sudden letch her "enormous diddeys." Later, it was brought to light in Bow Street General Court that she also tried to touch his "watering can" (sic). Spread abroad, this came to be known infamously, and looked back upon traumatically, as The Georgie Quaiff Incident (a name Dame Rehabilitation, in her infinite mercy, willingly altered for the poor jade's passport when she was rusticated to Australia the following week). But the tabloids had had a field day.

The boy was immediately posted, with a bag of sweets, a new pair of wellies, and his late father's interlinear Caesar, to an Anglican seminary in out-of-the-way Wem, Shropshire, where, it was hoped, he would come to look with horror on his first and hopefully last bout with genial carnality, guided by the Deanery of high repute there whose good example and instruction, it was said, would instantly mould and bake his volition from the moist ceramic it was into the Graecian Urn it should be. It took the eminent divine, Dr. Lushington—a prefect as old as the pre-Wren St. Paul's—no more than three months to tap his supply of angelic energies and decide for the lad that he had a vocation; it was then ordered that Which should be thanked and encouraged in this blessed, if factitious, decision to serve God, Whose emanations, it should be equally pointed out, caused minor, but unsettling, religious questions in the boy, and before the full Charismon, mandala of the Christians, could be imprinted on his soul with any degree of force, certain quodlibetical worries had to be resolved:

1. When Mass is being said at two ends of a church, where precisely is the Holy Ghost?

2. Was God the Father too embarrassed to become Man?

3. Had Eve a navel?

4. When Christ said "Teach my Gospel unto every creature," was the non-restrictive term intentional, viz., life on other planets?

5. May one pray to St. Polycarp and never be distracted by the name?

6. If the Monastery of St. Medard of Soissons has a tooth of Our Lord and the Abbey of Our Lady of Sudden Gladness the prepuce, then is He, in fact, fully risen?

7. Was Adam a hermaphrodite?

8. What are we to think of the Totality of the Godhead, given the fact that the Paraclete clearly might have moulted?

9. What tongue was spoken by Adam and Eve in the paradisiacal triangle with the serpent? Micmac? Rarotongan? Shelta?

10. Were the spittle curatives mentioned in the New Testament (a) less efficacious if administered from afar, or (b) ever—a curious paradox—fatally bacteritic?

Time passed. Which Therefore studied hard, won the approval of the faculty, and, some years later, was sent up to Oxford (BNC) to do his Austins, where he took a respectable Second (with thanks to St. Frideswide, patron saint of stout-hearted

Oxonians and the Old Boy network) with his highly readable
hagiography, *Saints Preserve Us*, later followed by its companion
volume, *Saints Alive*, critically acclaimed both (". . . two scrupu-
lously honest reassessments . . ."), then illustrated and abridged
as Puffins for general use in schoolrooms all over the British Isles.

Lady Therefore was firm on one point, however: he was *not*
to be sent to Africa, for, her husband's death aside—she was trying to be objective—she had heard stories from the very mission-
aries who survived that colour-blindness was inevitable, women
didn't know the meaning of underpinnings, and for Mass the
foolish nig-nogs did nothing but suck grass, bite chinch-bugs,
and transubstantiate stones.

Subsequently, Which was anointed, ordained, and, circum-
scribed with neither debts nor wifely compromises, eventually
given a parish in London. When he heard of his incumbency
(coincident with a contribution Lady Therefore had sent to the
Bishop), he decided to jump at the chance, for this was a rather
special church: St. Peter Perpendicular, the church known inter-
nationally for its reliquary, where on display were a pair of slippers worn by Enoch before the Flood; the thumb of Anastasius
the Cornicular; the coalrake that was used to broil St. Lawrence;
one of the columns Christ had leaned against in the Temple; the
stone pried from the forehead of Goliath; and a not inconsider-
able piece from the *medulla oblongata* of St. Face.

Act One began: Aurora pricked her finger, Carabosse cackled,
the Lilac Fairy entered, commanded a forest to grow, and just
as she brought Florimund to the palace to kiss the princess, Lady
Therefore sighed as a coda to it all, "I should have stayed home
and played pushpin!" Simultaneously, an enchanted Which was
curving his hand to impose pictorial composition on the final
tableau that he might commemoratively carry it home. The lights
came up.

"King Florestan's off, isn't he?" remarked Which, sitting up and wiping his fingers on a pansy-embroidered handkerchief. People, all around, stretched. "He *will* make those goo-goo eyes, dreadfully unbecoming, don't you think, seeing he has the thighs of a yak? No, not up to the magnet, I'm afraid. Not up to the magnet at all." But Which, passionate balletomane, burned for the dance, and, whatever the shortcomings, he could give intricate statistical descriptions—as he often did for his mother as they rode home—of every cabriole, fovetté, and soubresaut. In his delirious mind, even hours later, the milk-white coryphée spun and bobbed in stiffened net and graded frills as did the perfectly formed male *solistes*, in black velvet gilet or Greek chiton, who seemed to ride the wind.

"Trulls all," averred Lady Therefore, thinking of the wasted evening surely better spent in a good game of Bezique, in which, by the way, she always showed a wildly fated ability to win points even on the difficult Royal Marriage, never once forfeiting.

"Did you see Prince Florimund during that grand *jeté*?"

She yawned. "Vis-à-vis?"

"His satin de Lyon tights?"

"Charming, to be sure."

"Them's nutmegs," Which giggled into her shoulder.

"Actually, the Prince of the West looked he had a perfectly frightful case of nephritis," she said.

"The Prince of the Fat Fibula." It was a joke he couldn't resist.

"He looked as if he used nasal spray to comb his hair."

"That was hair?" Which asked, smirking into his hand.

"Furze, rather." She smiled a wave to someone somewhere. "As rigid as a barmaid's."

"Capital!" Which clapped.

"Ninette de Valois, pray for us," said his mother with a *paulo maiora canamus* expression crossing her face as she folded her arms. She needed a drink, she said. "Come, we're a cup too low" —and she and her son, upon whom she leaned, stepped nodding to no one out of their seats and moved processionally, with their co-religionists, up the main aisle, the mother all the while giving out with dry bitter cacks bearing on the wasted evening. Once in the foyer, Which stood in with a huge group of men at the bar, each one noisily advertising an overpowering thirst, and ordered when his turn came two iced vermouths; then, holding them high, he lurched back to where his mother was sitting, exhausted, in the midst of some haughty damson-eyed women and a crowd of stiff-backed men looking all remarkably like John Ruskin.

In the foyer, the chandeliers, all brightly lit, gave off the sheen of sunned snow to the winking composition of gems and jewels below, refracted in tiny burns from stickpin, necklace, diadem. Proud ladies in pelerine capes and empennaged hats and gentlemen in polished dickeys danced, and would forever, a minuet of good fellowship, poise, and a predestined alliance, passed on from generation to generation. Gay laughter echoed throughout the foyer like the high tinkle of ice-cream chimes as ceremonious introductions and reunions took place with the selected proems and soft enunciations impeccable taste alone can dictate—a pretty spindrift from the hard, mercantile conversations that broke only in private and unwitnessed crashes on the metaphorical shores of home, office, or within the chambers of Parliament. If one beheld the handsome crowd, ringed around in well-fed faces, expensive cloth, and rutilant mandibles from which emanated large draughts of self-assurance and the smell of good money, one also beheld a blessed crowd, aureate in the halo looped over only the singled-out and sanctified, those alone guaranteed, with quiet confidence and divine right, that boon so many seek, so few would know—the promenade from Life into Eternal Reward through the Doors of Paradise wrought with golden hinges by the Triune God, alone, happy, and breathless as He waited politely to meet and live forever with His peers, masters all of that heterogeneous collection of territories from Africa to Asia, Malta to the Zambesi, from the island of Anguilla to the reaches of Hong Kong. The Deity *was* given precedence; it was only fair —though it was understood equally, of course, as a *primus inter pares* situation that permitted the lower case D to be used and accepted as good form, for by employing the capital initial one feared, realistically, just the slightest dash of flunkeyism in the usage. Society worked that way. It did not work any other way. This was not a gathering of hatchet-faced couples or yodeling, country-bred herberts in cloth coats and hard brown shoes down from Scrabster, out for a night on the tiles. Neither was it a *Narrenschiff* of walleyed conventioneers slapping each other on the back and squeaking through horns. Nor, yet, was this a mere group filled with finicky whims, teasing each other with ineffectual velleities and social chit-chat. It was, in fact, an event, only another of those moments in the march of time that sent into the wide-eyed and onlooking world of nondescripts and churls the hunting cry of the *ancien régime*: "Floreat England!"

Suddenly, Lady Therefore burst out of her seat, much in the same way a frog will explode like a pistol when thrown into a fire; she grabbed for a railing and sputtered out, as if from infective breath, a poison blast of air that seemed to dampen and wilt the helix of shiny ivies bucketed in gold on the spiralling staircase before her.

"It's that whipjack black," she spat.

"Cyril?"

"I see no bone," snapped Lady Therefore, facing the wall, "but that *is* Jo-Jo, the Dogfaced Boy, isn't it? How sick-making!"

"Bone, you say?"

His mother pointed with little jabs in the direction of her clenched nostril as an explanation. She added, "Don't notice him." It was more command than advice. The victim always sees the difference.

"I won't see him," Which replied weakly, without conviction, in a flash of not-very-soundly-managed repartee as he noticed his choirmaster bobbing through elbows and arms, directionless, like a seal. He offered to get his mother a glass of hot black currant, an aid upon which he often relied in order to confect disparate matters simply. It was very like him, especially at such moments when he inevitably thought of St. Unencumber, patron saint of women in delicate predicaments.

"Is *he* habitué here, may I ask?"

"Well, that's rather the capstone of the whole thing, you see. You realize why he *is* here, of course." Which surveyed the long hall imperiously, drew some air through his nose, bent down, and stared deep into his mother's eyelash fixative. "The little coloured nosegay you saw up there in the burnt-umber tutu dancing the Fairy of Temperament is his Intended, coordinately seen, recognized, and proposed to within a fortnight, mind you." He paused. "Or so I've been told."

"Do you *say* so?"

"Anita," Which asserted in a voice full of mimicry, "which may rhyme with *muy bonita*, but I'd be the first to disagree, given I've had the redoubtable pleasure of seeing her without stage paint, which more or less puts her into the pure nigger bracket, you see. Grim?" he asked. "Grim," he answered. And he sought here to darken an unbidden picture now forming in his mind, the unmistakable image of St. Petronilla, patron saint of charwomen, who is always portrayed running about indefatigably with an arched broom.

"Nevertheless, she's a ballerina. Their private lives are worse than was Lot's wife's. They're all on the Soviet payroll. And they have the personalities of Medea, true. But they are not sales-girls, say what you will."

"I prefer Markova."

"Born Marx."

The patronymic was abhorrent on several levels.

Which looked up, surprised. "Is nothing sacred?"

"Yom Kippur, presumably," said Lady Therefore.

"For her?"

"Certainly not for me."

"For Markova."

"Born Marx," repeated Lady Therefore dryly. It was not redundant. It was clarifying, something to be kept in mind at all times, and invoked when necessary. The same was true of the Lord's Prayer.

"Anyway," said Which, "it appears the poor oaf knew her in the home country, wants to return with her. He's constantly at her beck and call, so I've heard. The calls are endless; she must have two strings to each bow. The becks are worse, and apparently she's been becking him right from those very first days in the thornbushes of the Tonga, during the transcontinental jump, and then all the way to London cum England without stop as if he were King Shrovetide, Monarch of Sneak Island. In any case, with me it's all too simple: no Cyril, no choirleader; no choirleader, no choir; no choir—well, you see how it goes. For her he leaves me flat."

"Why her?"

"Her," Which snapped. "Just her." He felt no compulsion to explain what he took no pleasure in recalling.

"A mopsy. A demirep."

"Hear, hear." Which yawned.

"Laced mutton."

"A temptress."

"A Jezebel to the eyeline," she remarked, looking at her gloves critically, "excuse that, but I'll give you she does pray with her knees up. It was the smile. Chaucerian. It evoked barbarities." Then Lady Therefore peered inconspicuously in the direction of Cyril, who was washing his hands in the water fountain. She sipped her vermouth. She was out of pocket, Which could tell; it was the stricken look that bespoke bad hands in their late-evening games of Pontoon. "And as for him, well, with a face like that, my dear boy, he'd as soon try to milk a pigeon."

"Well, there you are," her son replied vacantly.

"And, of course, all this serves only to show your average baboon would run up and fondle anything with a temperature of 98.6, animal, vegetable, mineral, or pound-note, the nincompoop. That's exactly what's happening on the other side, in the colonies. I say, *now* where are you with your half-dozen and three arguments to prove me their brainpan is any larger than a follicle on Hop-O'-My-Thumb's rubber leg." She sipped again, smuckered. "A darkman's budge who'd give his eyeteeth and the Channel Islands thrown in for even so much as a good-day-and-how-are-you from an English girl, bet on it, bet on it, dear."

Lady Therefore tried to make harmlessly unpremeditated and desultory what were, in fact, immaculately deliberate remarks, borne of those *mis en place* reflections that commonly point out what garden we should cultivate, that east is east, and just how birds of a feather should flock.

"Are you the woman to enjoy an irony?" Which suddenly asked his mother as if preoccupied with an interior joke. Lady Therefore's mouth sprouted into a valentine.

"The very." She moved closer.

"Well," Which began, with a ripple of a simper playing on the corner of his mouth. "On Queen's Accession last I had Cyril over for my Escargots Bourguignonne—candles, music, the lot."

"Don't say it. He filched the spoons."

"It was quite the evening," continued Which, shaking off the supposition. "Let's see, we started off with an *amuse-bouche* of Beluga caviar. Next, we had a ripping cream soup of imported German pfifferlinge mushrooms (here, he raised his thumb) and, for a touch of the bubbly, a nice wet Moët et Chandon; then,

fresh strawberries marinated in kirschwasser and covered with
an absolutely *scrumpy* orange sauce (here, he joined in a circle
index finger and thumb) and, and, and"—Which began to
bounce up and down excitedly trying to remember but almost
not wanting to do so, it was all so devilish—"oh yes, fresh chicory
coffee *and*, wheeee!, three or four snifters of Hennessy Extra,
which, let me tell you, nigger or no, he had little or no compunc-
tion in knocking back. A-n-y-w-a-y, the thing is, I had done my
bread that afternoon (here, he kissed the tips of three joined
fingers), and, this is the giggle, I pointed this out to him, 'Cyril,'
I said, 'this is called the kissing crust'—the part where the loaves
had touched in the oven, you see; well, may I be frank in telling
you that Miss Prunella over there in the ten-guinea suit leans
across the empty shells and tongs, listen Mother, and directly
says to me, 'I eat so good, I should kiss you.'" Which popped
his eyes and plugged his cheek with his tongue. "Kiss. *Me!*"

"Good," she took a massive breath, "heavens!" Then Lady
Therefore, for whom familiarity had always been a kind of im-
pudence, clamped her jaws together tight as a cowry; she sucked
her cheeks in and candidly nodded as a sign that she had clearly
divined the very act, so universal it was, years ago—with the extended meaning, of course, that it was a great if existential pity
that people like her son had to undergo those experiences which
were eminently avoidable, because ever foreseen, to the specially
endowed prophetic.

"Now *that's* bloody-minded." She grabbed for a cigarette out
of her vair cigarette case and fumbled it into her mouth. Which
lighted it, and she coughed out a rattle of tobacco fumes, adding,
"What infernal cheek!"—the last vowel combination making for
a not insignificant blast of exhaust which sent forth in smoke a
parade of crazy blue animals.

"Rather a pity, I suppose."

"That he's *onto* you?"

"Well, no actually, rather that he and the little titmouse who was golfing around up there in that perfectly clumsy *battement dégagé*—or that embarrassing *croisée derrière*, when you kicked the seat—will soon come home by weeping cross, shouldn't you think? What I mean is, when she'll bubble, he'll squeak. Wouldn't that be more bang-on?"

"Oh pooh," said Lady Therefore, chivvying him. "It's not so much he's a ruffler, Which, who wants to run around Greater London in the buff-tint until the reign of Queen Dick. Think, on the other hand, how extraordinarily tiresome it would be to be *married*"—she threw her eyes to the ceiling, maybe Beyond— "to such, to such an ostrogoth, never mind a man of colour." Given, she had heard that the Church of Rome had honoured one of them recently: St. Martin de Porres might—*might*—have been a man of virtue, perhaps (though the Bishop had rumoured he was a Sicilian), but to raise to recognizable beatitude a man the colour of a tarry bowel movement was a bit much, really.

"To my mind," she continued, her jaw creaking, "colour rhymes with trouble: always has, always will. It all goes back to Cain, doesn't it, who stole his brother's pottage, was turned black as a Newgate knocker, and, wrapped in his coat of many colours, was sent off in the direction of his face to Africa, the Wapping of the World, where gorillas wee-wee in waterfalls from the palm trees right in the wide-open, things go bump in the night, and where monkeys, so they say, could speak if they so wished but prefer to keep silent so they won't be made to work, the beastly things, just like the niggers—or the Wesleyans. I'll take my tea home, thank you." She flapped her arms. "But will you listen to me?" She glowered and snatched a long puff. "I'll rub-a-dub you will, my dear boy, and *that*," she reached up and snapped her fingers at his nose, "is your trouble."

"There *is* the parish obligation, Mother."

"That is to say?"

He looked away. "I'm to give him a marriage counsel tomorrow." Lady Therefore stood paralyzed; she had urged Cyril's departure too long now not to see it through to Test Match.

"Now *this* is something I haven't heard," she said with a sag that seemed to recognize the almost too late but implacably in time.

"I'm afraid it's true, you see."

Lady Therefore clasped her son's chin and pulled him down to eye-level. She narrowed her eyes. "Well, I'd simply tell him how we apples swim and have done with it!"

"I could be wrong"—the palliative seemed called for—"but, well, he mightn't understand," Which whined.

"Haw!"

"It rather brings to mind the idea," replied Which, marching into view on personal initiative a motive that seemed impregnable, "that broad-based under all is planted England's oaken-hearted mood." His fingers interlaced, neatly.

"Absolute bilge," she snapped. "You *will* read poetry. Well, I'd as soon baste his jacket for him, and then see if you watch his teeth smile on the other side of his face." She released his chin and shook her head in disbelief. "Was this well done?" she asked pointedly, aware, as she was, that remonstration was a privilege of motherhood, even if one's son, puffed up as youngsters can get, presumed on more important business in the Temple. Which skated his shoe along its edge and looked for just a smile of corroborative solace. "Let me answer for you," she said.

Which went rubbery to forfend disavowal.

"No!" came her answer, like a pea from a slingshot.

The two-minute interval bell sounded. Which directed his mother by the nose of her thin elbow back to their seats before the rise of the curtain, she a repository of racial declamation and torrential huffs, while he fanned from his mind thoughts that began to make manifest the easily accessible and not terribly new rubric that Life is a Bitch. He thought of St. Elmo who had his intestines wound out of him on a windlass. They sat down, but not before Which Therefore swivelled around in his seat and threw one furtive, almost pleading glance into the squash of the audience behind him to once more behold in the growing darkness, just before the Lilac Fairy blessed the marriage of the Prince and Aurora, the boy he loved.

II

Spring, so mellow, seemed an occasion of sin. The pale sky was tessellated into cirrus and white air, and the simple creases of hot sun that seemed the active gropings of a spiritual eye seeking to adjust the shafts of its focus on a country which self-assertively, almost capriciously, thwarted them with the not infrequent tesserae of thick clouds that this Royal Throne of Kings, this Other Eden, this Happy Breed of Men, this Realm, this England interposed as a disputatious sign it would reveal its infinite variety only in its own good time and would blot out with fluffy sullage any imposition, divine or otherwise, it did not ask for and consequently need not abide.

Cyril biked vigourously, in hoops, to a halt. He rolled his bicycle to the iron fence and peered up into the fanlight: dark. A card, embroidered in the margin with art nouveau squiggles, was tucked into the doorknocker under the stoop of the rectory of St. Peter Perpendicular, and a welcome message (*"Adeste, fidus Cyrilus"*) in vermilion ink told Cyril he need not bother to ring, simply to enter. He paused on one foot. He thought he heard music. He heard music. He loved music. Everybody loved music. These deep thoughts poured through his head. He wondered if he should simply open the door and go in. "Yes," he philosophized.

The door opened: a wrench of his mouth mimed the wrench of the door handle. He was inside—and eased the door shut; he walked into a large living room which was filled with pots of melilot, Solomon's seal, and prickly pear. There was an antique mortised faldstool in the corner, behind which was hung a burnished girandole mirror. Rows and rows of shelved books ran almost to the height of the high coved ceiling, a canopy so beautiful it harmonized only with that lowly self who stood below in proper dotlike awe and reverence. Such was Cyril: who then noticed a brown postcard of the Grand Hôtel, Cabourg, pinned to a wall, with a doily surround over the fireplace, and next to that was a large print of the famous Visscher Engraving of London, upon which was sellotaped a glossy photo of Marlene Dietrich, blue top hat, blue hose, inscribed "*für meinen Schatz, Lola.*" Music piped out from somewhere in the back of the large flat.

"Cyril," sailed a voice from the bedroom, "is that you, dear?"

"I am, Sir Reverend."

"Which," the voice corrected.

Cyril shrugged. "Weetch." He pulled off his bicycle clip.

"Have in here, honey."

Which Therefore was sitting up in his four-poster bed, flipping through some sheaves of paper, stretching out only to momentarily flocculate one of the mauve silk pillows spread around him. Upon seeing Cyril, he peeped mischievously over the sheets, like an homunculus through a jar. A gramophone within easy access to him was blasting out, on an old 78 record,

Fred and Adele Astair singing "Fascinatin' Rhythm," and he was kicking his feet up, keeping the beat, under a thick pink puff.

> Fascinating Rhythm, you got me on the go!
> Fascinating Rhythm, I'm all a-quiver,
> What a mess you're making! The neighbors want to know
> Why I'm always shaking just like a flivver . . . .

He scooped up a fistful of papers. "The Bishop's directives for Mothering Sunday, damn his canonicals." He threw them down, tittered, and spooned a globe of hippolyte from the top of a glass of Irish coffee on a tray beside him, slurping it in with a coy hunch of indulgence that implied that although he was such a bad boy, he really couldn't help himself. Which extended another creamfilled spoon, but Cyril deferred with a goofy arm movement over his head that signified either embarrassment or, maybe, new seismic rumblings somewhere along The Great Rift.

"Yum Yums?"

"Sweeties," Cyril said, "are being prohibited me."

Which looked perplexed, his spoon in mid-air. "Why, pray tell?" He hesitated a moment and then looked very closely at Cyril. "Dear me, Cyril, do you pluck your eyebrows?"

"Yeep, no," he replied. "I mean these nuts on my face are unsightly." Which peered curiously to see several offensive nubs like seventh-cadency marks on the dexter side of his stubbled, if heraldic, cheek.

"Blemishes," concluded Which in a bubbly, eupeptic tone, gulping the spoonful to show he was indifferent to any significance here. He waved the spoon. "But you simply must put aside those second helpings of foo-foo you're so keen on, mustn't you?"

The question was rhetorical, due partially to the played-out record, for Which quickly hopped from the bed, puffed dust from the grooves, replaced the needle, and, alive with hyperboles for the immortal duo, danced for Cyril a feathery tattoo through the room, with an old faded album cover, presumably Adele, possibly Fred, as his partner. But just as Which swooped away, humming to finality on his toe and arched backwards in a deliquescent swoon image, he noticed the empty bedroom. Cyril had disappeared. He had ducked from the room, not so much mortified by as unable to cope with a circumstance then unforeseen, critical only in that it had no particularly exact precedence in his relationship with the clergy: the priest was stark naked.

> . . . O how I long to be
> The man I used to be!
> Fascinating Rhythm,
> Oh won't you stop picking on me!

Which clicked off the machine. He slipped into a black kimono and some rope-soled canvas shoes, blaming himself for having embarrassed Cyril: a bad complexion, he knew, could be the very devil, but it would certainly clear itself up and was simply the result of his ravenous penchant for coagulate meals of half-rotten skate and greasy chips in those fourpenny ordinaries in the Notting Hill backstreets, for instance, and elsewhere in those teashops where the knives and forks were chained to the table and the gurry on the floor lay thick as an afghan. He thought of St. Rocco, patron saint of acne and skin diseases and, by extension, teenagers. Simply, the muse Hexachlorophene was not Cyril's. Lately, for lack of a care Which would have gladly provided, Cyril had come to show himself somewhat ratty: his eyes, once handsome, now looked like two rubber grommets; two brown shrubs of moustache looked like two small animals burrowing into his nostrils; and one had to look several times at his flaring bushy hair to ascertain for sure that he was not wearing a Russian shepka. On the other hand, Which was thankful that Cyril was a cut or more above the usual Negro who,

more often than not, took to the streets of London with more
cheek than Dick Whittington's Cat, showing feet the size of
shovels, soiled eyes, and a kind of paraphimosis of the nose. But
he did not want to offend Cyril. Not at all. That was the last
thing he wanted to do.

Cyril had appeared a quite different fellow before he got settled in London, that is, just when he had presented himself, at
Which's invitation, fresh from Negroland to the parish council
with only a tarnished pitchpipe, a tunable voice, and the chewed
manuscript for a "Kyrie" for wooden clackers and reed finger-
pipes in his back pocket. The vicar from the old St. Mary Ove-
rie's, visiting Rev. Therefore at that time, remarked, in fact, that
he, Cyril, actually had the beautiful Greek profile of Master
Ludovico Ariosto, though he felt he needed to add, lifting his
bumper of ale and squeaking with laughter and wheezes, that
he *was* "in his altitudes" and blamed that on Which's inexhaust-
ible cellar.

Which worshipped Cyril on the spot, thinking, as he was, of
the legendary beauty of the Hamites—tall stature, oval face, and
magnificent physique, each one to the last. And now, lethargic
and crablike, the poor fellow was crawling in a most unbeautiful
way toward that subterranean cave, demonstrably female and
the so-called apotheosis of the patently attainable she, which
shuts to with the speed of the Cyclades and the noise of thunder,
whereby the feelers snap and, unpincered, the shells shatter like
slate in an implosion of foolish microscopic crusts. Which, however, hoped with all his heart to exorcise him of this little chit,
and he thought of St. Equitius who once expelled a devil which
a nun had inadvertently swallowed on the duct of a lettuce leaf.
From that still pulsant body must the good curate of St. Peter's
now pluck those arrows, twanging still, shot from the hot little
hands of that hideous Cupidette who had forced him to his
knees and sent him into a blind, even ridiculously happy, vale-

diction to all good sense. His Dark Angel would sing again.

The Shilluks, the tribe of which Cyril was a member, occupied the country along the west side of the Nile, northward from about Lake No. Cyril's grandfather was a Bongo of the Bahr-el-Ghazal province and made enough money in the red and white gum business to send his grandson to the Gordon College of Khartoum ("Old C.G., eh?" Which once smiled in recognition), at which time he converted to Anglicanism—the angels, it was clear, were of the same persuasion—got interested in music, met Anita, and flunked out, in that order. His grand-father—for his father, whom God recompense, he never knew as that good soul, having one day carved a boat from a sunt tree for the Independence Day flotilla, suffered a rather embarrassing and inopportune cardiac arrest just at the moment of launching —refused to be demoralized and sent Cyril with his three stuffed carpetbags to London, or, as he said, The Land of the White Gums, with the express order that he was to translate into Tshi, Ewe, Efik, and Mandingo the company's multicoloured gum catalogue and not to come back until. Anita, still *à la barre* in a local dancing school, promised to follow and pressed a kiss into his palm that burned still.

Cyril's grandfather, the night before Cyril would leave to sail up the Nile, threw a huge outdoor banquet for him there underneath the stars and moon, having invited all the villagers to eat freely of all the roasted collops of bushbuck, dik-dik, and wart-hog, all spitted to a juicy brown, after which Cyril moved clock-wise around the guests and kissed them all—for it was in perfect accord with an old Shilluk rite to offer to rise and kiss everyone chastely on the brow, after each meal, as a post-prandial symbol of *agape* and goodwill. He found himself in a backwater of London nine days afterwards in a bed-and-breakfast with his dictionaries, a snippet of Anita's thermogene hair, and an acute case of homesickness.

Life broadened somewhat: Cyril had taken one long trip to see some of his fellow countrymen who were studying religion up in Thedwastry, a school world-renown for its plain chant, and one afternoon he spent all his time in the British Museum, not only the Areopagus of British culture but a building, it turned out, with long, long corridors where he loved to just sit around and bellow, the echo was so pleasing. But the guards, on that particular day, blew their whistles and told him never to come back again. Another spasmodic, but engaging, diversion for Cyril was found in the tunnels of the Underground, where, as a kind of Aeolean refreshment, he jumped against the warm rushes of wind. He waited. Wind blew. He jumped. He waited. Wind blew. He jumped. But this was a pastime not terribly over-reaching in its variety. That was when he began to spend his afternoons in Green Park, where, sitting under a tree by himself, he boomed out to stuff the void of longing with the shatter of flying muscles, a never before heard music beat either plaintively or rapidly on a zebra-hide drum he carried along with him and which, one day, caught the attention of Rev. Therefore, at that time walking his schnauzer in St. James. The music conveyed to Which what he felt must be the night side of Africa's consciousness, the pagan throb and delightful menace of rhythms that had thundered timelessly over a continent through the uncorrupted songs of strong, black giants he'd read about, dreamt of, but never met. A bead of sensation had now appeared on Which Therefore's faucet—and one, he felt, that could never stop dripping. "Where are you from?" Which had asked. "There," a voice announced in a single vibration from a dark, lovely body. Cyril was pointing across the park to Africa.

There were small, uncomplicated interludes that followed the first formal visit to the rectory: Which lent Cyril the odd pound, took him to an occasional play, and eventually convinced him to channel his talents through the rationally directed aesthetic of a High Church choir which for some time the priest had been trying to organize. And now his charge was about to forsake the merry servitude of God's Work for the corrosive and fugitive state the insufficiently self-reliant euphemistically called marriage. Dedication napped.

"You. Wicked. Young. Thing," announced Which, who entered the living room and moved through it like Henry pacing the Cloth of Gold. "Failing to show up at Evensong yesterday, Cyril, I should give you a jolly good hiding is what I should do." He threw up the shades. "Rather a dodge you've put me into, as well, may I add?" Then Which held up a bottle of cognac. "Drinkie, mmm?" Cyril slapped his hands together and gawked, nodding with delight. Which filled two tumblers; Cyril grabbed his glass, smiled, and rolled his eyes with satisfaction. "You will have an excuse, of course, fifty of them, but I shan't hope you imagine that will make me any happier." He tossed back his drink, smacked his lips. "It won't."

"It was imperative for me to will have gone to Royal Ballet to disgust this conference with Miss Anita," explained Cyril. He laughed. "Oh me, I have a scheme."

"Anita?" Which could be obtuse.

"Anita the girl," Cyril replied, turning away and selecting a self-conscious prop from the shelf in the form of a book; he opened it to the bookplate, a ferroprussiate reproduction of one of Rouault's mauled Christs, with Which Therefore's name in ten-point type substituted for Pilate's inscription (Which could not resist off-beat humour). Cyril began drumming his fingers on the plate. The priest, a booklover, saw the motion, owing to some strange sense of urgency, shift into a claw, a scrape, and immediately pulled it away and returned it lovingly to his collection, among which numbered: *The Compleat Adrian Beverland*; a facsimile of "The Porkington Manuscript"; Simon the Anker's *The Fruyte of Redemcyion*; *The Dramatic Works of Shakerly*

Marmion (1602–1639); Josephus Petrinus's *Pomettes*; Mrs. Beeton's Cookbook; *The Moral Basis of Fielding's Art*; Coryat's *Crudities*; Edward's *Gangroena*; a copy, in boards, of the Complutensian Polyglot; P.C.T.'s *Nosterel*; Sacrapanti's *Le Capucin Démasqué; A treatise of fysshynge, wyth an angle* (the first piscatorial essay in our mother tongue printed by Wynkyn de Worde); a stained codex of bromides from the not always reliable Nennius; Fuller's *Gnomologia*; Pierce's *Supererogation*; *The Wooden Works of Thos. Anonymous*; the rare *Whimzies* (1631); Geo. Coleman's *The Rodiad*; a black-letter tract called "The Nun in Her Smock"; E. Ramberg's *Die Zuchtrute von Tante Anna*; an extremely peculiar bisexual *roman à clef* called *Raymond*; the Church History of St. Benet Sherehog; *The History of Costume*; a few incunabula; and R. M. Ince's *Lipstick,* reputed to be the *locus classicus* of the dildo.

"Conference," Which said flatly. "Conference? Ahh, conference!" he suddenly exclaimed, holding his drink to the light to see the ruby dancing in it. He sipped, held on his tongue a puddle of cognac, then swallowed. "Your pending marriage, yes, of course." Which spoke the word marriage as if he had just then bitten into a year-old macaroon.

"I weel want to be married." Cyril downed the entire drink and looked up grinning. He looked like a Fuseli goblin, his eyes beaming like light bulbs.

"Yes," Which coughed. "Well. We'd best funnel it through a bit, don't you think? The wisest minds in history have told us repeatedly that haste makes waste, and those same minds would have it that marriage is nothing but a permanent contract based on temporary feelings, not that they're incorrect, not that they're correct, mark you, they are just the wisest minds, you see." He thought of St. Engulfus, patron saint of traduced husbands, improvident males, and/or the combination thereof. "No big thing," he pontificated, "but in *your* case, well, what about your case, my dear fellow? I shall go right ahead and put the question to you. Is this simply spring fancy? A crucial need?" He sat down and raised an eyebrow, the slimmest of. "Or just naked whim?"

"I want to wive."

Which stood up with a sigh, went to the large mirror, and, rotating his head, vacantly slapped his jowls as he did every morning to worry away some fat: *thap, thap, thap.* He could still taste in his mouth the Moselle wine he had used as a dentifrice that morning. Mornings, to speak of them generally, disoriented him, and on this particular one he did not really know where to begin. It occurred to him to ask Cyril where he was getting the money for all his plans, but he thought he might save that question for trumps. It would be a symmetrical *coup*, at the pinch.

"Why not knock the ball directly through the wicket and ask what it could be you really want from marriage?" He waited.

"I want to wive."

So we're going to be that elemental, thought Which. What a nasty mind. He poured Cyril another drink.

"To drag her about? To hold on to? To grow old with?" he asked exasperatedly.

"To hold on to," Cyril beamed.

"To hold on to *what?*" asked Which. Vagueness he abhorred.

Cyril siphoned in the whole glass of cognac in one suck and focused on a horizon somewhere beyond the room.

"Her tits."

Good grief, thought Which, wouldn't that be just up his street? The simplicity was shattering.

"Splendid," Which managed to say with a sedulously contrived chuckle. "A not uncommon predilection, Cyril, if a trifle, how shall I say, *nimis naturae?* Not to worry, there can be nothing whatever gained by frosting an eggshell, and, that by way of preface, I feel it's only fair to tell you that marriage is based on love, love faith, and faith, according to the mad tentmaker Saul—not only a Jew, but a treacherous pedant in sex matters as well—is defined as 'the substance of things hoped for, the evidence of things not seen,' the misunderstanding of which is invariably the first casualty of—but I've lost you." Which knew Cyril was in sight but out of hearing, cracking his knuckles, as he was, with sickening alacrity.

In a muddle, Which scratched his head. "Let me come to the point. Love, it might be said"—he scanned the ceiling philosophically—"has the same quality as good English toilet paper: it grips"; whereupon, he suddenly found an apt analogy in the plastic arts and pointed to the firm grip Dietrich had on her knee in the glossy behind his ear. "On the other hand, wouldn't I be the perfect sophist," Which added, "in failing to note for you that the word 'grip,' noun from the Middle English, is also connotative of spasm or seizure. Such, you see, is the ambiguity of love."

Which feared a lapse of tact, but he hoped to re-establish that private and joy-driven spontaneity they formerly enjoyed during the nights of choir practice when, directing, Cyril shook the chancels like the ghost of General Othello as he whirled his long arms through a red gown, and, a silhouette in yoking waves and natural mummery, he bounced his magic orphics high and wide, up to the very heaven. Then, for the first time in his checkered life, Which had seen himself as an epopt to those Eleusinian Mysteries that transfigured the commonplace and made of reality magic. All that now seemed a precarious memory, rifled, it was all too clear, by this recent misdirected charivari with a girl who could just as easily in two or three years be performing jack-flips on a runway in Great Windmill Street at a half-crown a go, a Salomé who'd divest down to the bone for a posy bag of shillings.

"Procedure," Which continued with an affectionate, and prolonged, squeeze of Cyril's femur, "requires that in every Pre-Cana conference, such as this is, the prospective groom be shown The Visual Aids. You may want to ask why. Then again, you may not want to ask why. Either being the case, however, I could only shrug and point to procedure."

Which sat down, crossed his legs, and drew from a nearby drawer some clipped sheets he had thermofaxed from a bulletin that had been printed with ecclesiastical approbation and filtered into the diocese in a very limited edition. The sheets were covered on both sides, much in the fashion of shadowgraphs, with pen-and-ink combinations of stick figures mimetic of The Act of Kind: each set numbered, captioned, and rubbed of all colour, physiological detail, and contour. They were clinical as opposed to emotional, and the object was to instruct rather than to incite. Which held them up high between thumb and forefinger like some perfected self disengaged from the tensions another might see in the little dramatic puzzles; then he wondered if he was showing them upside-down, a matter he quickly put aside, for doubtless it was an axiom in the positions of sexual union that there was, in fact, no dogmatic up, down, right, left, back, or front.

Cyril grabbed the sheets and sat bolt upright with a kind of kaleidoscopic goggle. He smacked a thigh hypotrophied from the abuse of his bicycle and shook with an inner storm of laughter and delight.

"Each one, of course, is considered an act of homage, Cyril," murmured Which with a kind of muffled dismay. "Or so they say, huh?" He gave a cluck of discord as he reviewed with Cyril all the pictures of these stick-couples upended in a network of oddly rendered limbs and protruberances. Even a perfunctory game of Ombre with his mother seemed a saner pastime. "That *is* what they say, isn't it?" Another louder cluck, like a pulled plug, drained the question of much of its power.

"Yes."

"If that's what one's looking for."

"Yes." Cyril's eyes gleamed.

"I'm not, you see."

"Yes."

"Perhaps you aren't either."

"Yes."

Which leaned over and up into Cyril's face and saw in his eyes a kind of cretinous stupefaction, the index, possibly, of a mind gone elsewhere.

"Yes yes or yes no?"

"I like to do this," said Cyril, and he pressed his large black thumb on Figure Nine, an interlaced squiggle of sticks that the Oriental imagination, Which knew, had affectionately designated "The Ripsaw."

"To be sure," answered Which with a gravely calculated coo bitten off sideways like thread. "And even if she wakes up of a morning looking a perfect fright, even when she's eighty years on, you see, you'll be obliged to, well, what shall I say, *wet the tea?*" Offering that contingency, Which sat back. "So will you?"

"God's blessings will assist. He watch out," replied Cyril, spellbound utterly over "The Loganberry," a position that required not only the imagination of a polymath but a body of Indian rubber. It looked like a cat's cradle.

Omnivideotic though God might be, Which reflected, how could He even bear to watch? Even in heaven, surely, must occasionally wave the Flag of Distress, and what better reason could there possibly be to run it swiftly up the pole? Which Therefore then noticed Cyril huddled over another diagram: his hands were rammed together as if frozen in prayer or at the moment of intense applause captured in still on a photograph. He was perspiring into his collar. Perhaps, Which inferred, Cyril had finally become totally repulsed (Which's intention), as was certainly inevitable, by the withering and terrible jests that man invented for his crazy ministrations: the dumb, primarily nocturnal formations that wired together, in a crucial grasp, Man and Woman in that wolfish scrimmage, born not of adoration, only greed. Figure One—"The Common Sandwich"—was distasteful enough. That was standard. The variations, infinite, were unbelievable—and those carnal acts were especially to be feared which did not have a name.

An ambiguous silence hung in the air. Which walked over and hovered behind Cyril who remained silent, still, excruciatingly poised, it turned out, over Figure Thirteen: "The Strutting Cusp." "The Strutting Cusp!" "The Ripsaw," yes, most everyone loved: it was direct, relatively planless, foundational. But was there man alive who would not gingerly flee to the ends of the earth rather than be called upon, not only to perform, but even to admit he had heard of "The Strutting Cusp?" Only a fortnight previous, one young husband-to-be stared upon that Medusine figure and, after retching all over himself, was stunned into an immediate indifference about his forthcoming marriage, while another couple, a few days later, instantaneously ran into separate rooms, where they stayed for almost three hours—and rumour had it that the groom, on the following week, bought an airplane ticket to Copenhagen where he was summarily docked like a puppy, an alteration perhaps explicable in terms of, and not surprisingly followed by, a radical obsession for angora sweaters, lisping, and eventually a job in the kick line of the Danny LaRue Revue at the Palace.

"Strong Medicine, what?" Which said with a serious, knowing wink, but, bug-eyed with wonder, Cyril then hurtled from the chair with a piping whoop of gayety and, on long autocthonic legs that looked like flexible ducting, flew around the room in looping skids, looking much like Proust's Agostinelli taking flight in his black rubber suit. The indication, it seemed for Cyril, was that life finally made sense.

"Whooooeeee! That were plenty plenty wingding, I tell you," Cyril gasped, dropping back flat as a flawn into his chair. The coon, Which thought, the absolute coon. Then, as if that were not enough, Cyril proceeded, with a frown of busy craftsmanship, to agitate his fingers into stitches and webs that attempted, by manual reproduction, a simulation of "The Teplitz Pretzel"; the just-about-manageable "Texas Roll," to which was added a list of erotic phonemes to be hooted at the moment of *crise*; and "The Granny's Knot" (contrived for the geriatric set); though he was quite unable to get around, as few could, "The Rajab Delay," which involved a fungo bat, two deck chairs, and, it was suggested, a jar of wintercream. Which noticed, such was his perspicacity, that Cyril invariably singled out for comment—and perhaps future use—the most convoluted positions, from which the medical profession, with the foresight characteristic of them, suggested the obese and puritanical abstain.

The priest pulled away the sheets and locked them up. He walked to the window, his hands locked behind him in the manner of a grave and deliberating constable.

"I want to ask you," Which cleared his throat and turned on a forensic heel, " I *must* ask you, actually, if you have had any carnal knowledge with—" He paused.

"Miss Anita the girl."

"So you have."

"Yes."

"Why didn't you say so?"

Which heard from the direction of Cyril a low snoach, very like sour flatulence.

"Could you help yourself?"

"She say help myself."

"And, of course, you did."

"I grabbed," asserted Cyril, and he followed this with a mischievous honk and peeped through his fingers. "Miss Anita, she show me jive, I tell you. She laugh so good. Not like with English girls who give you huge shindy."

Which winced, pulled back. "Have you ever enjoyed, enjoyed?, yes, *enjoyed* English girls?"

"They are afraid of our bananas."

Not really Grace, monocled and gloved, thought Which, as he stared wildly into his drink. "And Anita isn't, apparently."

Cyril bit off a laugh. "She say help myself."

"And you—"

"Grabbed."

What powerful expression there is in a limited vocabulary, the priest thought as he poured himself a double. He had a vision suddenly of these two expatriates, black as thunder, playing in silence you-show-me-yours, I'll-show-you-mine, growing as hot as an afternoon on the feast of St. Lubbock, and then rutting in lower-class bedrooms the size of matchboxes in Bayswater or Spitalfields until tomorrow come never. He emptied his glass.

"I must tell you," said Cyril straightening up, "Anita the girl is no tart."

"Perish the thought, my dear fellow."

"She shag only me."

"Of course," Which replied.

Of course, she *was* a tart, Which thought, but he was somewhat resigned to the impossibility of trying to resolve conclusively the distinction Cyril was trying to make. Which simply knew that the girl who laughed was taken already; the rest was a matter of logistics. What a tiresome process is the night excursion, he thought with horrified amusement, and how vulgar! People were so dreary, conventional lust so implex. He had a thought touching on those whom Milton called "the Corinthian laity." A ballerina, a princess, a meter maid: was not each merely a page in that chapter of world accidents that documented inevitably the fateful chain of events that made of invincibly ignorant girls mattresses? Perhaps there were exceptions. He called to mind St. Wigefortis who grew a beard in order to maintain her virginity. But he could never quite forget Dr. Lushington's vivid homilies to the seminarians and saw in his mind's eye streets filled with fat, painted prelatesses in grey sacks and slim anorectic queans with gamboge complexions guarded by cruel Maltese and blubberlipped Negroes in pinstripe suits, ca. 1950, who smoked dirty cigars, pushed opium up their nostrils, and loafed around the brothel doorways of Grant Road, Bombay, Sister Street, Malta, or the Wahdi District of Cairo. Sex? Love? The definitions were as tiresome as frequent. It was an intellectual gimcrack that merely raised the question similar to the one that sought the *ratio decidendi* between nude and naked. So much rubbish. Sex was only the bum crying out for suppository. Love simply supplied it.

The *tota errant via* tack in thos⁓ crusades whereby pastors sought to splash explanations of reform on the fires of mindless passion were, in fact, only so many sleeveless errands that eventually gave way to the more realistic and doubtless simpler absolute that love lost was really habit broken. It was a class problem, anyway—and therefore insolvable.

"How will you support your bride?" it occurred to Which as he heard himself ask the question. This money business bewildered Rev. Therefore. "You lost your position last month. At the jellied-eel stall in Bermondsey, wasn't it?"

Cyril extended and shook a long finger the size of a small tree. "This English proprietor, a damn fool, traipse over and say to me daily, 'Hey, chocolate face, you smelly! Hey, chocolate face, you smelly!'" How piquant, thought Which.

"How nasty," said Which. "But why, in the name of heaven?"

"His claim, the rogue, was that as I worked I was the devil for singing out loud. Drat on himself, too, I say," said Cyril who flagged his hand in a gesture of futility. "Then he hound me like you don't know, man, and call me vagabond and a big ass. I have eaten his salt, O boy. I make no headway."

"Did you call him any names?"

"You bet, what else."

"What?"

"An insolent weevil."

"And?"

"A forest pig who top his mother."

Cyril clapped his hands and shoved a tumescent thumb high. "That make chuckles for you? Is also chuckles for me. He say I pilfer. I say trash to that. But then, you see, I'm hot at mathematics. Before I come here, they tell us everything not honey. We in for shock. Chipped potatoes, fog, no spitting or pissing into the wall, mathematics everywhere you look, all that." Cyril smirked through a proud blush. "But I look sharp. I'm a Christian, I believe in Baby Jesus, sure. For English, man, you look sharp, else you just be like other prawns of fate, with no end. Push. Shove. Goodby, man. So much argy-bargy, I tell you."

It was a small Magna Charta. Which was almost amused. He pictured Cyril in his white paper hat, wearing a frayed undershirt that revealed swatches of axillary hair, and, cracking with happy music over the canisters of pepper and vinegar, scraping jellied-eels, cockles, oysters, and winkles into mounds on the trays, and scooping rotten whelks, in their turreted shells, into cut sheets for anybody with sixpence and an indiscriminate appetite.

"Anyway," said Which to console him, "it's all rather small beer, that."

Cyril suddenly burst into huge toothy laughter. "But anyway, I have told Mr. Proprietor to please go leak into his shoes."

"You told him that?"

"To piss off, yes."

"Extraordinary. But of course he didn't. He let you go is my point."

"He give me flap." Cyril licked his moustache.

"Then let you go is what I'm getting at." Which felt that in his guinea head there was a pound's worth of ideas sheltering a shilling's worth of knowledge.

"He get hot," Cyril shrugged. "He sack me."

"Yet that was all punchable money, wasn't it?" exclaimed Which, knowing in his heart that Cyril didn't, couldn't, was destined to never *know* what money was, and that should he, then and there, spread out a ten-pound note, Cyril would doubtless get up and colour it.

"By the by, Cyril, where are you, well, *finding* the money necessary to get married?" The question seemed direct, the problem vital, enough.

Cyril bit his lip. "Funds," he answered.

"Sorry?"

"Funds."

"Does this mean someone's seeing you along, a foundation, Oxfam, or, well, a close relative?"

"Funds."

The inscrutable African mind was this, Which wondered, or just pure out-and-out idiocy? Doubtless, the answer was as inscrutable. Or idiotic. And yet, in spite of it all, this was a wonderful specimen of man before him, uncomplicatedly black, a body hard as nacre, a sweet someone with the makings of a substantial epigone who preserved the forthright, if ingenuous, sense of compliance that both gladdened and provided maintenance for the Courts of England ever since the days of stately Jack Lackland. Here were the hands to lead a choir, stay a horse, bake a pie, card wool, hold a bridge hand, and—O Altitudo!—

give a rubdown. Here was a man with a voice like Farinelli, a body like the Apollo Belvedere, the strength of the Farnese Hercules, and the dedication of Gunga Din, and now, chances missed, he was about to be lost forever to some owlet moth of a dancer for a life of duncery and cold meals, this to be underwritten and clerically blessed, paradoxically enough, by the very man who stood to lose so much—and who was now extending a conciliatory tray of sugar biscuits and shortbread.

"Goodies?"

"Sweeties," Cyril said, "are being prohibited me."

So it was. The bilateral assault on Which's part, the trouncing stratagem that sought to insinuate reformation in two ways: to induce to stay on at St. Peter's the Cyril over whom he had lost so much unrequited sleep, and to reduce, by clarifying logic, his affections for a girl who simply did not count. From the very first day he had met Cyril, Which had hoped he could balance argument with invective that he might seduce him from the employ of the world and—before one grew old, rachitic, loose in the fundament, and weak in the sphincter—bring him to share in the small beauties, forbidden but forgiveable, that he had found when, secretly, he tiptoed into the privacy of his own heart.

The conference, along with the morning, would soon end. Rev. Which Therefore, somewhat diffident now as to his oversimplified and crude first attempts at appropriation, knew he must not mismanage any another opportunity to win Cyril over. Background music might be a start.

"Perhaps a bit of music to soothe the—" He hesitated. No, Which reflected, that might be just this side *de trop*. "To, ah, restore a bit of the hale and hearty, shall we say?" He skipped into the bedroom, past his flowers, and returned just as quickly to the strains of Blow's *Venus and Adonis*. Cyril cocked his ear, and, in response to the music, he weaved through the room on his large serviceable feet, swaying like a cobra and punctuating each high note with a modulated yip. Which feared that at any moment he might suddenly leap through a pane of glass or splinter a chair from sheer exuberance—breakage, Which thought, he could ill afford to restore. The money issue again.

"Now," Which took the it's-all-very-well-to-dream-but-this-is-real-life tone, "you're perfectly skint, old boy, poor as dace—except for the odd guinea I can see you, now and again—and yet you jolly well know, and with good reason of course, as soon as you are married, bang!, you'll wake up one day to find six to a dozen little creatures with their teeth on edge, barking way into the night for even so much as a smell of a marmite sandwich or else a mere thimbleful of that cheap stirabout on which you're so keen." He took Cyril's hand. "A man of your talent."

"I can cook," said Cyril, extracting his hand. The black nitwit, Which thought turning away.

"Given, you can cook. See? But what will you cook: snow? linoleum? your *trousers*? (imperfectly buttoned, Which saw)" Which walked into the bedroom, shaking his head, and shut off the gramophone.

There came a long pause.

Cyril whistled a dry note. "I have to contracieve, man. Centrecept." He squinted in confusion and nipped at the cuticle of his thumb. "Contrasumpt?"

Which leaned through the doorway. "Have to. . . ?"

"Bung her."

Happily, Which thought he saw light at the end of the tunnel, an intellectual slype now easily traversed, for, he knew, it was only a short step from abolishing the desire for children to making gratuitous the need for marriage. It was the Split Hair Aspect of Theology. Which thought of St. Drogo, patron saint of the "Chapel of Balances" in which persons who came to be cured miraculously were weighed, as a final test of sincerity, in order to ascertain whether their weight diminished when they offered up their prayers.

"There. Now, no one is punished in Dante for using contraceptives (an argument he once used to confound a seminar of forty mature nuns at a guest lecture at the Brompton Oratory), but, you see, it's a dicey little trick," Which said with a fussy gesture. "Or haven't you heard?"

"I have already try her with this trick." Cyril grinned.

"How, pray?"

"After we go boom-boom, I am making Miss Anita the girl jump backward nine times each." He did not hesitate. "Like this." He jumped backwards nine times.

"Good God, man, are we *jumping beans?*"

How dark the Dark Continent, Which realized, as he heard Cyril then promptly give a recitation of the time-worn abortifacients ("gree-gree," in Cyril's vernacular) which enjoyed popular use in his village: panax soap, sticklewort, chaste tree, calamint, house leek, and, given top priority, the application of burning prunes worn in a bit of linen as an amulet over the navel. They sat on their hands. They gobbled umbrella chestnut. They sucked rue seed, and they forced each other to sneeze with ostrich plumes. Cyril, finally, placed a great deal of stress, so effective it was, on the efficacious value of oiling the virile member with ceruse.

"Ceruse?" asked Which, picking up a pencil.

"But me, aaach! I don't like that. It burn my pipestem."

Which registered amused shock and made as if to strike Cyril; he swung a limp wrist and uttered a word like poo. He stood up and took from a shelf a toy plastic chicken, into whose colon he pushed the pencil, spun it, and pulled it out again, sharpened. Then the priest wrote out an orderly item-by-item list of the other possibilities available to his tutee, hoping, all the while, to reveal the inner mechanics of Woman—which he compared to the underground sewage system in Red China—and revolt him. Methods he touched on included post-coital exercises, I.U.D., *coitus interruptus,* and occlusive pessaries, to which he added, quoting a memorized passage from what he said was a directly revealed sermonette of St. Jerome, the holy Eusebius, on the Need for, but Impossibility of, Purification in the Inferior Sex, various jams, jellies, and foams—the very same commodities enjoying world-wide use, Which added, to kill rats, fire ants, arachnids, and, a more localized concern, to spray into belfries as a safeguard against bats and possibly vampires. The awesome polysyllables of the contraceptive techniques bewildered Cyril, however, and when Which asked him to give on-the-spot phonetic renderings, part of the tutorial, it sounded as if he were speaking futhark, and Which saw that it would take a good three days, something for which he had neither the time nor the inclination.

"Consider the elephant," Which said with a flagging sigh. "Such is his pudicity, according to the Great Cham, that he never covers the female as long as anyone comes into sight." He cosseted Cyril's fingers. "Such a thing we call prudence. Now. What can we learn from the elephant?"

Cyril giggled. "Not to shag one?"

"Go on." This was no time for humour.

"Look sharp, man, yes?"

"Righto, you see. And how does one manage that, you'll ask. My only answer is be true blue, old man, as I would be with you," Which effervesced. "You are not a chocolate face. You're not smelly, not by a long chalk. You smell a perfect rose, if the truth be known." He swallowed. "May I say you are the apple of my eye?"

"Yes," Cyril nodded. Which got flummoxed.

"Well, that's just it, you *are* the apple of my eye."

"I like to be your apple, Sir Reverend."

It was touching. "You mean that? I say, thanks awfully, Cyril. Apples just don't grow on trees, you know."

Cyril rolled his head toward Which. "Thank you for have asking me to be your apple."

"Don't mention it, old boy."

"Indeed," Cyril recoiled, taking him literally. "I am sorry."

"Heavens *why?*"

"Insisting for to be your apple."

"O larks!" Which gave a croon of admiration. How too divine! He felt he had him now. "You can be the perfect dear. I *want* you for my apple—and to lead my choir, I want to add. What I'm trying to say is, have done with this preposterous idea of marriage, for heaven's sake. You, a young man, why it's the purest bosh. A wider reader, you won't be insulted?, a wider reader, even one more widely read than *you*"—Which jammed out the beeps in a conscience that were now deafening, ferocious —"well, he is just absolutely forever tripping upon a proverb that has, goodness, just about become part of the language. Freely rendered, it is poorly put. The linchpin of it all is that women are like pianos, some are upright, some are grand, but a rather inviolate law is that eventually they all go out of tune." Which coughed earnestly. "The simile spares me a vividness that would embarrass us both."

At which juncture, the Reverend Therefore penetrated into the laurelled recesses of history and proceeded to set in motion, for Cyril, a caravan of celibates and soloists whose chastity, it was common knowledge, stood absolutely above reproach. He cited Dominic Savio; the castrated Abelard; Little Black Mumbo; Katerina Tekakwitha, the Virgin of the Mohawks; the Archangel Gabriel; the fifteenth-century monk, Bernardine, who, as a reason for avoiding intercourse altogether, wrote a treatise on animals who blushed; and, finally, the renowned St.

Asella who flattered herself at the age of fifty that she had never in her whole life spoken to a man.

"Is it for nothing that married rhymes with harried?" he asked pointblank.

"I have yet to know." Cyril seemed a shadow of his former self.

"Would I have you on?" the priest asked, desperately pressing Cyril's hands together in a gesture of exquisite bathos. He wanted to rinse out Cyril's soul. "To err is human, to repent divine," Which offered with certainty, "but to persevere is diabolical."

Cyril, not of the subtle school, was sucking his lower lip as he pondered Which's words; he smacked his wet lips, made noises, slurped. It sounded like the deglaciation of an ice-sheet.

Rev. Which Therefore drove on toward the breech. "Doesn't St. Paul, a veritable factotum in matters touching on the lower appetites, well, doesn't he give pride of place to the perfectability of the single life, which is to say, Supernatural Marriage?" The Pauline alternative to inflammability Which dismissed merely as a useless extension of the frying pan/fire metaphor or an interpolated palimpsest, applicable only to teenagers and the publicly intemperate, that had been written into the margins of Scripture by one of the monks of the Monastery of Carmina Burana, who, in what had been perhaps a weak, possibly waggish, moment, got into the cruets one night, took a few belts, and tried as best he could to become the Fifth Evangelist. "Nuns marry God, you see? Much as *I* serve Him in, well, the wifely duties, if you will: keeping His House in fresh linen, dusting away heresy, putting out the eucharistic napkin ring, et cetera, et cetera. By serving me, you serve the Church, which is only, in a way, the *dulce domum* God rents for His family. We can be wives together, as it were—to God. Lest you think

Him a bigamist, of course, I shan't explain *how* He proposes to us all. He simply does, that's all. It's a mystery."

And so Cyril was suddenly presented with an encouragingly domestic but rather atypical ikon: a Picture of God rising up at midnight in a rumpled nightie and bleary eyes, with uxorious requests, he imagined, that he, Cyril—transexualized, presumably, by an Eighth Gift of the Holy Ghost or the lonely but powerful magic of a despirited Bachelor, quondam Creator of the World—fill the toastrack, warm the teapot, or put out the cat. It all seemed rather beyond him, and, of course, his interests in Anita, if the parallel must be made, were something less than eschatological. The *ut infra, ut supra* reasoning was impossible; it gave Cyril a headache. An epithalamium on a pink cloud in the middle of Outer Space, if beatific, lost something in specificity. And it seemed an exclusive blasphemy to desire in Anita those compelling attributes, both concave and convex, which he simultaneously found less acceptable in the God Who created them. Complexities now arose between the spiritual and the physical, and the ultimate question, of course, was to which (i.e., to whom) should one be loyal—all this, quite naturally, raising the ancillary but parallel question sought after over the centuries by many an exegete: had David's lyre been less shaped like Bathsheba, might not there be now more than 150 psalms?

"Anita the girl has wifery in mind, I tell you," Cyril finally replied, striking a blow for humanism. Curse his eyes, Which thought, he's like a cushion: he bears the impression of the last person who sat on him. Sat on? Leaned against. Draped all over!

"So?"

"I have signified my promise."

"Literalist," Which muttered.

Cyril hesitated, his tongue protruding like a bell-pull. "My goodness, Sir Reverend, man, I don't want to rook you of your musics." He held his palms upwards to show how simple, he felt, everything seemed to be. "I am going to turn into a spouse," he added earnestly. The fool, of course, is thinking of "The Ripsaw," Which thought.

"May I suggest that you'll live to regret it?"

"Yes," Cyril nodded. Which got flummoxed.

"Well, that's just it, you *will* live to regret it."

The catechumen apparently did not think so. A last ditch effort on the part of the catechizer took the form of prophecies: that those who shunned the too-nimble and easily possessed alone could count themselves happy; that to be famished and to simultaneously refrain alone heightened awareness; and that marriage was the rummiest of mistakes that always put the coordinate partners into a fearful hash and sent them on an odyssey of tearful and wool-gathering reparation that would last forever; so it was in the days of Hungus, King of the Picts, so it would be When the Roll Is Called Up Yonder On that Final Day. Then Which grabbed the bottle and poured two more drinks, and, while he sucked the bubbles from his thumb, he threw out some lesser artillery: that amber, rubbed, acquires fluff; that the Churching of Women was not just hollow ceremonialism; then advancing notably Sir Thomas Browne's theory that man might soon procreate like trees, without conjunction, and asking all the while would it not seem more seraphic, more provably divine? All to no avail.

Which was spent. He stood up and held out his arms.

"I have revolved it in my head," Cyril said with a small but obtrusive smile that flowered into a rosy laugh.

"And you're going to see it through?" Which wimpered in a voice, orant, strained, cross-hatched with worry. It seemed a prayer. It was a kind of prayer, for what, in fact, is worry but prayer, that hoped-for conspiracy shot north by the constantly plagued and desperately hysterical? Here came a graphic picture of St. Ebba who chastised herself by spending her meditations and *lectio divina* up to her neck in ice water.

"God willing."

It was a knife to the very apostolic scrinium of his heart. Which turned slowly toward the mirror and noticed a face like a sad white moon speak from the reflection.

"But, can't you see, that is another matter *entirely?*"

And Which moped away from the morning window, stricken, like Agrippina bearing the ashes of Germanicus.

III

It was the day of the wedding. Rev. Which Therefore, in his *toga praetexta,* sat alone in the vestry. He was wearing sunglasses to make less bright a world he had seen, with sardonic awareness, become increasingly dark, for in these last few days he had taken refuge from his tribulations at the Athenaeum, where bottle after bottle of the house chablis had raddled him and did nothing to soothe what had metamorphosed, especially this morning, into a pair of loose, unready eyes. He was in a dreadful wax, aware that hangovers themselves constitute a kind of intoxication, and had sent the altar boys out, who were being perfect jackals. Their exit became Lady Therefore's entrance: she padded in, as punctual as Nemesis, armed with a box of headache powders and, upon seeing Which, pretended to jump out of her skin.

"Good heavens," she gasped, clutching her heart, "I took you for Dracula, the Vampire Bat!"

"Twaddle," Which snapped. He well knew she loved these

exaggerated dramatics, staged as they had been all through his life whenever she wanted to disclose to him his perceptible decline. How could someone so old, he wondered, be so juvenile? —though he was perfectly aware that this was her afternoon for cards, when, somewhere else, she might be playing for incommensurably high stakes (buttons), hour after hour, in crucial hands of Beggar My Neighbour.

"You rather put the wind up one, you do," she said. "I've never seen you looking so ropey. Drinking into the wee hours on these binges, you wonder you're all in a pucker."

"*Who's* in a pucker?"

"Say me, I dare you."

"I *so* hate a nagger, Mother," complained Which. He could not help but think of the not overly taciturn St. Poppo the Abbess, put to the sword by having the sword put to her.

"That means me, of course, doesn't it?" she said, filling a glass with water and splitting an envelope of powder. "Oh, I know. You certainly couldn't have in mind, could you, that horrid spider monkey out front, all gussied up in his tatty rumpled morning suit and looking quite the ponce?"

"Cyril?"

"No, Boris Godunov, the Czar of Muscovy."

"I am not amused."

"That insufferable little bounder, yes—and a bit high in the instep, I might add. He is mincing around out there like Lord Strutt." Lady Therefore took a knot out of the priest's cincture and gave him a sidelong glance as if from without a duckblind. "But isn't that more or less where the Church falls short anyway?"

"Short?"

"It shows, I fear, a dangerous tendency to equality."

St. Peter Perpendicular, in Westminster, was preferentially a church, of the High Anglican persuasion. A dark labyrinth of shale-coloured stone and traceried windows, doodled upon and saturated by centuries of rain, fog, and birdlime, into burnt black slabs of soot-caked realism, it seemed no less an irritant to the devil, if a boon to the tourist trade, for having been maintained over the years as a kind of damp mausoleum, an arsenal of arms and memorabilia: small unreadable tablets flaked to a smooth white; fat woodcuts of smiling bishops; old thumbed psalters; supine knights riddled in brass; clusters of shiny flintlocks and oiled knives; and draped high up near the arches, in front of the north and south ambulatories, old flags in faded tatters ("Jesus and No Quarter," etc.), many of them said to have been used at the Battle of Marston Moor or captured from the dissident Covenanters in the Scottish bogs in 1644. The pulpit, as in most churches, was claimed to have been carved by Grinling Gibbons (or his eighth son's nephew's oldest niece), and below it hung a little board showing several series of numerals in direct correspondence, it would seem, to the appropriate matching numbers to be found on the pages in the Hymnal, where, if only at Evensong, logic impelled one to believe the diversion of the Almighty seemed to take some precedence over, but not necessarily any charm away from, that equal but perhaps more universal diversion called "bingo." And yet, today, or on any given day, no matter how reverently those little figures are slipped into their slots by the minor canon, lives there a soul, possibly, who does not find himself sitting on the edge of anxiety, poised for that familiar disyllabic shout?

Now, however, one entered this church and immediately felt it a cenacle filled with the hebetude the Anglicans call peace.

The organist, invited from the Gabon Commission, softpedalled into the final bars of "O Sailor Infinite, My Lifeline's Frayed and Ratty" as an indication, inapposite perhaps, that the bride was now at the rear of the church. The choir began a hymn. The Thedwastry Baptist Choir was totally black. Many of them had been friends of Cyril in Africa, and, whether Bongo or Shilluk, they shared each other's friendships abroad. At the Bishop's invitation—for he had, they frankly admitted, invited them—the group had come down from its small college, where, as Commonwealth students, they were studying for the ministry. They enjoyed road trips for the singing on the bus and, as well, for the little stipends they could pick up to send abroad later as scholarship grants for potential vocations in Chad, Tanzania, or Basutoland. A tea had been given before the wedding. All showed up wearing name tags and happy grins. Which, caught in a clutch of a circumstance that necessitated basic decency, had to be civil; and, trying to smuggle in some kind of plus-value here, spent a short time seine-hauling the lore of Anglo-African relations as far back as he could go: he asked them if London's Zoological Gardens were as large as The Republic of Burundi's; how popular Eugene Stratton had been in Africa; were they aware that Henry VIII's falconer was black; and did they know that several Negroes ran out their trawlers and helped pilot the big boost when England packed it in at Dunkirk? But they merely stood around, shy, in mulberry-coloured blazers, sipping tea, while the bright teeth in their sun-fierced complexions contrasted with their dark, boxlike bodies, which gave to them the effect, if one looked quickly, of buhl furniture. Distributing surplices to them that morning, Which knew he was in the presence of irreducible man when a heavy lad with a bullet-shaped head—cherubic, if fleshiness alone characterize the angel —shuffled onto his knees and worshipfully kissed the elbow of the priest's sleeve.

A head bobbed up over the vestry door: Rev. Which Therefore peered out to the chancel and, for a fugitive moment, caught a glimpse of Cyril—dressed to the nines, rocking on the balls of his feet, and with the hair on his head pomaded and parted in so many places, it looked like a Scotch egg. There was an asymmetrical quality in two matters only: his left trouser leg sported a bicycle clip, and where should have been the carnation was pinned a "Hello, My Name Is—" tag, given to him by the visiting choir. The priest summoned the altar boys to his side and, with a sweep of impatience, brushed quickly past them toward the altar steps, where they then hinged together in a triptych—and waited.

The organ pipes suddenly thundered out in rich vibrations, joined quickly by the choir, the lovely hymn, "Lo! The Bride She Glideth Hie."

A frail shadow: Anita, the bride, scrubbed to a golden clean, floated in ribbons and white silk up the capacious aisle with the grace of a slip of flame on a penny candle, her sweet face flushed and radiant above a raceme of lilies held to her breast with a tremor of modesty. (Who is paying for this? Which wondered. Her dress cost a packet!) Cyril gave a lucid bleat of recognition and shimmied to her side with an obsessive and lunatic energy which the priest noticed with observable distaste while, at the same time, wondering fearfully whether or not Cyril might try to culminate the public ceremony right then and there by cutting the bride's stays with his eyeteeth and attempting to consummate the nuptials right on the chancel step. The moment of truth came—and was gone. They knelt down. Which shook a perfunctory sprinkle of holy water in the couple's direction and, as an afterthought, flicked a backhand splash at the smug groom to signify sacramental disapproval. Cyril, amused, licked the drops from his nose. It had begun.

"I require," Which read, "and charge you both, as you will answer at the dreadful day of judgement when the secret of all hearts shall be disclosed, that if either of you know any impediment why ye . . ."

Impediment? thought Which as he droned on. Why, the only impediment, of course, was this little Miss-What's-Her-Face, whose insatiate and imbecile fury had flung wide the doors of herself, only to shut tight again and imprison forever poor dumb Cyril, houseboy and commodious nigger, in her soft fleshy jail. Which, disabused of all wasted sentiment, x-rayed into her wiles and lack of scruple and accurately divined, he felt, a vicious scold in whom beat a heart black as jet, straight out of the unchaste jungle, and scored with a hundred dirty crimes against him, the frump.

The words, read through spleen, jumped into morris: ". . . and keep her in sickness and in health; and forsaking all others (that hurt, that hurt), keep thee only unto her, so long as ye both shall live?" Which Therefore paused and threw Anita a look that would have frozen a snowberry. Cyril, far away, staring affectionately, as he was, into the intricate porches of Anita's ear, jerked to attention, remembered where he was, and quickly handed the priest his passport, alien registration card, and a smudged wallet-sized photograph he had once taken of himself in a machine at Gamage's for 2/6. Which cooly handed them back.

"State 'I will.'" Then he added in a whisper which sounded like a bit of advice, "Or 'I'd rather not.' Either way."

"I want to," declared Cyril.

"Now, you see," said the priest, "that's precisely where your wicket gets sticky. You want to? Or you will? A minor distinction, notice, but a distinction all the same."

"I weel."

"You verify it, then?"

"I weel."

Rev. Which Therefore marked his prayerbook with a finger; he went unceremoniously slack, rubbed his sunglasses clear, and stood static, smiling all around, as if waiting in a doorway for a capricious afternoon cloudburst to subside. Then he decided

to turn again to Cyril. He shook his miter'd locks and stern
bespake.

"You're dead firm on this, no second thoughts?"

"I have revolved it in my head," he replied. "I weel"—as had
apparently Anita, "revolved" it in her head, who gave a low,
almost inaudible, but very affirmative answer as her turn came.
The roll was up and counted.

Fugat Petrus: debate went voiceless, hope hopeless, and, dead
to life-inducing surmise, the sheeted ghost of Retribution gib-
bered and flapped through his brain on its infernal errand to
whip up anew a thousand devils and all the old mockeries, now
pinched from their filthy slumbers to billow up and wreak havoc,
havoc, and more havoc in the furnace of his wilting soul. Man
is a match, Which thought, and then an ash as quickly. And yet
the inescapable premonition he had had of late still caused a
buzz of intrigue within him. It was the suspicious twinge that
someone had subsidized this wedding, a feeling especially con-
comitant with the formal letter he had received from the Bishop
"suggesting" he proceed with the nuptials. (Genghis Khan,
making "suggestions" from an episcopal seat, need be no less
Genghis Khan.) A rebus of random events linked into order:
a bishop's intercession, expensive clothes, a rented organist, a
large choir, a rushed church date, flowers, and, doubtless on the
same tab, a sweaty spree into the Cotswolds where they would
rut like ducks for a fortnight. Of worldly pennies are such
things bought? No, there was a predestinative force shoving the
whole show along, and Which was damned if he knew who it
was. A patron? His absurd grandfather trying to hustle the gum
catalogue into translation? Or had a kitty been taken up at the
ballet? Who had assisted was the question; that Cyril was
married was not.

"Yaaaaabooooool!" There: suddenly one wild boom of enthusiasm flew from within the large choir in distinct counterpoint to the wooing gale of song. Which winced with a twitch of dubiety and thought of St. Fiacre, whose intercession is invoked particularly by persons suffering from hemorrhoids.

Thrums, evidence of an echo, ceased. The choir was ranged in rows just off the north aisle between the columns that supported the vault behind which stood the Lady Chapel, famous not so much for having withstood the Blitz—there were still small piles of chips in view, kept visible by a die-hard and resolute sexton (one arm, Benghasi, 1941) who, with a cud of longing in his throat, nightly swept the transepts—but because it was said to be the domain of King David's ghost who walked there every year on St. Swithin's Day inveighing against bumptious and uncircumsized giants.

Next to one of those columns sat a small table where one could purchase, for a shilling each, leather bookmarks embossed in pinchbeck, shiny postcards of the Family Windsor, and small pamphlets which stapled together the church's history: records of notable baptisms and deaths; mottled photographs of the old clerestory, sedilia, and cloister (the area, it was pointed out, where the locals queued up for gas masks during the War); and prose accounts of various legends more than willingly enlarged upon, as was usual in these churches all over London, by little old pie-faced but dedicated shawlies who sat lost in their mufflers, blueing in the cold, chatting with Japanese businessmen and troops of German girl scouts, and recommending this or that with chirps of delight and sad smiles—grumbling mercilessly only in the off chance they should be locked in overnight, a not infrequent hazard for the napping octogenarian placed in the same corner with long dead ladies and snipenosed, marmoreal queens.

Cyril faced Anita: two rings, woven from the hair of a giraffe's tail, were exchanged, and then Cyril chewed through the Lord's Prayer like a plum and spit out the Amen. "Bestow upon these thy servants (Which snorted ironically), if it be Thy will, the gift and heritage of children . . ."—and he read on with that wooden severity and grey inexactitude of speech that ran the closing benedictions into a mere recitation of inconclusive parentheses, washed of every feeling and inflection.

"Yaaaaamaaaaak!" Without warning, one figure bounced into the aisle like a rubber ball, an elastic rebound whirring with song. The shout boomed the length of the nave.

A frightful vision rose up before Rev. Therefore, simultaneous with two or three cold triumphant shouts from the direction of the choir (from whence the figure), each one screwed a pitch higher, then followed by a trill of volant notes which snapped off in shivers and spontaneous barks of ecstasy. Which flipped his sunglasses to his nose, turned to one of the altar boys, and, closing his eyes, quickly jerked his head as a sign he would speak; as quickly, an altar boy, small as a rock pigeon, stood below him. He touched the boy's pale neck (noticing his raspberry-coloured lips).

"Bumpass, what's that vile thing doing in the aisle?"

"Please, sir?"

"He's squiffy. It's written all over him." Which stamped his foot, hidden beneath the alb, while the hymn with drumbeating insistence grew louder and wilder with strange, almost pre-lapsarian vigour.

"The man down there, sir, you mean?"

"The nigger, Bumpass," the priest said. "Yes."

"He's singing, I think, sir."

"He wishes," replied the priest, pushing the boy aside. Which recalled that he and his mother had once seen this very choir several Christmases ago in Trafalgar Square, where, together with the Society of Pan-African Wives, they had sung a selection of carols in their tribal masks and costumes: bright robes, bone combs, sashes, stripes, and paper flowers. ("Are they elves or lollies?" Lady Therefore had asked, dragging Which away.) His memory was composed chiefly of the highly ornamented males, natural and quite lovely, the aesthetic capacity of the females, he felt, having been advanced—unlike the male—in perfect accord with the Darwinian theory, through exercise or habit in the same manner, he had read somewhere, as our own taste is gradually improved. Walking away with his mother, he remembered, he had flatly denounced the peahen.

"It is not insisted upon," Which said, blinking dim reproaches at Cyril, "but you may kiss the bride."

"This is permittable and not being prohibited me?"

"Though not insisted upon."

And he who doted on Sensations, Pulsations, and Exquisite Moments had to stand passively by and watch both of them, with highly censurable vim, fumble together like cheap dummies in a long, vulgar kiss that smacked out a loud report. A shriek of endorsement from the choir pierced to the very roof: "Waaaaaiiiieeeee!"

It had been explained as the original intention, during the collation of watercress sandwiches and tea that morning—as the young men were snapping on their cassocks—that through its cruciform arrangement the choir would try to reflect, as well as somehow ritualize in platonic copy, the order and pattern of what theology saw as The Greater Symbolic Design and, notwithstanding its reputation, humbly try to duplicate it. The Recessional, however, seemed to recapitulate a Zulu puberty rite.

The choir, during "How Mature Is Jesus, Very," began to come apart—just as Cyril and Anita left the altar, hand in hand. The marginal positions gave way first when, in happy agitation over a few too-long-held polyphonic bursts, several choristers mambo'd over to the pews (vacant, vacant), and, snapping their fingers as if on the giddy crest of some tumultuous crisis, they swooned in fits of piglike hysteria. It was now a map of passion, totally lost to the concept of boundary; and vocal deformations, heated with wheezes and amazed whistles, were followed by physical. Rev. Therefore thought immediately of St. Tatwyn, patron saint of the costive in devotion. The hymn, more chased away than come to an end, left the choir hanging out in fealty a series of tongues frothed in pink. One boy found himself gasping for breath in the cobwebs of the loft, where, in the fervor of unabridged passion, he had tried to run into the steeple and ring the bell. Ring the bell!

"Epilepsy, so brief of horror," Which exclaimed, alone on the altar, as the bridal party left the church, "wherefore is it thou canst not die?" He was an omniverous reader.

The howls ceased.

The church hung in dead stillness.

The lights had been extinguished some time before Which, more grey than eminent, slipped from the shadows of the vestry, where he had quietly kept station as an escape, a sanctuary, from the constantly renewed consignments of the living, in this case—unbeknownst to him—his mother, who, waiting at the main door, looked like a little poisonous toadstool that had sprouted through a crack there in the moist darkness, exuding spurts of bitter venom that fell drip, drip, drip from its network of close wrinkles and shadowy bracts—a liquor Which had gladly drunk to shrink, drugged, into perpetual dullness, even death. It seemed either that or a soaring dive in a plummet from the turrets of Tower Bridge. He thought of St. Phocas, the market gardener who dug his own grave, and patron saint of those who suffer from uterine nostalgia.

"Punctuality," the mushroom announced, "is a sign of breeding."

As he heard the voice, Which jumped in fright and caught
at his throat. He staggered backwards, his face the colour of milk
glass, and slumped into a dark pew.

"I had hoped—"

"Vainly," she replied.

"And yet I fancied—"

"That the squall and catspaw of those perfectly foul Abys-
sinians sent me running?" She harumphed. "Pray build no hopes
there, dear. You are speaking to a woman still as yet undefeated
in the game of quinze, with which acumen, I might remind you,
has something to do."

"My hopes, if you must know, Mother, are dashed quite."
Which, dispossessed of Cyril, sacrificed to expediency, and
stooped over, even as a young man, with an obstinate distaste
for the ways of fortune, reached over and took his mother's hand.
He was miserable. He thought of St. Swope of Croquet Island,
patron saint of the twentieth century, who was decollated in his
twenty-fifth year for claiming he had invented the symbol for
nought.

"Luddites, Costermongerers, Evangelicals," she said, eyeing
him through her veil as she thought of the tumultuous kick-up
the choir had caused. "Each one, notice, an antonym for Good
Taste, to say nothing of the cement of moral imperatives."

"Then, so *primitive.*" He seemed diffident. "Or did you think
not?"

"Ugly races are always primitive. It's their form of sour grapes.
The lower classes," Lady Therefore whispered, confidentially
pushing his head into her shoulder, thin as a wishbone and suf-
focatingly perfumed, "have been the raspberry seed in our wisdom tooth for a long, long time."

"I am the victim of rather hoping that were not the case."

"Then you are, my dear boy, the victim of hypothesis."

He felt an inward groan come from within him, a volley of

sighs, faint but clear, light but poignantly sad, like the flutter
of laughter echoing from the past. "They *were* rather utterly
too too, he answered in an eggshell voice as he remained un-
moving, slumped against his mother. And so they sat together
in the hollow of the pew, surrounded by the intimidations of
eerie darkness, a jumbled Pietà.

Although it was her constant maxim, Which reflected, that
the Church should never be polluted with irreverent combinations, he was extremely surprised that his mother had not only
patiently tolerated this wedding but had not whistled in Scotland
Yard to insist they impound the choir, whose rubbernecking,
even obscene, performance sounded like a Mau-Mau circumcision
ceremony or some kind of hallucinogenic gang-bang performed
on coconut matting in some out of the way Tibbu village. With
relish, he had once assumed, would his mother have happily
meted out to them that condign but infinitely more deserved
punishment through which St. Primus, patron saint of the con-
genitally mute, so singularly met his end, i.e., by having a few
dollops of moulten lead poured into his mouth—a curious *non
ex ossibus* relic which was then extracted and eventually placed
on a wand as a commemorative ball-cum-sacramental in the
garden of a devoted Franciscan tertiary somewhere in Goose
Rocks, Maine.

Suddenly, an idea fell into his head like an errant pinball
sped precipitately on its way, through targets and obstacles,
down the slanted surface of his mind.

"You know," Which began, his hands clasped, the knuckles
standing out sharply, "I have a nagging suspicion some chap is
playing the deuce with me?"

Lady Therefore sat up. "What *could* you be talking about?"

"You saw the groom?"

"In his best bib and tucker—and no less the kind of Lascar, to
my mind, who on any given dark night, pick one, would bolt

out from a tree and pinch you blue as a blushing dog, or worse, just to write home about it. The boy has a screw loose."

"And, of course, you saw the bride."

"The veriest sillypop," answered Lady Therefore, whose face filled with ruminant, sly fun. Then, she frowned. "A rude shock, yes. A complete surprise, no. I've met the type, my dear boy. May I suggest her sisters became aunts rather young?"

"Oh dash!" Which snivelled petulantly, assuming his mother had for some reason brought to mind the memory of Georgie Quaiff (q.v.). "I meant her gown. Had you a look at *that?* Schiffli embroidered organza, if you will, with val lace insets, and a venise-edged mantilla. *Au courant?* Let me say so. I'm certain it was Courrèges." The detailed description indicated preoccupation, perhaps a willingness to experiment.

"What did you expect, dear boy, to see the pert baggage march up to the altar in her stocking feet, wearing mosquito-netting and dishcloth?"

"I expected," he grizzled, "no such thing, Mother, and, though a bracingly unorthodox thought, it's rather off the point. I'm talking about *money*—and lots of it. Just where did it all come from?" The pinball gained momentum, wheeled, clanked helter-skelter.

"To my mind, that sort pans out well enough from the money standpoint." She reviewed her fingernails.

"Welfare, you think?"

"General monkeyana," Lady Therefore yawned, patting her mouth with the rapid flutter of her glove. "You know, dustmen, bus drivers, bumbailiffs. They're not really the unacknowledged legislators of the world, but there's a living wage there for any-one, be he who he may, though the taste for such kind of work is special and, I gather, acquired."

"Rot, Mother," he replied with an unprelatical boyish whine. "Somebody has his foot in the dish, I'm certain of it."

"You *are* in a pickle," she said and tweaked him on the knee
to try to dispel the sullen sense of injury in his heart. "I suppose
we all are, what with all the whim-wham in the world today.
Violence, guns, Baptists, devaluation, mustard gas, an American
on every corner, and everybody having to take off his clothes
to have a good time. I blame the horrid brat of historicity."

"Cold comfort that," he sulked.

"You used to be so happy."

"DeQuincey used to be a dopefiend."

"Not to hate, my dear boy, there's just so much to *resent* in
you. You are so thoroughly tiresome when you're like this," she
snapped. The grumpy exchanges ebbed, a long effortful brooding
flowed. Quibbles seemed useless. He no longer, it seemed, could
find himself in arguments for some time now coating him over
in layers, and he lost his tooth like some sloppily, heavily leaded
canvas. Then she looked at him, not smiling, but pressing her
small chin slightly into her neck. She took his hand, while
snapping the last buttons on the pair of white dog-skin gloves
she wore. "Come dear, don't mind me. The driver is waiting on
us out front."

"The driver?"

"An old woman needs her leeways. I had hoped for a game of
bumble-puppy with you tonight. Or a nice evening of two-
handed euchre. Now, will I be disappointed again? You know
what you mean to me, so come along dear, please." Which
looked up wistfully into her pinched, wintry face that now
seemed animated with a tiny sparkle and detected there, he
thought, a trace of intractable sureness, a triumphant glow, as
Lady Therefore, preoccupied with the power and advantage of-
ficially established at Cana, led him through the dark church
door. She was in the tradition of those brave, long-suffering
mothers—tiny, gimp, stiff as buckram—stumping across the
eternal pages of Scripture in their sweet old exponential shoes:

Jochebed; the Mother of Ichabod; Rizpah; Hannah; the Widow
of Sarepta; the Great Lady of Shunem, who gat heat; and, not
least surely, the innominate but for that no less estimable Syro-
phoenician Woman, she of the vexations.

Which stopped short on the steps of the church; he perceived
himself a fool, a butt of fate, a sappy and ineffective degradand
riddled with foreign matter: questions, guesses, speculations. He
felt like a bottle of cheap wine filled with bits of cork. Everything had happened so fast.

"Did you know, by the way, that the Bishop cut me in this
whole affair?" The pinball rattled into a post, jolted free on a
swirl. "I rather thought he was one to keep a straight bat."

"What *are* you on about?" asked Lady Therefore, hobbling
along, unperturbed, tapping her cane. "The Bishop?"

"Correct. He wrote to me and told me, you see, *told* me, to
get on with it."

"It?"

"Do the wedding," he waved his hand maniacally, "hire that
humpty choir, the lot!"

"Sad fudge, I'm afraid," said Lady Therefore.

"Him with his rent-roll, new tennis courts, and pomposity,
the big ninny! To pull the rug out from under me, such as he
did, is unforgivable, quite." Which squinted away. "Un. For.
Givable."

"Why would he do that?"

"Good God, had I the foggiest, would I bring the matter up?"
His imagination stampeded. No law or agency could be identi-
fied. Nothing, it seemed, could escape the prowling and eruptive
forces of pursuit and arrest in a world daily lost to new guaran-
tees and privileges. And now Cyril, *Caton Infidèle*. He had a
vision of the world as the Ultimate Panopticon, the perfect
prison so designed by a rhyparographic God that He could, just
for His Own amusement, send His minions to distress and

thrash away from men even the least of their paraplegic opinions, their most harmless and unspoken dreams. Then spontaneously rose before Which a horrible reality: God Himself as an inflexible, fault-finding precisian, as warty as Cromwell—the subtle Dr. Irrefragabilis, with psalm book, inkhorn, and pale candle, blinking over His brittle parliamentarian docket to oversee at a singularly aseptic distance the poor human creatures, with whom He sports, humiliatingly dunked into ponds in cucking stools, pilloried by their fingers, and locked into thumbscrews as if each was of no more worth than the smallest flitch of bacon. Ours was merely the life between splashes: doused, gasping away, pneumonic. Time finishes the job God started, Which thought, but why had Man been dragged in to watch? The dehumanization was bloodcurdling. We were merely formulas, each an index of peeves, hopes, joys, and grudges, and our formulas were on file in a secret cabinet somewhere in the last recesses of the Eternal Mind.

The late afternoon darkened. A dirty fog settled in and seemed to stain everything in anthracite: anthracite trees, anthracite buildings, anthracite people. A large silver-and-glass limousine, plush and sleek and shiny, was rolled up to the kerb and alone seemed sealed to the dullness spreading through the streets. Lady Therefore took the wet steps in paces, like a holy fowl. She turned and gave Which her arm as they trod down the steps, over the small flakes of wet, coloured confetti, down to the waiting car.

"As I said, dear, I am *so* looking forward," she announced through the window as he eased the door shut, "to having you steady again and back with me just as it always was, fine as fippence."

"Well," Which answered half-heartedly, "I shan't stay all night, Mother. It's been a day. I'm rather thumped in, spoony, you know." He entered the car and sat in its expensive gloom.

"There's a good boy. But I don't refer to only tonight, Which. I'm just pleased you'll be with me *always*, you see. Remember your antecedents," she said, her eyes now growing mistily autoreminiscent, "so be a gentleman, be a dear. You know what they say."

Which rolled his head lugubriously toward her. An amused *sic probo* smile, Which noticed, seemed to flicker across her little mouth. "No," he asked, "what?"

"Not important."

"What?" he insisted.

"I was going to say—"

"Yes?"

"Pay up," she said, "and look pretty."

It was like a flute note blown across a pond.

The pinball plunged through its fast action, rolled smoothly over the grooves, rung a glass bell, and, lighting up a bright series of bulbs on a mirror, it tilted into a final hole with a loud click.

Paralyzed, Which Therefore felt a terror, a vast humiliation, grip his hair, and, wide-eyed in utter disbelief, he turned slowly toward his mother. But she was talking.

O where, she asked in an almost hypnotic dream-reverie, her eyes moist and shining through a mask flushed with old distant thoughts, O where had flown that quaint and merciful fidelity that bound Mother and Child together in a lifetime of discovery, that cozy shipshape world of Used-to-Be, when the waterfalls of Cremorne splashed along in runnels, and rivulets bubbled through trimmed gardens and pavilions of oaks on those long, never-ending autumnal days when the blackthorn showered down its petals and the lowing herd wound slowly o'er the lea? When last seen those moments of peaceful vagabondage when handsome rakes, all of English nativity, sat high and lovely in the saddle and took a turn, on a cob or palfrey, through lush country fens or dashed in hunting pinks across the rolling hills in point-to-point gallops to the cries of "Tally Ho"? Had they gone forever, those gay Lotharios—with rue their hearts were laden—who once held lovely ladies balancing in the *pas de pour suite* of the Redowa Waltz and then, in chests of medals and strong black boots, sat lovestruck and poetic in the filigree gazebos, drenched in moonlight and musky blooms and made one sob with the long, dark looks that sparked a cheek to redden and caused a downcast eye? How bring back those mild, halcyon Sundays, filled with promenades and the darkling thrush, when craggy, high-collared Men of Principle gathered together in Palladian mansions, behind thick curtains, before rich tapestries, and sipped sherry in earnest, while fresh, ivory-cheeked girls in snowy pinafores played battledore among the white roses of a Jacobean garden? Why nevermore the People of Quality who tripped through cold mornings to Kensington Palace or rode to visit the Queen in high-swung barouches with immense armorial bearings on the panels? Why no longer in evidence those strawberry girls from the little villages of Nether Lipp and Tooting Horn who looked to a one like the Blessed Damozel and ran barefooted through the sweet dewy grass to the music of lovesick pigeons, or avidly cheered, with lilting voices, the balloon races at Vauxhall on those brown-sunned, unforgettable summers when the skies were sailboat blue? Shall all this have been lost forever: the stately rooms at Osterley, Marble Hill, and Knole; the weekends down to Cowes, when bold-hearted men, smelling of leather and ancient sack, strode out from the feudal donjons of their fathers, across the avenues and coppices of their estates, shooting grouse and stalking golden deer; the copses and thickets of Glastonbury, rich in holy thorn, where Christ had spent so many happy days in His teenage years with his uncle, Joseph of Arimathaea? And what of Arthur and Avalon, the tinkle of the muffin bell, the merrie pieman, and the whistling knife-grinder in his wide, fat apron who trod the cobbled streets? Who remembered the old English games and festivals of bun-throwing, apple-howling soaling, the hare-pie scramble, pancake tossing, wassailing the apple trees, mumming, burning the ashen faggot, and clipping the church? And what had happened to the kind, paternal lamplighter, smiling down a benison and flaming up the lampwick to only once again reassure the quiet village, and forevermore, that "All Will Be Well, All Manner of Things"? The Lion and the Unicorn would always boldly guard the door that led to that paradise, the land of sweetness, light, and transforming prevenient grace, and yet, asked Lady Therefore, could she at last unto that sacred portal, into that sacred land, one day bring her son to spend their final days together, only themselves, alone?

Which, however, was not listening. He was staring flatly through the closed car window into the remorseless darkness, helpless, lost, alone to himself, shrunk into the cushion in the back seat of the car—only the small dot of his head visible— like the last hemophiliac son, a titled heir in his nonage, to the long privileged dynasty of good blood, begun with William the Conqueror, that, over the years and down the stretch of centuries, had thinned, weakened, sterilized. He opened his mouth to speak, but he could not move a muscle. His tongue was like soft white rubber. Neither was the car, the early night air, nor any momentum of future resolve within him moving. All was quite, in fact, at a standstill. It was nightfall. And, remorselessly, the characteristic of nightfall, only once again, was its blackness.

London 1970